Hong Kong Rocks
Peter Humphreys
Proverse Hong Kong
2019

I0615893

Though rooted in experience and influenced by real-life events, this novel represents an alternative version of Hong Kong's recent history and takes regular liberties within this parallel world for the benefit of satire. The book was completed after the Occupy protests of 2014 but before the escalation of protests in the territory beginning June 2019, the action taking place in a notional 2018.
—Peter Humphreys, Author.

Nick Powell, arriving in Hong Kong with his soon-to-be-ex-wife Lennox, finds himself drawn into the political machinations affecting the city as the Occupy movement of 2014 takes root.

A fatal accident exposes the factions vying for control of the SAR and gives Nick the second chance desired by many Hong Kong expats. Will he make the most of the opportunity, or find himself on the wrong side of history?

Shifting between a variety of unique voices, HONG KONG ROCKS (a Hong Kong Proverse Prize finalist) is part thriller, part creative exploration of the challenges facing a special administrative region punching above its weight.

PETER HUMPHREYS has been working as a writer and editor since 2004. Currently based in Lancaster, UK, he combines his role as a freelance editor for a large educational publisher in Hong Kong with a part-time position at Lancaster University's "Imagination Lab".

Peter began writing committedly while studying for his MA in Creative Writing at Manchester Metropolitan University (2002–2004), achieving a distinction, and being awarded the Dawson Jackson Prize for his first, self-published novel, *The Blaggard*.

His short fiction has been published in Manchester, Hong Kong and Shanghai, while his stories and poems for young learners of English have appeared in numerous Hong Kong course-books and on the British Council's "Learn English" website.

While a member and then Joint Chair of the Hong Kong Writers Circle (HKWC), Peter twice co-edited the HKWC's annual fiction anthologies and was a contributor to four of them.

Hong Kong Rocks

Peter Humphreys

A Proverse Prize Publication

Proverse Hong Kong

Hong Kong Rocks
by Peter Humphreys

Alternate first edition published in paperback in Hong Kong
under sole and exclusive licence
by Proverse Hong Kong, November 2019.
ISBN: 978-988-8491-72-8

First edition published in paperback in Hong Kong, November 2019,
under sole and exclusive licence
by Proverse Hong Kong, P.O. Box 259, Tung Chung Post Office,
Lantau, NT, Hong Kong SAR, China.
Email: proverse@netvigator.com; Web: www.proversepublishing.com
ISBN: 978-988-8491-83-4

Cover image: Peter Humphreys
Cover design by Artist Hong Kong.

British Library Cataloguing in Publication Data
A catalogue record is available
from the British Library

PROLOGUE

Perhaps you don't know the way people kill themselves on Cheung Chau? Let me enlighten you. They check into a quiet hotel or hired room with some barbecue coals. They have a last drink, cigarette, or whatever else they may have enjoyed in this life and then, having sealed the doors and windows, light the charcoal and wait patiently to die. This is why most hotels and hired rooms on Cheung Chau will only accommodate guests in pairs, the theory being that no two people, bonded by an inclusive room rate and unlimited seafood, would want to slip away together in such a way.

And perhaps they're right. When I was a happily married man, barbecue coals were an existential menace only when taking an eternity to heat up during summer networking events on the roof of our apartment block, thereby delaying the greeting, eating and double-kiss departures such that my will to live was occasionally threatened. My estranged wife never seemed to mind. Lennox has a need to feed and nourish people, and no desire to make them disappear – even those she ends up despairing of; in contrast I wonder how my Hong Kong friends put up with me when I reveal so little of my inner life to them.

Not that I am alone in this regard: scattered across the islands of Hong Kong live a small band of anti-social individuals of my acquaintance who exist outside the world of bankers and lawyers into which Lennox and I were first initiated. These inveterate expatriates, of varying degrees of respectability, represent the flotsam and jetsam of a long-receded empire of which little remains but the common language the world has chosen to document its own demise. But now I'm depressing myself. Why so glum? I suppose it's the white lie I've just used while checking in.

"Mr and Mrs Powell. First names? Nick and Lennox. That's right, Lennox. L-E-N-N-O-X. Yes, it is an unusual name, isn't it? My wife will be joining me later – you can ask her about it then."

In our top-floor room I pluck a miniature whisky from the drinks tray on the dresser and raise a tiny bottle to the suitcase in the corner. Then I go out onto the balcony and look down at Tung Wan beach. Not a bad turnout for a Saturday afternoon in early spring. A group of grinning teenagers flop and roll off a circular dive platform within the bobbing circumference of the shark net. Family units try to give dad a well-earned rest from work until the urge to bury him overwhelms them.

Rainclouds hang over the skyscrapers across the water. We've been luckier on this side territory today. The bright red Macau hydrofoil emerges from the gloom and prepares to bypass Cheung Chau on its way to the former Portuguese colony. It moves at a rate of knots but if you're in a real hurry you can take the helicopter that appears to fly directly into the sunset. Soon there will be a bridge linking Hong Kong's Special Administrative Regions – nothing stops progress here. Escape routes are plentiful but all lead somewhere else.

I turn to the smaller, less touristy beach, beyond the Wind Surfing Club and beside the Mini Great Wall. The last outing we made together – Paul, Frank, Fenton, and myself – was to the bar on Kwun Yam beach, to watch the New Year fireworks at a respectable distance. I wonder if the lads will miss me? One of the first things Frank said to me when I met him at the Yellow Brolly three years ago comes to mind: "Living abroad, you're always on the edge of a precipice." How right he was. No backup. No support. Not that you can assume the locals have it any easier. The owner of the beach bar had one day watched his father kayak into the spray, never to return.

I zip open the top of the suitcase, and take out the charcoal I bought earlier. I check for possible seepage from case to carpet. There is none. I fish out a cigarette from the pack in my breast pocket and try to decide which spirit to partake of next. Is this how it ends – choosing between brandy and rum – when at one stage life had promised to be a bottomless cocktail of possibilities?

I know, I should be grateful to have made it this far. Even as I dragged my heavy load up Peak Road just now a schoolgirl flew down the hill on her bicycle, closely followed by her equally irresponsible mother, missing me by inches. There are no cars on Cheung Chau but there must be at least a couple of fatalities each year caused by cyclists hungry to meet their maker. I found myself recovering beside the stone that once marked the place beyond which no indigenous Chinese could live. Parties of schoolchildren are sent there to learn about the racist past. So is it true that I was born in the right place at the right time? And if so, did I make the most of my opportunities?

Growing up in a succession of small, northern English towns; attending predominantly single-sex schools, I was always aware of certain boys my age who'd become men more quickly than everyone else, either through nature or circumstance. These informal protégés – underground DJs; philanthropic drug dealers, or casually brilliant footballers – exhibited a cool worldliness that impressed their peers more than any teacher or parent ever could. They rarely went on to university, though they were often brighter than the rest of us. They didn't try to be funny, fashionable, or fearless – they simply *were* all of these things and more.

These young men were our guides as we prepared to enter adulthood. Some were dads before we'd lost our virginity. Others became disillusioned, then destitute, in the course of a few short years. A few died and were afforded a paragraph in the local paper. Now I wonder how they squared their ambitions with their accelerated life paths. I suppose I did okay, without ever finding the answers to the questions they seemed to know instinctively: girl next door or wanderlust? Friend or foe? Moral stance or hedonistic stagger? Life: meaningful or meaningless?

The cemetery to the west of Cheung Chau offers stunning views of the South China Sea to the occupants of its steeply terraced rows of graves. Instead of a horizon cluttered with ferries and pleasure craft, the ancestors of today's fishermen and tourist traders are treated to a vast watery nothingness flecked with gold, upon which the occasional sampan of their youth still offers a solitary silhouette against the sinking sun. However, that is not the place I find myself in. Not yet. Instead I must bide my time at the Gloucester Hotel, with its loud carpets and buffet breakfast threat. Once more I raise a finger of liquor to the suitcase (rum, since you asked), and to you this time as well. Thanks for listening.

CHAPTER ONE

The deal was he would speak English all day, every day. That suited him fine. Like most expats he only had a few words of Cantonese, pronounced differently each time he used them. They were at the Central Star Ferry terminal eating ice-cream in the rain. May wore a purple winter parka with the hood all the way up. He noticed her bright black eyes had started to dull.

"What's the matter?" Paul asked.

"Been here before," said May, kicking at the promenade.

"Not been here before in English though, have you?" he grinned.

In truth he wanted to kill her. When he was growing up they still had grammar schools. At the grammar schools they played rugby. Going to grammar school had been his start in life. Now everything had stopped. Still, he was quietly confident he could dropkick eight-year-old May between the two tallest skyscrapers on the opposite side of the harbour with ease.

"So boring," she said, "you bad teacher."

He couldn't deny it. He might have been a good teacher once, when he first arrived in Hong Kong with his book of Liverpool poets and dreams of the exotic East. Now he was a bad teacher. Perhaps even a bad human being, though it was hard to work out how much of his self-loathing was tied to his hangover and how much he would have recognised unassisted by stomach-churning queasiness and chronic dehydration.

"Shall we go to the Maritime Museum?" he asked. "Read about the pirates that used to sail the South China Sea?"

"Pirates are boring."

"You wouldn't be saying that if there was one here now, would you?"

He binned his ice-cream wrapper and turned back to her in character.

"Ahaaarrrrghhhh," he growled. "Shiver me timbers. You'll be walking the plank afore the sun sets on the old empire."

"You are stupid," said May. "Very stupid man."

Undeterred, Paul began to wave an imaginary cutlass.

"I'll cut ye to ribbons and send ye to Davy Jones' locker!"

"What is locker? What is Davy Jones?"

Paul wondered if he should tell her. She had to know sooner or later.

"Davy Jones was the little cockney singer in the Monkees. But 'twas also Davy Bowie's name, afore he changed it so as the listenin' public didn't get 'em mixed up when they was readin' their Melody Makers."

"Mama says you drink too much."

"Every pirate's allowed his rum!" Paul yelled. "Now I'm coming to get you."

She squealed as he wrapped his arms around her. He could smell the fuggy dampness on her padded cotton coat. The damp that made everything rot here – clothes, books, notes, pictures; even the walls of your poky apartment. As compensation, he got to inhale the perfect freshness of the long, black hair she had carefully folded into her hood when it began to rain. Yes, he could smell the caffeine shampoo that her mother chose for its alleged brain-enhancing properties, but there was also the scent of May's perfect skin that existed in defiance of the sourness of its owner. It was the scent of the future and it made him want to cry.

"Stop! Now!"

The words had been flung at him by the maid, sitting twenty yards above them in a green-fringed concrete enclave, smoking on a NO SMOKING bench. Mrs Ho wouldn't allow him to take her precious daughter out on his jollies around the city without an escort. She thought the Filipino helper, Sophia, was too soft on him so instead sent a stick-thin nameless *amah* who wore sunglasses in all weathers and stared coldly at the pair of them when she wasn't fixated on her iPhone.

"We're just messing around," Paul smiled up at her. "Don't worry, love."

"It's cold," snapped the angular *amah*.

"Don't you start," he wracked his brains. Where to take May next? In another couple of years she would be released into the malls where she would graze contentedly until her mother identified a suitable mate. But today the world was still their oyster, and he was being paid by the hour.

"Come on," he said. "Let's catch that ferry."

"No want museum," May sulked. "Disneyland."

"We're not going to a museum. Or bloody Disneyland," said Paul. "We're going to get a curry."

Sensing movement, the maid tottered towards them. Her expensive-looking heels, a gift or bribe from her mistress, didn't fit properly and threatened to catapult her into the harbour.

"Speak more to her," the maid snapped at Paul. "Teach her good words."

"Try this," he cleared his throat. "Ladies, I would be honoured if you would accompany me on this short, historic ferry ride across the harbour to Kowloon."

"No singing," May frowned. She knew what her tutor was capable of.

Ferry, 'cross the Mersey
'Cause this land's the place I love
And here I'll stay.

In more idealistic days, Paul had convinced himself that having a regional identity and distinctive accent would be assets to his teaching. He thought he might be able to teach the kids here about difference and diversity by sharing his own experiences, and those of his birthplace idols. At the same time he had been braced for the worst-case scenario and rehearsed it in his head on the plane over.

In that scenario, a stuck-up school principal with an Oxbridge background would order him to refine his voice and speak the Queen's English to his students. "Over my dead body," Paul would retort, but the line and the rest of the unfolding scene, in which his snooty superior was tied in knots by his heavily barbed sarcasm, were never to see the light of day. No one cared where he was from, so long as he was a native English speaker. Mrs Ho thought he was Australian.

"Tell me place," said May, as they stepped off the ferry. "I find."

Paul sighed deeply at the sight of May's tablet, retrieved from her Hello Kitty backpack. The ten-minute ferry ride had been dominated by her creative insults but at least she had been practising the language he was being paid to transmit. The child scuffed a Croc against a wooden slat on the darkened ramp-way and he seized his chance to remove the computer from her chubby hands, slipping it into his own bag.

"No," she screamed. "Not fair!"

They left the dank green womb of the Star Ferry terminal, pausing to let their eyes adjust to the daylight. Tourists and locals were locked in battle, their faces hidden beneath cheerful umbrellas as they sought food, shelter or clothing.

"Today, you're going to ask someone for directions," Paul explained. "In English."

"No!" May reiterated then turned to the maid. "Give me."

The maid scowled but apparently felt she had no choice but to hand over the child's phone.

"Don't you dare," said Paul. "It's high time May learnt to fend for herself."

In private he was already feeling sorry for the poor mug destined to be on the receiving end of her charm. At least the directions themselves wouldn't be too taxing. The place they were heading for was easy to find – too easy if you had a fondness for smuggled smartphones, counterfeit watches, or getting high.

"Where Chungking Mansion?" May shouted at a Mainland couple.

They paused to admire the cute little Hong Konger, cooing at each other in Mandarin before ruling out a photo opp due to the conditions.

"Stupid Chinese," said May as they departed.

"Don't be so bloody rude," said Paul. Rain was dribbling down the neck of his Hawaiian shirt but he was determined that May would acquire at least one life skill before they ate. "Choose a western couple this time," he told her. The maid passed Paul her umbrella while she lit another cigarette. Eventually he spotted an elderly American couple and shoved May towards them.

"Hello, little girl," said the woman before turning to her husband. "Harry, do you have a few dollars?"

"I not beg," said May.

"I am not begging," Paul corrected her, prompting the craggy-faced husband to look him up and down.

Ignoring Paul, the wife lowered her hood and bent down to look May in the eye. Paul saw that the woman would have been very beautiful just a few years before. Her big blue eyes looked capable of seducing May. Maybe the kid had met her match.

"How can we help you today?" she asked.

"Please missus," May fingered an opportune raindrop as it nestled on a peachy cheek. "That man 'n lady take us from me mama and say I have to go live with 'em."

"What?" the woman stood and faced Paul. Her husband stepped in front of her. He also had faded film star looks. Even the overhanging skin that tempered his once perfect cheekbones was honeyed and cured like continental ham in a Christmas hamper.

"Do you mind telling us," he growled at Paul, "exactly what is going on here?"

Paul avoided mirrors these days. The last few years of heavy drinking had left him with puffy eyes, rash-red cheeks and a stomach that he could no longer hold in. Imagining himself through the angry American's eyes, he added some greasy twists of grey-brown hair plastered to his flaky, worry-rutted scalp, until he sank to his lowest point since waking between musty sheets that morning.

"We're having," he mumbled, struggling to summon up the words, "an English lesson."

"Oh I don't think so," said the woman, with flawless conviction. "Harry. Call 911. We have got to rescue this little sweetheart. And if we have to take her back to Maine with us then so be it."

May looked up at the adults.

"Wanna go Maine," she said.

Harry fumbled for a phone in his waterproof cape and Paul realised there was the very real possibility of him getting arrested or of May being kidnapped by do-gooders. With nothing, or perhaps everything to lose he grabbed May with one hand and the indifferent maid with the other before barging past the Americans and diving into the uncharted forest of umbrellas.

"Mind your own bloody business," he yelled over his shoulder.

"So rude," said May, satisfied with her work.

At the Indian curry house in a hidden armpit of Chungking Mansions, Paul sipped on his bottled lager and felt partially restored. The maid was taking tiny sips from a can of Coke, having made it clear she wasn't going to eat anything served in such a place. That left him and May.

"Hungry?" he asked.

"Yes," said May.

She finger-combed her hair, slick from the invasive rain, while humming to herself. Her eyes were bright again.

"Am I pretty?" she asked him.

The waiter brought over a basket of naan bread.

"Course you are, kid," he said, relieved to have escaped the crowds and happy for his beer.

"Am I prettier than your daughter?"

Comparatives – she was using comparatives. Good. Progress. But how the hell did she know about Poppy? Had he mentioned his estranged daughter to Mrs Ho in his interview? Perhaps he had. What a fool.

"Yes?" May raised her eyebrows hopefully.

"You're both very pretty," said Paul.

"Liar," May scowled. "Mama says I'm the most prettiest girl in the world."

"Prettiest," Paul corrected her, feeling tired again.

May took advantage of the waiter's fond gaze to list her demands.

"Chicken and pork and ice-cream and…and…"

"All together?" the waiter crinkled his handsome brown eyes.

"No, not together, stupid," said May, slamming shut the padded menu.

Paul turned to the man in sympathy.

"She'll have the veggie curry with rice," he said. "Like mine, only smaller."

"Want meat," May wailed. "Meat make May strong."

"God help us," Paul murmured, sending the waiter away. "You're lucky to be getting anything at all after your performance today, madam."

"Vegetables make May smell," she fanned her wrinkled-up nose. "Smell bad, like *gweilo*. Stinky *gweilo*!"

The maid stifled her laughter.

"Vegetarian food is good and natural," Paul explained. "It's what the monks eat in the temples. The monks that think about stuff deeply instead of shouting their heads off or making things up, like you do. Like the politicians do, come to think of it."

"Mama says we can eat anything under sun. Anything we want."

"Yes, that's what an old Chinese emperor said. And that's why you end up eating chicken hearts, shark's-fin soup and slow-cooked terrapin in this part of the world. But he was speaking a long time ago, you see, when people didn't have enough to eat."

"I'm hungry!" May shouted, flinging her spoon and fork to the floor.

"You wouldn't eat your dog, Mitzy, would you?" Paul asked as he picked up her cutlery.

He couldn't help himself. He knew the suggestion that her beloved lapdog might one day be lunch would send her into symphonic overtures of grief. Yet from what he could gather she tortured the poor animal almost as often as she tortured him. The curry arrived and he added May's to his own and ordered another beer as the maid tried to console the demonic brat. A group of West African men took a nearby table.

"We're not safe here," said the maid.

"You're a racist," said Paul, sipping his beer.

But while the first beer had eased his pain, the next had him musing on Poppy. Was her mother creating a child more or less monstrous than May? Were the displaced Africans missing their own children as much as he missed Poppy? It didn't seem possible – they were smiling, joking. But then he knew more than most about hiding his feelings. He had learnt long ago that teaching was a form of acting. Back then he had no idea that his whole life would become part of this act. He swallowed a final spoonful of spiced potato.

"Shall we go?" he asked, burping softly.

On their way out he stopped at a couple of shops in the muddle of small businesses that existed opposite the Peninsula Hotel, within yards of the designer couturiers. It might have seemed dangerously multicultural to the older Chinese population but he welcomed having somewhere in Asia's so-called "World City" where he could pick up a phone charger at a reasonable price or a bag of samosas to accompany his evening wine binge. May was fussed over by traders from the four corners. He hoped that by the time they reached the red-tiled entrance to the nearest MTR station she would have softened slightly, but there was still one final indignity awaiting him as they segued with the crowds on Nathan Road.

"Goodbye, May," he smiled at her, thinking of the money. "Don't forget to practise your English with Sophia."

Then he turned to the maid. "Tell Mrs Ho that I need the bank transfer to be on time this month. I have rent to pay. And bills."

"Whatever," said the maid, a phrase he had inadvertently taught her.

Paul turned his back on the pair and began walking towards the ferry. In thirty minutes they would be safely secreted behind a seven-foot sliding gate in low-rise Kowloon Tong and he would be ordering his traditional post-May pint at The Yellow Brolly in Sai Ying Pun.

Just as the thought of her was receding he felt a short but meaningful burst of pain blossoming across his denimed backside. He turned immediately, thinking someone might be snatching his wallet with a casual – and frankly unnecessary – brutality. Instead, he found May standing there with a goofy smile on her face. Quite clearly she had just kicked him up the arse.

"What the hell do you think you're doing?" he asked.

The maid was slouched, hands on hips, some metres back. May didn't say a word. Instead she put a finger to her lips in a wanton display of ignorance. Paul looked around for witnesses to his humiliation. If anyone had seen what had just happened they were already well on their way to wherever they were going. This was TST. Everyone was wrapped up in their own glassy-eyed urban adventure. He would let this one go.

"Time to go home, May," he said, turning again.

Five paces later the same thing happened. He looked appealingly towards the maid but she hadn't budged from the underground entrance. May looked up at him with the same stupid smile. Time stood still. The noise and the lights and the faces of Kowloon disappeared. It was just him and her in a mismatched face-off. He prepared to do something he knew he would regret.

CHAPTER TWO

Fenton Wilkes wondered why he had regained consciousness. In moments of rage he speculated on how it might feel to crush a man's head using his workshop vice. Tonight he knew how his imagined victim would feel. The explanation for his arousal slithered past his legs and into the globular shadows at the edge of his vision. His spectacles had abandoned him during his three-metre fall into the drainage channel. Practically blind, he decided to assume the vanishing portent had been a rat snake and not a many-banded crake, whose cheery insignia signalled death out here, alone in the jungle, miles from anywhere – the way he liked it. Yet from walking beside this ditch day and night for the last fifteen years, he knew it provided somewhat of a highway for snakes of all varieties, and that it would be a good idea to shift his battered body up and out of there as quickly as he could.

Not so easy. His knees and elbows were cut and scraped from the fall – that he fully accepted as par for the course. What he failed to grasp at first were the pins and needles in his wrists. He felt one and then the other. Blood. Tacky, some of it already dried. How long had he been out cold? Ouch. Fucking bastard. There was glass in the wounds. What the hell had he done to himself this time? He looked up at the stars, usually so generous with their light over Lantau but tonight hiding from him. It was dark and he was blind and he appeared to have been trying to continue a family tradition of deadly misadventure.

But this fractured theory wouldn't hold. Everything his family had done, Fenton had done the opposite. No amount of booze would have persuaded him to follow in their tracks, of that he was sure. He wasn't a risk-taker like his great uncle, the wartime ace, or his father, who gambled his last penny on stocks and shares. Had he been trying to kill himself, in the vein of more melancholy ancestors, he could have done it in the comfort of his own home, a few hundred metres down this winding path and a short tiptoe through the jungly substances. It didn't make sense

He sniffed his wrists. Wine. Thick, sweet red wine. Of course. He had picked up a bottle in Mui Wo to take home with him. One for the road or the sofa or to find half-drunk next to the sick bucket beside his bed the next day. It would have been swinging around in the long, loose pocket of his mackintosh when he fell. What else? Oh yes, the taxi.

"Why do you people never speak to each other?" he had asked the two prison guards sitting in the back of the cab.

Silence. The men were tense, understandably. The high security prison between the coast and the enormous green hills behind it had a reputation for brutality and death. The worst of the worst were put there and few got out alive – worn down by the years or eviscerated in short bursts of lethal conflict on the dry-as-a-bone football pitch or in the showers. Fenton had drunk too much and his private thoughts spilled into the car as their driver sloshed them around corners and up tight, winding roads into the bosom of the island.

"It would have been different in the old days," he explained. "The British may have been heavy-handed at times, but they knew how to keep the triads apart."

One of the guards glared at him. Fenton hiccupped.

"No offence intended," he reassured them. "Just don't be scared of using the whip – insert modern equivalent here. I got caned at school all the time. Didn't do me any harm."

In no time at all they were at the dam and the guards got out and took a moonlit path towards the floodlit prison.

"Miserable buggers," Fenton remarked, checking the coins they'd given him as their contribution towards the shared journey.

Then what? It was self-explanatory. He had stumbled out of the taxi. The moon had gone in and he had fallen down here. Perhaps he had been trying to walk home with his eyes closed to prove it could be done in the event of a random apocalypse. It wouldn't be completely out of character.

"Shite," he retrieved a shard of glass from his forearm. Bloody fucking cheap thin glass. Asking for trouble. He should sue the French as soon as he'd finished suing Hong Kong's Water Supplies Department. He wrapped a monogrammed handkerchief around his most seriously damaged wrist and clogged the other with tissue and a gingerly positioned shirtsleeve. He shifted his aching buttocks and began to palm the damp concrete in his immediate vicinity. Anything sharp, even a clump of crispy foliage, caused him to retract his hand. Damn nerves were shot but eventually he found his specs. One lens had survived the fall; the other was nowhere to be seen.

Finding his feet with difficulty, he grimaced at the memory of the tall tales he had told in the Yellow Brolly since it became his pub of choice. In one he was an ex-SAS operative able to survive in the bush for weeks on nothing more than lightly seasoned grubs, in another he was an RAF veteran who had ejector-seated himself to freedom during the Falklands conflict. All in all, he had a lot to live up to. Fortunately, what he needed in this case was just a biscuit-sized foothold in the convex wall. This crumble in the concrete that in normal circumstances would have invited a tirade against shoddy Chinese workmanship allowed him to haul himself back onto the path, boosting his chances of survival exponentially.

Shuffling towards home, he reached into his wine-soaked pocket and retrieved his pack of cigarettes. All but one was snapped, and that was thoroughly rouged. His hands shook as he tried to light it with his three remaining matches. Shock. Delayed shock. He flung the smoking gear into the ditch. Let the snakes get cancer. Then he remembered the python he had seen the week before, easing its way along the high road, positioning itself beside the slowing cars, as if assisting its human inferiors to gauge its immense length. Had it been eight, nine feet?

"Nice snakeys," said Fenton, trying to speed up without inflicting further pain on his limbs. "Leave old Fenton alone tonight. Go find yourself a nice fat cat in the village."

By the time the moon returned the sun was almost up. Fenton had the best view in Hong Kong, perhaps the world, at dawn on each new day. He could sip coffee on a bench outside the abandoned house he had made functional through sheer bloody-mindedness and admire the small garden he had hacked out of the jungle. Here he grew oranges, avocados, crab apples, sweet potatoes and some unidentifiable herbs that Miriam had cultivated. But his small patch paled into insignificance compared to the magnificent, mountainous view to which his eyes travelled next, different every morning yet always the same chunk of nature, unconquerable by the follies of man.

But first he had to get past his own lines of defence. A sign at the start of the rough trail that led to home insisted TRESPASSERS WILL BE SHOT and was displayed next to a cartoon image of Robin Hood loading up an arrow. He still wasn't sure about the sign. It gave out mixed messages. Perhaps he was trying to amuse the few friends that ventured out this way; but in doing so he may have been risking the lives of any intruders who also saw the funny side – he really did have a crossbow, and he would use it if necessary, though perhaps only when the banks collapsed and the idiots finally discovered that all the riches of the world belonged to him, Fenton Wilkes. Yes, he would be willing to kill to protect his way of life here. Which sane person wouldn't?

"Bloody heck," he spluttered, shimmying under the chest-high cheese wire which ran from tree A to tree B. It wasn't taut enough to decapitate the postman but he had neither the strength nor urge to grapple with it now. His feet kicked up loose earth until he could finally raise himself again. His hands were stinging. He looked down at himself. Filthy. How fortunate that Miriam wasn't here to see this – she wouldn't have let him over the threshold.

The snakes would be back in their burrows by now, he hoped. And if they weren't the smaller ones at least were likely to have been scared off by his moaning and groaning. It amazed him that people actively searched for them. When Paul last visited he had been stunned to learn that the idiot actively pursued the things – seeking out their hibernation spots in winter; taking photos as they yawned themselves awake and wondered what they should have for their first meal in months.

The man was unhinged. When Paul rolled up his sleeve as they shared a joint, Fenton had half-expected to see a series of puncture wounds, but instead his friend revealed a tattoo of a cobra that encircled his arm, the digestive spasms of the beast tastefully recreated by Paul's serotonin-pumping veins. Scousers. Hopeless romantics the lot of them – something to do with Liverpool being a port city, but then the same couldn't be said for Hong Kong. He could only tolerate people staying with him for two nights max, but he would have given his last yam to see Paul's chubby face about now. Instead it was his marauding black-and-white mongrel, Hunter, who came out to greet him as he tried to unlatch the gate with his gammy fingers.

"Hello boy," he said. "Daddy's been a fucking idiot."

Fenton missed the dawn – sleeping for ten hours straight and waking in the afternoon, devoid of liquid and with a headache like a series of precisely planted head-butts. He rolled over on the sofa, his skinny frame sufficient to squash every minor injury against skin or bone until he became a burning cocktail of pain.

"Help me," he wailed. "Kill me now."

Had he been dead already, who knows what might have happened, but seeing his master was still alive, Hunter waddled over from his basket and licked Fenton's grazed knuckles. Like him, the dog was old and stupid. If he had tied a note to its collar and sent it on a rescue mission, it would have wandered through its modest territory chasing butterflies then returned hours later expecting dinner. He needed to find his phone. A painstaking search of his coat, during which his fingers were pricked on more crumbs of French glass, revealed he had his wallet (empty) but no phone. He must have left it in the drainage ditch, or perhaps even the taxi. He declared it lost, presumed broken or stolen.

At the window he looked at the light on the hills. It must have been raining most of the day. Now the greenery was letting off steam. Kites circled high and wide between the two gradually sloping peaks nearest to him, half a day's walk away. He considered going up to the road and hitchhiking his way to Tai Po or Mui Wo until he saw himself in the bathroom mirror. Cars could only travel with a local's permit here. Even someone he hadn't officially fallen out with in the surrounding area would think twice about picking up an angry-looking Fenton with a half-closed eye and purple forehead.

"Bastards," he muttered – a pre-emptive strike.

He assembled a first-aid kit as best he could; finding blister plasters in his workshop and Miriam's PMT tablets in the bedside cabinet. He filled the sick bucket with soapy water and located a half-clean hand towel. He took the Buzzcocks off the record player and replaced them with early Hawkwind, then proceeded to slowly operate on himself.

By early evening he was feeling better in all but two significant ways. The raw pain of his wounds had – for the most part – been replaced by a healing itch. His head throbbed only if he got up too quickly or turned it suddenly. The next part of his tailor-made aftercare programme was – indisputably – a celebratory cigarette and a drink with which to toast his unlikely survival. Neither was possible. He made several painful circuits of his small home to no avail. The kitchen drawers were rifled, the empty packets and bottles from his dustbin thoroughly exhausted. The wood glue in the workshop might have appealed to his younger self, but he was fifty-five this year – solvents had no hope of resolving this feeling of entitlement.

"I damn well deserve a blasted drink," he told Hunter, who smiled up at him with his tongue out.

At dusk he took the crossbow off the wall and went outside to shoot something. No beasts stirred in the half-light so he aimed for the target at the far end of the rough patch of scrub he liked to call his lawn. Here a range of photocopied images painstakingly copied and blown up from the *South China Morning Post* were pinned to the flaky bark of a half-dead tree. Fenton fired off a bolt then limped over to remind himself who his latest victim was. He raised his eyebrows and chuckled soundlessly.

"Sorry Hilary old girl, you've been through quite enough already."

Hunter barked him indoors, demanding food. After feeding the dog, he fired up his blackened wok and cooked up some random nubs and spikes of veg in soy sauce with a touch of chilli. The TV was snapped on and quickly muted when some campaigning politicians appeared on screen. He slipped into unconsciousness muttering something about things never changing but when he woke up the next morning he was a new man.

CHAPTER THREE

The noise propelled him out of bed but Frank Taylor was not yet ready to burst into the open-plan living space of the flat. Normally he could think himself out of the darkest hangover – just as he could think himself through the days of unemployment familiar to most artists – but the black dog that smothered him this morning was unusually friendly. It led him to doubt the quantity and quality of fire in his belly as he stood tensed at the edge of the mattress. Sure, he was unusually fit for a man of fifty-two. The belly in question was nothing if not flat and rigid. But on most days he woke with back pain of some description. He had seen better people than him in their forties and fifties escorted urgently from the building by cancer. A total abdication of physical legitimacy could never be ruled out and might occur at any time.

There it was again – a careless banging from the kitchen. The burglars evidently thought no one was home. He cursed himself anew. Not only had his so-called drinking buddies led him up another piss-stained cul-de-sac the night before but he had insisted to Kim, just weeks earlier, that a ground-floor apartment in a village house would be preferable to a more expensive first-floor or rooftop residence. Since then they had both been bitten by the same bloodthirsty mosquito (executed at dawn after hours of painstaking detective work), had a spider move into an unreachable corner of their bathroom, and a drug-addled neighbour staying the night after locking himself out; and now this latest invasion from the ungovernable Lamma landscape. Kim was either going to kill him or leave him – both of which she had tried to do before.

"Coming – ready or not."

And with that he charged into the body of the flat in nothing more than his grey boxer shorts, armed only with a sense of extreme righteousness. Yet his friends from the Yellow Brolly knew Frank had a little more up his sleeve than would be immediately apparent to any interloper. A distant ancestor was alleged to have been General Francis "Loony" Leopold who had fought with wild abandon for the losing side in the Napoleonic Wars. A great-aunt had taken delight in dressing young Frank as Napoleon, while his older, taller brother was always Wellington. He called on this uncertain pedigree as he formed his piano-playing fingers into fists and prepared for battle.

"Jesus Christ, you look terrible," said Kim, sipping her coffee.

"What the fuck...what the fuck are you doing here?" asked Frank, unable to stop himself completing an aggressive circuit of the small downstairs.

"I don't work Saturdays anymore. Remember?"

"It's...it's the weekend then?"

"Have some coffee," Kim sighed and clanked around some more with the coffee pot until it was full and on the stove again. "Tell me about your night."

This was a better reception than Frank might have expected. Most live-in wage earners would take exception to their partner waking up, stinking of booze, with no idea of the time or day of the week. Perhaps he deserved this reprieve. There had been blazing rows aplenty when they still lived in the city. When he lost his teaching gig at the university and decided to focus on his own work, it had driven them to the edge of poverty and almost split them up. Kim had to give up her guitar tuition and go back to pole-dancing in nightclubs under the stage name Kitty Chow. All her smiles were used up by the time she got home. A change had been required. They were happier here, despite the intrusions, and the rent was cheaper by half. Which made her black eye, and the rumours surrounding it, all the more ironic.

"Weird night," he said.

"Who was there?"

"The usual suspects – Nick, Paul, Fenton."

"Three very boring people. Why was it weird?"

"Well," Frank wondered how much he could say. "It was the ferry home more than anything. Another three, four familiar faces – people who shook my hand and said "Nice to meet you" when we moved here – totally blanked me."

"Maybe you were scary-drunk."

"I don't get scary-drunk."

"They don't know that."

"They don't know anything, which makes it ten times fucking worse when they accuse me of being a wife-beater."

"You have to be married to be a wife-beater."

"Funny. Anyway, I get off the damn boat – incidentally, why's there so much graffiti around this place? There's no graffiti on the sea walls at Cheung Chau."

"Cheung Chau smells bad."

"It smells of fish, like an island should. So, I leave the pier and I'm about to head up the jungle path when I see that gormless woman with legs up to here – Molly, is it?"

"Molly Ransom."

"That's the one, and she's with her kids – Christ knows what they're still doing out at 1am – and she sort of herds them away from me while giving me a look."

"What look were you giving her? Did you think about that, Frank? Ever heard of mirroring?"

"Bullshit," Frank slurped his coffee, renewed – pumping the ammunition amassed in the bedroom into a new target. "It's the self-righteous posturing. The cold-shoulder loftily administered like we give a shit about these people. Why can't they come out and say something? If they had an ounce of integrity they'd ask, 'What really happened to Kim's eye because we don't believe your story about her tripping over a box of LPs when you moved in?'"

"Well, actually," Kim was making French toast in their cast iron pan. "Someone did say something at the café yesterday."

"What?"

"Promise not to get angry."

Frank slumped into their soggy sofa and began to massage his temple.

"Okay, promise."

"First, tell me what your plans were for today."

"My what?"

"Tell me what you were going to do today, if I hadn't been here."

"You know," Frank gestured to the books piled up around the flat, many of which they had bought second-hand from Scampi, a hippy who regularly toured the island with a supermarket trolley full of variable literature. "Research."

"Okay. Anything else?"

"I might have walked down to the front and—"

"—had a beer?"

"Sometimes a beer helps me finish a poem."

Kim slung a chipped plate with two unsliced pieces of toast into his lap. For the first time he realised she was dressed in her thigh-hugging jeans and black leather jacket, as if she was on her way out.

"Strange," she pursed her red lips. Frank didn't like to say, but in the morning light it was clear that her black eye needed a little more concealer applied to it. "You haven't read me any new poems for a while now."

"I've hit a dry spell."

"Do you know what's also strange?"

"No – I don't. Not this morning."

"That I work in a café in the middle of Lamma and when you take a break you don't come to see me, but instead hang around with the single mums at the wine bar."

"It's not a wine bar, it's—"

"Which makes it all the more difficult to know what to say when I have people – nosy, interfering but well-meaning people – coming to Vegasaurus specifically to ask if I'm okay."

"They did what? Do-gooding pension-hoarding bastard retirees."

"I swore you hadn't touched me," Kim continued, ignoring his slur. "And they swore they see you down at the wine bar by 12pm every other day."

"We all have to manage our relationship with alcohol," Frank told her firmly. "You have a rum and coke and you start sticking your tongue down every fella's throat on the dance-floor."

"Not true."

"I have a bucket of beer and it's water off a duck's back."

"Ever wondered why that is, Frank?"

"What do you mean?" he asked, wondering if he could persuade her to stay.

"You're numb," she said quietly, putting her guitar in its soft case and slinging it over her shoulder. "You have been since we moved here."

"Maybe it's the power-station."

"It's not the power-station, Frank. Any more than this black eye is from a karate chop."

"Off to see your other man?" he asked as she opened the door and let in the dank fug of day.

"I'm going to give Jess's son Felix his first guitar lesson. He's eleven years old."

"I see. Kiss?"

"Maybe later," she sighed, closing the door behind her.

He tried to eat the rest of the French toast but it made him feel sick so he went into their tiny kitchen and flung the slices out of the back door. Outside the scenery was starting to twitch and chirrup. God knows what creature would find his breakfast in the long grass and use it to strengthen and embolden itself. The door was stiff and he made a fuss of shutting it. A neighbour appeared in the better-tended plot opposite – a middle-aged Chinese man in vest and shorts. Frank waved but didn't wait for a reaction. He made sure all the doors and blinds were closed and turned on the air-con. He would lie on the sofa and treat himself to ten minutes of icy gusts and then he would open his notebook and write today's date.

Hours later he woke up, freezing. His old-fashioned mobile was honking from the bedroom. Was it always so loud? He snapped off the air-con and went to find his phone. "PAUL" was flashing on the display. He let it ring a little longer while he located a T-shirt and sweatpants. It was really fucking cold. What were you meant to do in a place like this? "Isn't it great to be in Asia but still have seasons?" people never tired of saying. Not really. Not if three of them were unbelievably hot and humid and every year eighty per cent of your vintage suits, paisley shirts and suede shoes rotted.

"Hello?"

"It's Paul."

"I know, I saw your name on the thingy."

"Oh yeah."

It didn't sound like Paul. The man was a sad sack par excellence but he usually had enough of what passed for scouse wit to see him through basic conversations with friends as old as him.

"What do you want, Paul? I'm working."

"Thing is…"

Paul sounded distant, echoey.

"Where are you?"

"Cheung Chau."

"That explains it."

"Explains what?"

"You sound like you're trapped in a K-hole."

"I'm here because…the police rang."

"The police?"

Booze-induced paranoia suggested he was being busted for some long forgotten bar-room brawl, witnessed by pedantic Paul who struggled to tell a lie. But why would the cops have asked him to report to the Cheung Chau station? Had they mixed up their outlying islands?

"Nick's dead."

"Nick's what? It sounded like you just said Nick was—"

"I've just identified his body. He was at the Gloucester."

"You're kidding."

The silence told him it was no joke.

"You okay, mate?" he asked. "Want me to come over?"

"No point. What's left to do?"

"How did he die?"

"Take a guess."

"Suicide?"

"Didn't manage it first time. Lit some charcoal but ran out of patience. Took a running jump off his balcony."

"My god…Nick."

"Can't say we weren't warned."

"I know but we all say things, don't we? After a few pints."

Frank lowered himself onto the mattress. What he had concealed from Kim he couldn't hide from himself.

"Has this got to do with what he said last night, about him and Lennox getting divorced?"

Another pause. A click on the line. An intake of breath. Chinese voices in the background.

"Maybe," Paul said at last. "Look, I've got to go. Brolly tomorrow? Post-mortem?"

"You always did have a way with words," Frank regurgitated a short, bitter laugh. "See you there at eight."

"Bye, Frank. Sorry you had to hear this."

"Same here."

The phone battery died that instant. Frank took a pillow and punched it across the room. Then he found the small penknife with a mother of pearl handle on their bedside table, thumbed it open and pricked his little finger with the blade. A bubble of blood was his reward. The pain felt good. He began to feel more human. Today was not a day to be numb. He went and fetched his notebook and began to write.

CHAPTER FOUR

What a great bunch of friends. Not without their faults, but who is? I was lucky to know them. After spilling the beans on their foibles and drawing back the curtain on some raw and private moments you probably feel I should be telling you a little more about myself. That's not how it works, but I take your point so will concede a few more facts, such as they are. You already know I'm around a decade younger than these metaphysical greybeards. Maybe you don't think I've achieved the same level of disappointment with life. I would argue against that assumption. For although none of the men concerned are currently pulling up trees in their fields, they have in the past achieved a level of success that in me – tell no one – strikes a melancholic cord of envy.

Take Frank. At eighteen he had travelled the world on merchant ships, back when the globe was an unread book and you didn't inherit air miles, orgasm over Airbnbs, or download heat maps of hipster hotspots. If you were lucky, you remembered a newspaper article or found a well-thumbed guidebook before disembarkation; otherwise you went in blind. Frank and a companion got caught up in a riot in India. When the police chucked the protestors' rocks back at them, they returned them with interest to the police. Why not? That's what punks did. He was lucky to get out alive.

Then there was the time he tried to disrupt the running of the bulls in Pamplona by intercepting the charging animals and urging them to rise above human provocation, lay down their horns and strike. That saw him hospitalised for three weeks. What did it matter? He was young, and scars were sexy. So far as I can tell, Frank returned to education only to pick up the fundamentals he needed to embellish his adventures. Studying English at SOAS, he devoured the reading list in days; then moved on to publishing his own poetry in self-bound pamphlets. His tutors were astounded. He cleaned out the trophy cabinet, or equivalent. The reason he isn't a household name today? A healthy dislike of networking and unwillingness to compromise, if you ask me. But what do I know?

Nothing I do could be described as artistic. I can hear Fenton saying "same here"; arguing that the aesthetic affectations of impractical art forms are the product of over-education or parental indulgence. Yet quite clearly the things he crafts in his workshop, in that damn mysterious place of his in the jungle, are nothing if not minor works of art. I have seen his family dining tables, on the one hand immensely practical, built to last for generations, on the other hand – or rather, carved into the buttery wood at the foot of each tapering leg – a three-dimensional heart, suggesting that he wishes these families to have a better time of it than he did. I won't embarrass him further, but Fenton has also been known to create ingenious clockwork toys for his friends' kids at Christmas. When have my hands ever shaped anything that might delight another living soul?

Paul is a slightly different story. In the lexicon of our forebears he would have been described as "artless". In other words, I've seen nothing to persuade me that he isn't the nicest guy on the planet. Apparently, he ran a small community theatre in darkest Merseyside back in the day, but the way he's expressed his fellow feeling and optimism for the species since I've known him is through teaching. How many people could do that job? I remember being dragged along on a field-trip he'd arranged when his support teacher pulled a sickie. It was around the time Lennox had persuaded me to sign up for numerous job agencies specialising in accountancy and insurance. Being supremely unqualified for any such roles, I was twiddling my thumbs, and my thumbs were twiddling other parts of my anatomy, while waiting for a call.

As you can imagine, the prospect of escorting thirty teenagers to Sai Kung Country Park wasn't much more appealing than being home alone, but this was soon after I'd first met Paul and I suppose I was trying to impress him. At the time he was at the top of his game. The kids remained indifferent to me but Paul was like a magnet to them. They swirled around him, asking questions, or showing him the latest bit of crap they'd found while we were beachcombing. I felt like a spare part – a six-foot lump of fleshy detritus in a rather nice suit. I was profoundly envious of Paul that day, but I was realistic too. I knew his glowing countenance had much to do with the profound connection he was enjoying with his daughter, Poppy. Lennox and I had ruled out kids as a viable option, for now at least. How could I compete?

Let me tell you another story about Paul. Two years on, and a lot of water has passed under our respective bridges. We sit as single men on a burnished stone bench sipping beer at the edge of a Wan Chai park at 2am, unwilling to return to our bachelor hovels. Sharpened fronds emerge from the darkness behind us, scratching at our necks, urging us to leave. But what's the point? Hong Kong is peaceful at this hour; almost otherworldly. The daytime crowds and evening shoppers have long since departed to their coffins. The 7-Eleven is open all night. No Hong Kong policeman is going to tell two harmless white dudes to move along.

"Do you know what the worst thing is?" Paul is asking me.

I know what the worst thing is. It's so bad I can't even interrupt him to say that I know what the worst thing is, because that might deny Paul whatever slight relief he gleans from sharing it with me for the fifteenth time.

"Her grandmother."

"Her grandmother?" I take another sip of Tsing Tao Draft. It tastes watery after our nightcap whiskies at the Yellow Brolly.

"The mad bitch beats her with a bamboo cane. Know where?"

"Where?"

"On the soles of her feet. On the soles of my poor Poppy's feet."

This isn't like Paul. He's too conscious of other people's wants and needs to dwell in self-pity for long. It's the alcohol that's making him dwell. I wonder how much he drinks each night these days. Since moving out of the flat Lennox and I handpicked in Sheung Wan and into my illegal rooftop apartment round the corner from here, my average has increased threefold. I tell myself I can take it, but at other times I worry. Last weekend I used bug spray to kill an insect interloper. The poor thing stood on its hind dozen legs and twisted and turned in a prolonged death dance for me as I watched from the bed with hot tears rolling down my face.

"Killer Powell" they called me after I confessed to my crime in the pub.

"It's okay," I tell Paul. "We'll find you a better lawyer. We'll get your visiting rights back."

Paul shakes his head, shakes his can and prepares to fetch us another.

"You don't understand, Nick," he tells me. "This place is cruel...heartless... If Poppy wasn't here I'd—"

There are cracks here, it's true. The secret is not to fall down them. If you do, you will be consumed. A young man is running down the middle of Queen's Road, dodging the sparse, medicated traffic. He is barefoot. He is panting convincingly. There is a red welt across one side of his face. This could be a birthmark, or he may have been smacked across the face. If anything is going to snap Paul out of his melancholy it is the sight of someone in greater need than him running directly towards us.

"Oh shit," I see it coming a fraction too late.

"Twenty dollars," pants the youngster. Paul is already reaching for his wallet – the sucker.

"What's happened?" I ask.

The boy's face is sallow, the neon from the nearby shops rouging his pronounced cheekbones but failing to bring his features to life. His eyes shine black like Neolithic tar-pits. He is a creature of the night.

"Need money," he says. "Bad men."

Later I will ask Paul if he thinks the stranger is deliberately hiding his language abilities. Even relatively uneducated Hong Kongers speak better English than the mute, Wi-Fried Brits I encounter at home these days. In any case, it's my right to be suspicious, lest we forget George W. Bush's deliberate dumbing down to win the votes of the defiantly ignorant that Trump so graciously inherited further down the line. Paul says it's hard to tell, but he thinks the lad is the real deal – a genuine dumbass.

"Where have you come from?" I ask, putting a stiff arm between his outstretched hand and Paul's gaping wallet.

"Restaurant," he points in the direction of Stone Nullah Lane.

"Nowhere in the new development," I tell Paul. "He's been somewhere subterranean. Somewhere up a back alley that's escaped gentrification, possibly by supernatural means."

"You're drunk," Paul tells me. "He's just a lad in trouble. Had a fight with his Mrs or his mum or something."

"Where are his shoes?" I ask Paul, and then the boy. "Where are your shoes?"

He shrugs and smiles and in the same languorous movement manages to extract a fifty-dollar note from Paul's elastic reach.

"Christ," I despair.

The youth turns to me expectantly. I reach for my own wallet and open it. I ignore the neat row of 100s and instead extract a business card.

"If you give me a call," I lock him with my negotiator's eyes. "I'll buy you a new pair of trainers, okay?"

He snatches my card, pockets it, and glares into the semi-darkness from where he's run. Just a couple of winking indicators, dormant traffic lights and lines of shuttered up shops – so far as we can tell – but he seems spooked all over again. Without another word he sets off in the opposite direction at speed, disappearing beyond our 7-Eleven and heading towards the nearest shut-up MTR station.

"What did you do that for?" asks Paul.

"Your round was it?" I smile sweetly.

"Fucking hell, Nick," he grimaces. "You really are a tight arse."

They say we only tease those we love. Paul's insult suggests I'm as beloved by my friends as they are by me. Lennox never teased me, not towards the end anyway. She became deadly serious – and deathly dull. Eventually I realised a person that vivacious couldn't possibly be corked so effectively by little old me, and her unstoppable social energy must be finding release elsewhere – in another bed, in another country perhaps. By this point she was flying around the world as the youngest partner in her law firm. She was beyond dealing with the likes of Paul and me, however much we might have needed her for our own reasons.

"Time for bed then," I say. "Too much excitement for one night."

We trudge east along Queen's Road together. Soon I will take a right towards my walk-up with its 360-degree windows on the world; where artificial light seamlessly merges with the dawn and the first bus rumbles you awake at 5am. Paul will continue to his studio apartment in Causeway Bay where he's staying on a week-to-week basis while he works out what to do. We're in limbo but remain undefeated. We only have to think of the Brits sent to this outpost in their scratchy woollen uniforms, struck down by disease and buried in the cemeteries of Happy Valley and Stanley, to know how lucky we are.

"Teaching tomorrow?" I ask Paul as we prepare to part.

"New job," he tells me. "Private tutoring the daughter of some hot-shot single mum. I'm looking forward to it, Nicky. I rarely get that one-on-one time in the classroom."

"Sounds right up your street."

"We'll see. How about you, job hunting or freelancing?"

"Same difference."

"Heard much from her?"

"She's busy."

"Give it time. Not like she's going to divorce you. Both of you needed a breather, that's all. You see, my ex – she hates me."

"How could anyone hate you Paul?"

He shrugs off my condescension.

"You and Lennox, you've still got a chance," he explains. "Just be patient with her, Nicky. She'll realise what she's missing soon enough."

"Perhaps. Goodnight Paul."

"Night, mate."

My leg muscles burn as I tackle the near-vertical road home. Ship Street, Schooner Street, Moon Street, Star Street. Before the land reclamations, most of this area was underwater. Our old Brit forebears didn't all die of cholera or dysentery. Plenty fell into the harbour while unloading boats right here. Others died on the sea when howling typhoons arrived unannounced. There was an exception, there always is. Constable Ernest Goucher, mauled to death by a tiger in 1915 – a tiger, in Hong Kong! Can you believe it? If I'm going to go, I decide I'm going to go like him, between the jaws of something wild and untameable.

CHAPTER FIVE

The Yellow Brolly was entering its third act. Fortunately for the purists, it had taken its surviving fixtures and fittings – including its unusually diverse clientele – from one location to the next to the next. Established in Lan Kwai Fong, within range of the shot-toting teenagers who maraud through the nightlife zone as a rite of passage, it demanded a certain tolerance of its older punters. First known as Think Tank, it was little more than an outdoor patio with barrels for tables and notoriously wonky stools for the drinkers. A video from the time shows a youthful Jeanie outlining the pub's aspirations to a local news team while taking and delivering orders. "This is somewhere people can relax and be themselves," she yells above a lost weekend's cacophony, her cheeks a little rosier back then – her short spiky hair not yet silver.

After the handover in '97, when debate about the future of the former colony began in earnest, Think Tank became somewhere intellectuals could hide themselves amongst wannabe-intellectuals and discuss what could be done to help preserve Hong Kong's fragile autonomy. Leading figures from the pro-dem movement took the barrels at the back where Jeanie manned the bar, while facing the street were tourists who wanted a break from the neon madness. In between sat the long-term expats, discussing the latest news items in the *South China Morning Post*. When the government tried to implement Article 23 of the Basic Law in 2003, a bill that threatened to outlaw even mild forms of subversion in the city, the bar closed for the day so that Jeanie and the regulars could join the protests – a tradition that continued in its next two manifestations.

When Paul and Frank had first known Think Tank, it was located down a Sheung Wan backstreet and about to change its name to honour the memory of 2014's Occupy movement, during which umbrellas had been used to fend off the teargas expelled by panicking policemen. They had been aware of it before by reputation, but had only recently found space in their lives – their partners being sufficiently understanding, or absent – to take over from the previous generation of regulars. There followed a few years of bonding on their part as a small social circle of mature men – equally prone to flights of fancy and crashing fatigue – emerged. Bromances were discouraged but a certain comradeship was formed between half-a-dozen or so expats, of which they, Nick and Fenton represented a controlling interest.

"Drinks are on me tonight," Jeanie insisted, positioning two chilled steins of Tsing Tao beside them at the table unofficially reserved for regulars.

"Cheers Jeanie," said Paul. Frank nodded in agreement.

"I didn't know Nick very well," she continued. "But I know he meant a lot to you."

She pointed to a photo of the gang above the communal bookshelf and smiled in sympathy, then retreated diplomatically to the bar.

Latterly the Yellow Brolly had moved west down Queen's Road to Sai Ying Pun. Despite the escalating rents, Jeanie had snagged the first three floors of a walk-up neither prohibitively expensive to rent nor condemned to regeneration – yet. The drinking zone was smaller than that in Sheung Wan. Four stools at the minimalist bar, behind which she and her staff quartered fresh limes for mojitos and tended a tangle of wires for phone recharging purposes; three tables in the snug, one wall of which housed the colourful bookshelf and unisex water closet, the other two the often garish art created by grateful patrons over the years. To subsidise the drinks, Jeanie ran a hostel on the floors above and maintained a separate desk and matrix of pigeonholes to this end at the new entrance to the Brolly.

"Did you get in touch with Fenton?" Paul asked.

"Couldn't get through," Frank told him. "Phone's off. He'll still be recovering from Friday. Never seen him so hammered."

"We were all in pretty bad shape by the time we left here."

"I walked Nick to his cab." Frank still hadn't touched his beer. "I said goodbye. I told him things would be okay – that you've got to experience everything at least once in this life. Divorce being just another one of them."

"Don't blame yourself."

"I'm not blaming myself," Frank squished the condensation on the handle of his glass. "I'm blaming you maudlin bastards."

"What?"

"You and Fenton with your woe-is-me love lives. Filling Nick's head full of doom and—"

"Cut that out Frank," Paul spoke with a quiet authority he rarely managed to achieve; his attempts at discipline being routinely parried by friends and students alike. "It's no one's fault. Nick was his own man. Since when did anything we said have any effect on him?"

Frank took a slug of lager.

"You're right," he wiped his mouth. "How old was he? Not yet forty. Young and reckless and with a wife who—"

"Not her fault either."

"Tell me what happened, Paul."

Paul coughed nervously. He didn't like having this level of responsibility. Though he wasn't afraid to speak his mind he had never thought of himself as a spokesman.

"It's like I said. I get a phone call from the cops after lunch. I'm at the ferry piers anyway so I catch the next boat to Cheung Chau."

"Why Cheung Chau? What was he doing there?"

"Checked into the Gloucester yesterday lunchtime, apparently."

"Must have been looking for a change of scene. Too many memories at their place. Where's Lennox?"

"On a business trip, South America somewhere. Cops are trying to reach her. They only had my number 'cos I got those new business cards printed – "Private tuition to potentialize talent" – and he'd put one in his wallet."

"Right."

"There's something else."

"What?"

"Cheung Chau. It's famous for suicides. You know how Nick was reading up on local history? Maybe he thought it was apt."

"He was a pragmatist alright," Frank mused. "Saved every spare cent from the shopping money Lennox gave him. Worked out exactly how many pints he could afford with it. But still, it all seems so…"

"I know."

"What did he—?"

"Look like?" Paul took a deep breath. "He looked at peace. Isn't that what you're meant to say? He looked dead anyway – dead as a doornail."

"I'm sorry," said Frank. "Can't have been easy."

"No."

A half-pint silence settled on the table. It wasn't only caused by the tragic circumstances they found themselves within. Like most members of the group, they struggled to operate as a duo – instead needing a quorum of at least three to fan the flames of conversation sufficiently. They kept half an eye out for Claude, Jonathan, Wei, Briggs, or any other members of the extended gang, however lowly – but Sunday was a quiet night.

"Who else have you told?" asked Frank, at last.

"Jeanie, of course. So the other girls will know by now. No one else."

"Not your ex?"

"We haven't spoken for months."

"I'll have to tell Kim. What about Nick's parents?"

"You don't remember, do you?" Paul's face darkened, the raspberry continents mapping his excesses appeared to glow crimson.

"Remember what?"

"Nick's parents were killed in a car crash in the '80s. He was brought up by his grandparents. Then they died."

"He never told me."

"You don't listen," Paul scanned a minor influx of newbies – French, like so many of Hong Kong's recent immigrants. – "Everybody nods but nobody listens in this place. It's a talking shop. That's the top and tail of it. A talking shop full of hot air. Nothing ever changes. No one gives a toss."

Frank wracked his brains. He couldn't remember Nick ever talking about his parents, but neither could he recall receiving any suggestion he was orphaned. Either way, he wasn't going to let Paul get sanctimonious about it.

"I suppose you remember every detail of our pasts, do you?"

"Your father left when you were twelve," Paul told him. "You and your Mum have had your ups and downs but you've grown closer over the years and now you Skype her every weekend.

She's in her mid-eighties and sometimes hits the wrong buttons."

"Shit," said Frank, suitably humbled. "You're a good listener."

"No," Paul corrected him. "You're a good talker."

They were interrupted by a new arrival. By the time the glass front door had banged shut Larry, the thickset Canadian cartoonist from *Hong Kong Uncensored*, was upon them.

"I just heard the news, at the office," he explained, planting his hairy paws knuckle-down on the tabletop. "I'm truly sorry boys. Whisky?"

"Whisky," Frank concurred.

"You're a gentleman," said Paul.

Meanwhile, Fenton was sitting on his sofa, sipping lemon tea and reflecting on his day. There had been ups and downs – unquestionably. That much was to be expected on the first day of the rest of one's life. Fans of living in the moment would have given him top marks. Sunday morning was traditionally a crime scene bearing witness to his worst hangover of the week, but today he had woken with a clear head and set to work immediately. True, more wincing emanated from his workshop than had been heard since he accidentally locked Hunter in there, yet he could tell himself – quite reasonably – that this was simply the crackle and hum of healing wounds. By 8.30am a wooden puzzle he'd been frowning over for weeks was done and dusted and he was feeling restless.

"Neighbours," the song entered his head from nowhere. It was the theme tune to a soap opera he had despised in London decades earlier and since then effectively suppressed. "Everybody needs good neighbours."

He had a dim recollection of his nearest neighbours – a German schoolteacher and her Chinese engineer husband – having a child of some type. Perhaps the child would like a wooden puzzle. Did children still do puzzles? Yes, they liked phone apps. They were puzzles of some sort, judging by the constipated expressions people wore while using them. This reminded Fenton of his own lost phone. If he was going to walk two kilometres to his neighbours' he might as well go from there into Mui Wo. Of course, they would have to lend him a few coins for the taxi for the onward leg....

Fenton patched himself up all over again. The yellow pus on the underside of his old plasters reminded him of childhood custard. He managed to find a clean grey T-shirt and a pair of Wranglers with less conspicuously placed holes than most. He put the wooden toy in a plastic bag, slid gingerly into his oil-stained denim jacket and set off limping with Hunter at his heels. Keeping well clear of the drainage ditch demanded his full concentration, but once they reached the main road his spirits lifted.

"Hello snakeys," he called out. "How are you today?"

Not a car nor snake passed them before they reached the path that led to Magda and something-in-Chinese's isolated cottage. As they walked slowly towards their destination, Fenton grew increasingly surprised. Where was their security? In place of fences and tripwires wild flowers had been corralled into some kind of order; trees clipped back to assist rather than deter the casual visitor. And here was a lawn. Bumpy, yes, and hardly the green, green grass of home, but a lawn nonetheless. Before he knew it, he was smiling. And what luck! The parents were reclining on deckchairs outside their modest, tin-roofed property, hanging baskets either side of their doorway, and a little girl was skipping around the garden, singing:

"*Eins, zwei, drei, vier – Ich möchte eine katze hier.*"

"What ho!" cried Fenton. "Neighbourly favour required."

The family's reaction was instantaneous. Later, Fenton would wonder whether this was a drill that had been practised many times over. The blonde woman – Magda, presumably – ran over to her daughter, scooped her up like a rugby player collecting a wayward ball and scuttled inside the house. The father – thingummyjig – covered their retreat with wide-eyed vigilance then backed through the door himself, slamming it firmly shut behind him. As Fenton approached he heard at least two locks being twisted shut.

"Look here," he said. "This is your neighbour, Fenton Wilkes. If you're worried about Hunter, you needn't. He's completely harmless."

"We're not worried about the dog," Magda's muffled voice explained.

The hanging baskets were really quite charming. He decided to get some of his own.

"Then what are you worried about?" he replied.

Silence. What the hell was going on? Hunter sniffed at the deckchairs. Then another voice escaped from the family's bolthole.

"Please go away."

It was the husband. The engineer. Fenton felt a little of his familiar old anger welling up. He looked at the drinks beside the deckchairs. Gin and tonics, possibly.

"Listen," he called back. "I've brought a present. A toy for your little one."

He held the plastic bag up to the nearest window, through which he could see shapes moving cautiously around.

"She doesn't like presents," Magda told him.

"Every child likes presents," Fenton insisted, taking the puzzle out of the bag.

"*Ist es eine katze, mutti?*" he heard the child whisper.

He sighed and put the puzzle on one of the deckchairs.

"I'm leaving it here," he said.

Silence.

"I'm afraid I need something in return," he explained, scratching his salt and pepper scalp.

No reply.

"You see I had a bit of an accident recently. I don't have any money. Or a phone. And I really need to get to Mui Wo. Today if possible."

He heard the couple conferring in urgent, hushed tones.

"I wouldn't normally ask…"

"Please go back to the trees." It was the man's voice. "I will leave some money outside. And a phone. Take the money, call a taxi and leave us alone."

"Really?" Fenton looked to the heavens. What had happened to trust, to respect, to loving thy neighbour? He was left with little choice but to take what he had been offered, consoling himself with the thought that there would be plenty of time to solve the world's problems now he was on the straight and narrow.

"Very well," he called through. "I shall withdraw. Please be assured that I am forever in your debt."

With that he took his leave, bowing slightly at each backward pace. Hunter looked at him in total confusion, but fifteen minutes later they were in a taxi with the windows down, speeding towards civilisation.

"You'll never believe what happened to us," Fenton told the driver, who failed to muster a reply.

Things didn't go much better in Mui Wo. After using his regular cash machine, and sealing a deal at the corner phone shop, he called in at the Wellcome supermarket to buy a medium-sized box of chocolates. These he took to the Italian restaurant where, three months before, he had attacked the last in a succession of crappy cars with a cricket bat when it failed to take him and his takeaway away. That night he had dim memories of being restrained by waiters; children crying, a bucket of cold water, an old woman wailing. Today no one was answering. Figures appeared to be shuffling in the shadows when he peered through the smudged glass, but he couldn't be sure, operating as he was on a single spectacle lens and with the possible side effects of abstaining from alcohol for thirty-six hours.

"Come on Hunter," he said. "Let's go and get a coffee."

Despite the disappointing lack of company, only once did Fenton feel like caving in and finding himself a beer and a tab. Staring out to sea from his outdoor table at the Vesuvius café, Fenton's eyes defocused as his mind sharpened around a particularly unwelcome memory. Miriam. Leaving. An event over which he had insisted, for more than a decade, he had no control over, and yet – there had been a chance. On the day she packed her bags and prepared to leave their jungle paradise, a siren had ricocheted off the bosomy hills and sharp crags: a prisoner had escaped. The police created roadblocks. No taxis would be running that day.

"Maybe it's a sign," said Miriam, as they walked back to the house.

"Of course it's not a bloody sign," he snapped.

That night she had taken their bed and he had slept in the workshop, drinking whisky till he passed out. When he woke up she was already gone. Hunter brushed against his leg and he snapped out of his reverie. His coffee cup was empty and the waitress was asking if he wanted another one.

"No," he said. "I mean, no thank you."

She smiled. The first smile he had received all day. But it was time to go, before the wind changed and he found himself blown into the nearest 7-Eleven. At home he was safe from temptation. In the taxi, he found his transient thoughts jolted from Miriam to more recent events. He took out his brand new phone and scrolled through the contacts transposed from his address book. His thumb hovered over the usual suspects – Frank, Paul, Nick. Something had happened on Friday that hadn't made sense. Not his falling into a drainage ditch. That made perfect sense. This was something else altogether. Should he call Frank? Check that everything was okay? No, they would be in the Brolly, and the new, improved Fenton wasn't quite ready for the old Brolly yet.

CHAPTER SIX

So how did I end up in an illegal rooftop apartment, euthanizing bugs? The truth was I didn't realize the place was illegal, any more than it occurred to me when I left the flat Lennox and I shared in Sheung Wan that we would be kissing goodbye to our relationship indefinitely. To be fair to my landlady, I still don't know if my corrugated iron and glass open-plan, insect-friendly, studio, topped by a crow's nest of TV aerials and sitting on the brow of a hippopotamus pink walk-up, was an illicit addition to the Wan Chai skyline or not, though the lack of my own letterbox and the way in which I was discouraged from identifying myself to the downstairs tenant suggested nefarious deeds.

The finer details didn't matter. It was only a temporary measure. I signed up for six months, figuring that by the time my tenancy was up, Lennox and I would have patched up our differences. Hell, by then I might even have a fancy job with a business-card embossed in gold. I imagined it would be stiff and off-white, like the post that arrived for my unseen downstairs' neighbour from the yacht club. But instead of getting better things carried on as before – intense arguments followed by prolonged overseas absences on her part, and prolonged sessions in the Yellow Brolly on mine. Eventually I had to accept that I might be there for a stretch. I even attempted entertaining once or twice.

Unfortunately, after seeing my first guests – Dirk, a recruiter at the job agency which had come closest to finding me work, and his wife – react to the vertiginous views and basic amenities to which I had become accustomed, I realised the place wasn't fit for human habitation; or rather that it had been conceived and (sloppily) constructed solely for someone as unworthy as me. The polystyrene ceiling was too low. The only source of hot water was the shower, the only cooking facility a single hob. You could see cockroaches figure-skating under the kitchen units when you sat on the plastic stools that passed for furniture.

To top it all, the toilet-cum-shower cubicle bizarrely located in the centre of my few square metres was of insufficiently clouded Perspex; thus when Dirk's admirably cheerful wife needed a pee, we had to take up a perch near my sweat-stained bed and offer bombastic commentary on the traffic way down below on Johnson Road to cover her personal audio. "Busy, isn't it?" "Yes, really busy!" "Is that a Ferrari?" "Yes, that's a Ferrari!" etc.

After that disaster I was either to be found at the Brolly or sitting alone outside the door of the apartment, drinking under a raggedy canopy and facing out onto the collection of oversized pot plants cared for by my fellow rooftop-dwellers. Not that I saw much of this Hobbit-like community. They were either enveloped in layers of tin, plywood, tarpaulin and other mummifying tat, or deep within the echoey antechamber of the red ship's container someone had hefted up here to retire within. Occasionally I saw an old man washing himself with a hosepipe outside. What do you say to that? "*Jo san,*" of course.

One sultry September night I had unexpected company, and it almost broke my heart. A young Hong Kongese couple appeared on the rooftop while I was reading Nabokov by dim electric bulb. Dressed in little more than swimwear, their excited breathing suggested they were here spontaneously. Perhaps they had heard the rumours about the herbal remedies to be found on top of the sole remaining walk-up in the district. I was no expert – my main interaction with the plants was righting them after heavy rainstorms – but the couple quickly identified a pot containing Aloe vera and used its sap to tend their sunburn, unconscious of my presence.

As they disrobed in the moonlight, my forehead started to cactus-prickle with sweat. They hadn't noticed me, but were I to move an inch they would immediately spy my hunched-up presence in the gloom. I should have coughed politely but by the time I remembered the dark arts of English manners they were kissing passionately. Out of options, I simply closed my eyes and waited for it to be over. When I opened them again they were almost fully dressed. He whispered something and she giggled. Then she took his hand and led him to the stairwell. From there I was forced to imagine them nimbly descending seven floors, their limbs shiny with balm; moving lightly from fantasy to reality, whereas my reality was up here with the pollution and the pot-plants, and my fantasies had leapt from the hippo's puzzled brow some weeks before.

At low times, a childless man entering his forties can feel more like an elephant than any other beast: if not the one in the room then the one cast out by the herd to the very edge of the forest to contemplate the end of their line; to think about extinction. I was forced to remind myself of the hypothetical discussions Lennox and I had indulged in when we first met. There was little hope of any significant, long-term human future on the planet, we agreed, so why bring kids into a world so obviously doomed? Talk is cheap. I guess I'll never know if it's a good or bad thing that the kids I might have had, or the kids that the kids I might have had might have had, won't be around to see what happens next.

My drinking mates expected Lennox and me to get back together sooner or later. A month passed. No problem. They had met Lennox when we arrived in Hong Kong. They had met the old Lennox, in other words. Yet the fact was, she was only the new Lennox with me. If one of them ran into her in the street, she would still be the old Lennox, stroking their beards flirtatiously and throwing her head back with laughter at their mumbled jokes. They would be reassured. They also underestimated the extent of my impotence. As a man prone to a certain amount of healthy jealousy, with potential love rivals – real or imagined – everywhere, I was glad they hadn't detected my diminished sexual appetite, but it also meant there was no one with whom to discuss this delicate matter. Perhaps if I had reached out for help; found some form of therapy at that stage, I wouldn't have gone on to do what I did.

Incidentally, I succeeded only once in persuading Lennox to the walk-up. As far as I remember, she didn't even stay long enough to use the Perspex toilet. We had been out for dinner nearby. Administrative matters dominated our conversational menu and allowed us to tolerate each other over three unfulfilling courses. This at a fancy new place in Wan Chai that serves "bite-size" hamburgers and equally joyless "fun fries" alongside full-size pints of fortified dishwater. It didn't take us long to get drunk.

I presumed it was the flat that put her off, but later it occurred to me that Lennox would have seen worse. In her wild youth she would instigate affairs with mechanics, gardeners, labourers and fellow students on a "no talking" basis. Surely their abodes had been no less basic then mine? As I uncorked a bottle of wine, I think she realised my plan before I did – processing the data leaking from my subconscious and calmly accepting the challenges it posed. Because instead of grabbing her and kissing her, as I had so many times before, I was going to withhold my affection – to show her what it was like to be ignored. Her solution, I see now, was a pre-emptive strike. She would fight fire with fire, only in the cold war declared between us there were no battles, no gunshots; only ragged holes into which mere months before we had discharged our unrealistic expectations.

"I'm getting a taxi," she said. "Work tomorrow. I've drunk enough already."

"You've changed," I gave her a watery smile. "Good thing about being a freelancer is you can get up when you want, work late."

I was only making things worse by perpetuating the white lie of my self-employment; attempting to cover up my own embarrassment with no regard for hers. But then there was no need to cover for her – Lennox is one of a lucky few who will remain forever unembarrassed. I offered to walk her down the stairwell but she politely declined.

Even after ruling out *Country Life*-inspired snobbery, there were plenty of reasons to point to when Lennox stopped answering my texts shortly afterwards: apathy, work pressures, or because she felt her occasional replies only bred more of the passive-aggressive diatribes I would send her way towards the end of boozy nights at the Brolly. Passive because my messages often asked after her health and meekly requested her company; aggressive because unlike our softly-softly conversations they usually exported a prime cut of personal beef directly to her phone.

There was the unresolved row about me flirting with X or Y; there was the unresolved row about her flirting with X *and* Y.

Let's face it, as newlyweds in a hot, strange and unforgiving city; self-medicating on booze, we'd had the opportunity to stockpile a whole warehouse of grievances. Perhaps the most damaging for our relationship was when, after a boozy night out, we agreed to pay for my plane fare for an upcoming holiday using our wedding money; an amount to be replaced cent for cent when I began working. Not a big deal. Except when we came to review the accounts a month later and it transpired – to my horror – that Lennox had forgotten all about the arrangement. More than that, her immediate reaction to the minor deficit was to accuse me of stealing from our shared bounty. From that moment on, I felt like a criminal in her eyes, so breaking into our flat six weeks after leaving it didn't seem like such a big deal.

Although our lines of communication were down, I was able to charm one of Lennox's colleagues into revealing she was away. It was time to find out if my wife was living as chastely as me, or if someone self-made, decisive, gym-fit and with ten times my potency had already moved in. The entry code hadn't changed and once inside the elderly security guard waved me impatiently towards the lifts. The door to the apartment would be the tricky part. Fortunately, the place had been renovated specifically for western expats. This meant a kitchen with an oven and shelves all the way up to the ceiling – so the seven-foot *gweilos* had somewhere handy to store their oversized plates – but no metal grill across the front door. Unlike their Cantonese neighbours, these transient ghosts weren't stashing gold or family heirlooms in their abodes.

"There we go," I breathed a sigh of relief while inhaling the dim scent of her perfume and the potpourri she liked to pepper the place with. Lennox had slammed the door on her way out but hadn't double-locked it. Lucky me. Before handing over my keys I had managed to get a spare copy of the Yale but the others would have taken too long to replicate.

Inside, the place was relatively tidy. Certainly the pictures of us as a couple had been discreetly stashed or destroyed forever; replaced by photos of Lennox with her girlfriends. Like her, they were attractive career women with a low threshold for the men in their lives. That was their right, of course – most of them were the main or sole breadwinner in their relationship; the men deferred to their beauty, money and ambition.

The picture of Lennox's family remained centre stage on a bookshelf liberated from my reading material. There they were on the boat she was born and raised on. Not a super yacht in a Monaco marina, but a converted coal barge on the Thames. Dad was a successful property developer, brother rising high in the navy; Mum kept everything shipshape, while Lennox – the brightest – was expected to fly. Again, it was hard to argue against this tableau – at least until I found some evidence of wrongdoing.

I went to the bedroom first but the sheets were clean – suspiciously? Had she been staying elsewhere? – The number of condoms in the Hello Kitty toilet bag in the bedside cabinet had neither expanded nor diminished – at least not significantly. The blackout curtains were closed. Compared to my light-drenched digs her tiny sleeping quarters represented the cosy woodland set of some nocturnal creature. I was almost tempted to take a nap but instead moved next door to the study where our old laptop dozed on an IKEA table, surrounded by fresh washing that appeared to have been slung onto wonky clothes horses seconds before she left.

Washing – it could be argued – was where our problems began. Call it paranoia, but labelling it as such doesn't stem its insidious effects.

First, there were the socks. Odd socks had constantly appeared in our laundry – her laundry – whenever I stayed over at her shared house back home; and now here too. Not that I could remember which socks from her jumbled, multi-coloured collection we brought with us; only that by size and design they clearly belonged to men I hadn't met before – or perhaps men of my acquaintance who had been careful to cover their bare ankles in my company.

Second, there was the new underwear. The sepia twists of gauze suspended limply before me would no doubt become undeniable items of lust once entered into by her elegant thighs and well-defined calves. Never had she worn such things in my company. Maybe she wasn't a jet-setting lawyer after all; perhaps she was an undercover underwear saleswoman?

I brushed aside her washing like so many imaginary cobwebs and tried to log into my trusty old computer. Access denied. She had changed the password. Undeniable relief – not only would I be spared the pain of finding emails from her new lovers, but it seemed she had finally taken on board some of the well-meaning tech advice she had found so cloying when I attempted to transmit it person-to-person.

"You win," I whispered, adjusting the study door to the angle at which I'd found it.

Sitting on the sofa bed in the lounge, allowing myself a few seconds of self-indulgent remorse, my eyes fixed on a plethora of items arranged on top of the Victorian sea-chest she had found at Cat Street Market. The rest of the flat appeared to have been minimised in my absence, so why was there a bento box, empty vase and psychedelic paperweight balanced on top of its varnished wood and metal hinges now? I took a photo with my camera phone in order to record their locations, and then removed the pieces of bric-a-brac one by one.

Here they were. "Nice set of lungs," I remember her saying in a broad northern burr when we went for the medicals that would allow her to work, and me to be available for work, in Hong Kong. The memory of her mimicry made me simultaneously smile and secrete a sentimental tear. The framed photos of us as husband of wife might have disappeared from public display, but the X-rays of our lungs survived one atop the other in our communal chest, guarded by various trinkets she had bestowed with mystical powers.

But there was more. The X-rays and our skeletons were perfectly see-through; lurking on the seabed, as it were, I could see a wodge of foolscap. Divorce papers? No, not yet. I reached in and retrieved the pages. They were freshly printed, warm and sharp. I sat and read the entire document, but in fact its opening paragraph told me everything I needed to know.

CONFIDENTIAL
Legal response to upcoming CCP congress item on "former colonisers"
Once the anticipated article becomes law, only highly qualified British expats with proven political neutrality and a spotless criminal record can expect to have their right to live and work

in the territory upheld; those who fail to demonstrate their usefulness to, and support of, the new Hong Kong will face immediate expulsion.

CHAPTER SEVEN

Jeanie missed the cats just as much as Star, Ditzy or Beryl, but she mourned them less openly than her girls. It was her job to protect the staff, and with it the business, by projecting her fair but formidable presence onto Hong Kong's nightlife scene. There was no point cracking up and confessing how she too would like nothing more than to be trying to entice Ginger, Chump and Devil's Breath out of the undergrowth beside their old Sheung Wan location, instead of apologising to the owners of a neighbouring *cha chaan teng* about a Swiss backpacker who had thrown up on the pavement after trying a spam fritter.

The case of the unfortunate Swiss reminded her of the discretion essential to her role, and the thousands of secrets she had been entrusted with over her three decades in the business. Although the bar had officially left Sheung Wan to "diversify the brand" (ha!) there were other, darker reasons too. Everyone knew about the evening police patrols, regularly cutting through the alley and issuing formal warnings if the discussions inside spilt too readily onto the tarmac and small park beyond. While Jeanie accepted that some of her neighbours, mistaking Hong Kong for a pastoral idyll, disliked having Think Tank so close to their homes, it seemed to her that plenty of other bars disturbed the peace from time to time while avoiding the same kind of scrutiny.

Eventually, the threat of losing their license became real. After one too many happy-hour hollers, or political pronouncements, they were put on six-months probation. Cool, calm and collected for most of the time, the pressure eventually got to Jeanie. The night that the formal threat against their license was issued she found an axe in the storeroom, called Star outside and between them the two women hacked the outdoor tables and chairs to bits, preserving only those used by the old men for checkers on Sunday mornings. The horrified punters could only look on aghast; to them the destruction of perfectly good pub furniture was something akin to the burning of books in Nazi times, but to Jeanie it was business. What choice did she have?

The threat of losing their license slowly receded, but there followed a less public trial for her to deal with. One Sunday morning, Jeanie agreed to open up Think Tank for a student art exhibit. On arrival, she found Ginger sprawled outside, a creamy substance coating his gums. Poisoned. Taken in isolation, this incident was no stranger than the noise complaints from disgruntled neighbours. Deliberate animal poisoning was common in Hong Kong, hence the high-profile police campaigns against it, but Ginger could just as easily have nibbled rat-poison left out by a backstreet restaurant. Still, Jeanie wondered why all this bad luck was coming their way. She disposed of Ginger's body before Star arrived from the wet-market with a bag of limes; when the girls asked where she thought the shy old tom had disappeared to, she said he had probably moved on to a better place; while quietly researching their own relocation to somewhere new and improved.

The young Swiss came to apologise once he'd cleaned himself up, assuring Jeanie that he hadn't been drinking – rather the taste and texture of bright pink processed meat had unsettled a digestive tract busy adjusting to the intricacies of Asian cuisine. She believed him about the drinking. This new generation was different from the last. Frank, Paul and Fenton had just arrived. However formal their upbringings, whatever problems they were going through, they could at least open up to each other by their third or fourth beer; experiencing a kind of catharsis until the next morning at least – the young men and women she marched with these days were admirably principled but sometimes wound so tightly she feared they might snap their brains in two.

"Go relax," she would tell them after a well-attended protest. "The work is done for today. Have a beer. Get laid."

They looked at her as though she were mad. Was Auntie Jeanie – famous firebrand feminist and unequivocal activist – really telling them to have more sex?

She thought of the expression she had heard so many expat boozers use down the years: "Everything in moderation – including moderation". That shouldn't be too difficult to translate. Perhaps she could put it in writing behind the bar? When she turned to seek a possible space she found herself facing two-dozen pigeonholes. Wrong desk. Daydreaming again – stupid old woman! She covered her embarrassment by shouting at Beryl who was bent over a bowl of cat treats at the doorstep; silhouetted by the spring sunshine streaming into the Brolly.

"No more cats, Beryl! They're nothing but trouble."

Beryl smiled and nodded shyly but didn't pick up the offering. Jeanie thought of comparing needy cats to needy men but hesitated. If it had been Star or Ditzy who now stood, stretched, and resumed collecting empties, she would have made the comment unthinkingly, but Beryl was her newest employee and her romantic preferences – if any – weren't yet clear. She was short, boyish and seemingly subservient, though could sometimes be spied laughing uproariously with lecherous barflies famous for their bawdy humour and so circumvented by the other girls. Yes, hard to work out what might cause offence, or misunderstanding, with Beryl.

Besides, Jeanie had come to the conclusion that there was nothing wrong with neediness in men – or people in general. For this she blamed the ex-boyfriend who had looked her up only last year, wanting to reminisce in his final days. Before the cancer got him they had become closer than ever they would have allowed themselves at twenty, or thirty. She ushered him away for now. Too busy, too busy – he had it easy up there in heaven on his cloud!

"Cover the bar for me," she instructed Beryl. "I still need to check the post."

Jeanie flicked through the morning mail. Finding nothing new for her guests, she felt a little disappointed. When she asked Mr Wu to build a set of sturdy wooden pigeonholes, numbered to match the digits painted on each guest's bed or bunk, she imagined that as well as receiving airmail envelopes from afar, her young visitors might leave notes for one another at her makeshift reception desk, affirming friendships or suggesting dalliances, which she could deposit in the correct cubbyhole.

Where had she come across such a foolish idea? From the television, undoubtedly – the dreams of England's ivory towers that hooked her generation early and wouldn't let go. It was the kind of thing that took place in the halls of Oxford or Cambridge. Did it still go on, or had their contemporary students swapped love letters for emails as ruthlessly as her international guests?

As her eyes wandered the rows, gifting a flyer for a comedy night to the long-stay guests she thought might be interested, another mild source of disappointment reared its head: the undelivered package with the UK postmark. What was she going to do with the thing? There was no return address, yet the delivery address was handwritten and it was heavy, both of these things suggested importance. Three months it had been sitting there, unclaimed. She had cross-checked the addressee against the names of every subsequent westerner who decided to make the Brolly their temporary home. No luck.

TO COLIN SWOON-PATS
C/O THE YELLOW BROLLY
SAI YING PUN
HONG KONG

The surname still sounded like a brand of salted butter that might have been advertised on the side of a tram in her youth; but Jeanie found she had warmed to the forename. "Colin" sounded sweet and innocent compared to the truncated monikers kids preferred today. Although a smattering of younger Brits had just arrived for an evening's booze, she felt Frank and Co. would have more of an idea about the kind of creature for whom the package was destined – but only if she asked them now, before they consumed another round. Reaching their table, Jeanie realised it wasn't going to be as easy as usual to get an audience in her own pub. Frank was on his feet, his crimson shirt and notebook open; swaying to the rhythm of words as yet unspoken – an aged Byron transplanted from the Med.

Nick, Nick – you little prick
Lost overboard
Receding quick
By your own hand
You chose to die
With charcoal fumes

And salty sky
And unlimited sea
Rather you than me.
Nick, Nick – you silly sod
Impatient boy
Meets confused god
Sought oblivion
And eternal night
The libertines say
It was his right
Sod them, man down
Please raise your tankard
To Nick – the suicidal wanker.

Frank grabbed his glass, raised it sloppily and took a hearty swig. Paul and Fenton followed suit but it seemed the poem had left them unmoved.

"Bit harsh, isn't it?" said Paul.

The poet crashed down into his seat looking exhausted yet exhilarated, the way Jeanie had seen him at the end of many a long night. Perhaps he was a couple of drinks ahead of his friends.

"Harsh?" Frank rolled his eyes. "What do you want? Hearts and flowers and 'We miss you sweet knight'? If you can't be upfront about those you love…"

"I still can't believe he's gone," said Fenton, sipping his mineral water.

"Jesus," Frank considered his other audience member. "You look like you're going to cry."

"He's only just found out," Paul reminded him. "Great poem, Frank, but can't we save the histrionics for the wake?"

Frank, energised by art and apathy, wasn't going to be calmed so easily.

"What the hell are you drinking?" he prodded Fenton. "You can't still be recovering from Friday. If you won't have a drink with us now, for Nick, for God's sake—"

Jeanie saw her chance.

"Fenton's given the girls his order," she told Frank. "It's water for him all night. Dentist tomorrow, right Fenton?"

"What?" Fenton looked up at her, eyes almost unnaturally bright. "Dentist…yes, that's right, Jeanie…water…good for the soul and the…gums."

"If you gentleman wouldn't mind – I have a question," said Jeanie.

Frank unburied his head and looked at the package she had placed amongst their glasses.

"What is it?"

"That's what I want to know," Jeanie smiled. "I've had it a long time now but I'm not opening it until someone can tell me something – anything – about Mr Colin Swoon-Pats. Does the name ring any bells?"

"Double-barrelled," Paul bristled. "Never good. Bad enough in a shotgun – worse in a human being."

"Really?" Jeanie looked at the name afresh.

"You're double-barrelled, aren't you Frank?" Paul continued.

"You know damn well I'm not."

"That's right – you've got a middle name instead, haven't you?"

"Maybe."

"Leonard, isn't it?"

"Leopold."

"French," Fenton nodded gravely.

"Don't start."

"Tell us about the uniforms, Frank," Paul urged his friend. "What did great-great-granddaddy do at Waterloo?"

"He did whatever the hell he liked," said Frank, his poetical sheen sliding off him like a silken cape. "You don't get to be 'Loony' Leopold, scourge of the Low Countries, for nothing, do you?"

"But he was fighting for the wrong side," said Fenton, remembering the joke.

"I'm trying to imagine your ancestors," Frank fired back. "Mercenaries, probably. Unprincipled, angry little swine, herded from one battlefield to the next covered in mud, shit and gore."

"Language, please," Jeanie acted shocked. "This is a respectable establishment."

"Tell us about the uniforms, Frank," Paul began quaking with laughter. "Tell us about your great-aunt and how she used to dress you as kids."

Fenton had caught the bug too. He wasn't capable of Paul's belly-laughs, instead producing a gasping cackle that whistled through the gaps in his teeth.

"She was a batty old sow," Frank grumped. "Suspected transvestite."

"But a true patriot," Paul insisted.

"Didn't she dress your brother as Wellington?" Fenton asked.

"And you," Paul delivered the coup-de-grâce amid much hilarity, "as Napoleon?"

Frank puffed out his chest defiantly. His pride was hurt – but far from fatally. Despite having no great knowledge of European history, nor proof of Frank's connection to it, Jeanie saw something of General Francis Leopold in him; wondered if it was age or breeding that prevented him from stooping to their level and using his fists to allay the insult.

And talk of the devil, here was Claude (de Paris) with Wei and Briggs and Frank was suddenly ordering them all drinks and making Beryl laugh while doing so and opining about Nick and soon another night would be lost in the mists of time. Jeanie sighed and took the package back to the pigeonhole matrix beside which a pretty backpacker was looking interestedly into the bar and waiting patiently to check into the hostel upstairs. *C'est la vie.*

CHAPTER EIGHT

I have to remind myself not to be surprised on seeing Lennox's long limbs bursting out of the shiggy terrain in the valley below. All that pent-up energy and frustration, fermented on the long-haul back from Latin America; compounded in some hostile security hub in the States, had to find an outlet somewhere. And wasn't part of the hashing code – for these "drinkers with a running problem" – about catharsis and recovery; more often from the weekend's excesses, but perhaps also from the unexpected death of an estranged husband?

"On on!" come the distant cries of her fellow hounds as they crush another chalk-marked arrow underfoot.

Forward. Forward! For the living, where else is there to go? For members of the undead, like myself, a more circumspect view may be taken. Here in limbo there is no need to exist in a narrative straight line. I can amble through the past, present and future without fear of messing them up any more than I have already; at the same time aware that even small actions and events resonate indefinitely, and our perceived histories are as much subject to change as our fragile futures.

For example, the tall, pale woman with the ensnared red hair in the white vest – SQUEAKY BUM – to give Lennox her honorary hashing name, must once have had a settled rear view of me and her as lovers; romantic in our way as we flopped into bed together, as easy in our interactions as two old soldiers in a familiar foxhole. Likewise, her future imaginings – like mine – must have hinged around a leisurely continuation of a love that would prove all too easy to take for granted.

Inevitably those memories and projections have since changed within that distant, bobbing cranium; to what extent and in what ways I do not know, but the fact remains that hashing codes and ancient rites aside, the woman I love is out there tearing up the Sai Kung countryside instead of sitting at home weeping over what was and could have been.

I strain to see the hare, scooting ahead down the trail, stooping to slash a chunky chalk stick across the ground every thirty metres or so. The parallel trails – one for Rambos, one for Wimps – are usually set out on the morning of the hash, or even the night before, but the rain means BIG BITCH (I don't know her real name) is having to re-mark the tougher course, incorporating false trails designed to tease the runners, while her co-hare, PANDA PUSSY, plots 3km less pain and suffering for the runts of the pack.

They better watch out – this duo of large, sexy, confident women – Squeaky Bum is gaining, along with three or four others. No men. This club is indelicately known as the HASH WHORES; my own outfit goes by the misleadingly mellow name of PURE HASH. While it would be glib to claim that the couple that "runs together stays together", we had no choice but to go our separate ways. The unspoken decision was made during our regular Bowen Road outing, one steamy summer morning.

I was pushing it, trying to sweat out the previous night's booze while enjoying the crow's-nest view that suggested a more compact and manageable Hong Kong than was possible in reality. As I glanced down at Happy Valley slumbering in the haze, I was surprised to see Lennox at my shoulder; shocked when she eased her way past me with a wordless apology made in shallow breaths; eyes on the prize and scarlet stripes patterning her cheeks like war paint. It wasn't only the age gap that had caught up with me. This was about her eating better, giving up smoking; spinning on a static bicycle to techno beats under disco lights over consecutive lunchtimes. All the things I should have been doing as the senior partner.

Checking my tank, I realised I had precisely nothing left. All I could do was watch her well-oiled bum round the corner and then open up on the home straight like a thirsty gazelle bounding towards a Wan Chai watering hole. A year before I would jog on the spot, waiting for her to catch up with me, now she had quietly surpassed her own expectations in this and most other aspects of her life. What of my expectations for her? I'm ashamed to say they were few and far between, and at their core was the assumption she would stay by my side and look after me no matter what.

Well, I won't make that mistake again, I promise myself, waiting for Ray's signal. Better to have your allies instilled with more than an amorphous, fleeting affection that might burst like a flatulent raincloud on a spiky hillside at any time. Ray is a case in point. We barely know each other but the money and status I provide him with – the sense of importance that his small-fry triad bosses so spectacularly failed to deliver – means he has my back indefinitely. Had his gangster bosses kept faith in him, the bright lad would still be providing them with his almost involuntary guile and morally-exempt instincts.

In the absence of sunshine, Ray is unable to flash me with his mirrored sunglasses from the hill opposite; instead waving a piece of florescent tape he must have found marking something significant in the area. I urge him to keep down and only when satisfied none of the hashers has seen his signal point to Big Bitch, confident Squeaky Bum will choose the Rambo option every time. While I remain squat in my bushy hide, Ray raises himself from his.

Despite his natural running ability, Ray still looks strangely uncomfortable in the fluttery gauze nothingness of his navy sports shorts; tugs nervously at the shiny yellow running-vest peeling off his skinny frame. But once he starts his descent, those sinewy legs propelling him effortlessly onwards, he rises through a hierarchy of perception to become top dog in the eyes of any old pros in the vicinity. Yes, I have seen their grizzled faces marvel and felt strangely proud – almost paternal. None are in evidence today. I get the exclusive view of Ray entering the shig and switching to a light trot some thirty yards behind Big Bitch; his languorous technique suggesting he might actually be floating an inch or two above the trail. Soon they are both obscured by the tropical canopy. I follow the burnished red of Lennox's hair, surely too long and thick for purpose these days, before two minutes later it likewise vanishes into the green.

Each hash ends with cold beers – a lot of cold beers. Plus soft drinks for the particularly wimpy who will be berated for their choice whether or not they happen to be recovering alcoholics. Snacks are also a requirement. A hare may be run out of town if he or she fails to provide the necessary refreshments to the exhausted yet exhilarated hounds. I wonder how Big Bitch has arranged things today. She probably has a flunky carting a cool box or two towards the site of the "hash bash" as we speak. She's too experienced at all this to make a mess of it. Perhaps her first attempt to be a leader ended in a similar way to mine; though I doubt it could have been as humiliating.

My route was well planned – fairly imaginative for a virgin hare, I was told. But in an attempt to save money, I provided the Pure Hash boys with a woefully inferior beer at the post-run hash bash; worse still the nearest 7-Eleven was out of ice. Warm, cheap beers are the antithesis of a reward in sweltering Hong Kong; the ragging I received from the Pure Hash crew was worse than anything I'd witnessed during my politically correct education. I realised then that the British expat scene in the city had elements of public school sadism that I would have to study and – perhaps – use to my advantage.

Walking to the nearest minibus stop without shorts, cupping my shrivelled manhood while dodging hikers, gave me a lot of time to ponder such things. The local passengers didn't bat an eyelid as I attempted to spread the damp bum cotton of my mini-briefs over a shiny, leatherette seat before belting up. They had seen it all before – their ancestors too, for at least a couple of generations. Maybe they forgave the hashers their indiscretions because some of their original number were rumoured to have joined in the defence of the territory against the Japanese in 1941, an operation that proved as madly defiant as their running and drinking. I bought a pair of oversized Hawaiian shorts at Stanley Market and told Lennox my runners had been snagged and torn on a stray branch – I didn't tell her they had been torn off my body by drunken bankers, re-enacting some ancient rugby rite.

The hashers far ahead of me, I feel confident enough to assume the guise of a respectable walker and stroll along the spiny path that will take me up and down the next three or four hills towards the site of the hash bash. To my right, far below, tourist towns, golf resorts and secret getaways cling to a craggy coastline before a bright grey expanse of water barely punctuated by pleasure craft on this muggy day. More in evidence are the dark brown kites that glide around the rocks twenty metres below me, looking for snakes and small mammals amongst the scrub in their unhurried manner. Never fond of heights, I turn back to the juicy green hues to my left; catch a flash of pallid limb a good half-kilometre ahead of me. My elevated path is much easier to manage than their hydra-headed route but I will still have to pick up the pace.

What do I want? Fair question. Just to hear her voice, I suppose. It's been a few months since I was within earshot of her quietly authoritative tones – by which point they had transmogrified into a crescendo of frustration and bitterness. Should she utter a few words of regret or remorse to her fellow hounds regarding my fate, I won't complain.

Eventually, my path begins to vein its way down from my vantage point, towards the thickets preferred by the semi-secretive hashers. I stoop as I continue and the high road threatens to merge with the low, my appearance switching to that of shy mountain hunchback vaguely ashamed of his deferential appearance. In fact, my only true source of shame is my raggedy red tracksuit pants and shrunken, colourless T-shirt; neither of which I have any intention of allowing Lennox the merest glimpse of. A clearing up ahead has me tidying myself into the surrounding foliage, but I can see no fresh smoke rising from the public barbecue area that appeared to be – on the map at least – the perfect spot for a Hash Whores' hash bash.

"What would a lion do?" I murmur, spotting a stray sausage in the claggy earth beneath the burnt-out pits.

Lennox would ask me this question whenever one of us dropped an item of food on the kitchen floor – our excitable, booze-fuelled cooking procedure making this an everyday hazard. Then she would force the piece of veg, fish or meat into my reluctant mouth: a lioness feeding her cowardly lion. But this dusty old sausage has been down there too long. The picnic area has a tired, neglected and slightly sinister feel, despite the evidence charred, scarred and occasionally skewered into the blackened earth of many desperately happy teenage parties. Crinkle-edged aluminium trays that once contained chilled and salted animal flesh now hold only a few crumbs of unused charcoal, rattling from corner to corner when not encased, amber-like, in vintage grease. A rustle in the bushes has me hissing stupidly.

"Ray?"

No reply. Safe to say I've upset some scavenger with my presence and it has withdrawn to the undergrowth until I'm on my way. I'm happy to move on. The place has the feel of a razed village post-pillage or gourmet Pompeii. I let the descending path suck me further into the valley. The light is beginning to fade. This is no gradual, stop-motion process in Hong Kong. Soon it will be dark – too dark for all but the wildest, typhoon-chasing hashers to run through. The bash can't be delayed for much longer. And there he is, not a moment too soon: Ray, glowing yellow in the twilight; motioning to me from outside a ruined cottage about two hundred yards ahead. The finger over the shoulder means the hashers, including my estranged wife, are taking shelter within the old stonework. I smile congratulations at loyal Ray but my off-white teeth are not displayed for long. I hit the deck, my movement urgent enough for a look of puzzlement to cloud my teammate's face. Big Bitch has blindsided him. Nothing I can do but watch what unfolds between mucky fingers and wild grass stalks.

"Pervert," says Big Bitch – loud enough for me to hear. She's holding something in her hand, a canister or flask maybe. T-shirt sleeves are rolled up, revealing a huge dragon tattoo on a chunky upper arm.

Ray protests in pretend-crap English.

"Sorry, I lost. Tourist. Where is the…um…fish and chip shop?"

"Fucking Peeping-Tom."

Big Bitch isn't buying Ray's excuses. I don't like her tone. I don't like Ray's chances.

"Caught you just before you started wanking, eh?"

For a second it looks like Big Bitch is going to grab him by the balls, but then she seems to think better of it. It's unlikely she's found evidence of any voyeuristic excitement in Ray's petrified nether regions.

"Well, there ain't nothing to see here," Big Bitch continues, gesturing at the cottage then calmly raising her can of mosquito repellent and spraying its contents directly into Ray's eyes.

My God. I've never heard such screams. Poor Ray. His wide-eyed innocence had presented an easier target for Big Bitch than his retracted testes, but the results appear to be no less painful. I scramble backwards, crab-like up the path, tearing my eyes from the sight of Ray, slumped to his knees, howling in agony as Big Bitch walks briskly round the outside of the cottage – no doubt returning to the beers and bonhomie within. I can't risk being nabbed too. The best I can do is to take a small bottle of water from my backpack and toss it towards him like a nervous grenadier.

As it bounces heavily a few yards from him, I know Ray will be grateful to have some eyewash at hand in his moment of need.

"Sorry buddy," I whisper, before reversing and retracing my steps at a steady pace, stumbling occasionally on thick tree roots but making enough ground for Ray's moans and stifled sobs to be slowly replaced by the melancholy cawing of Hong Kong's night birds.

I meet Ray two hours later at our prearranged bolthole – a concrete bunker near the start of the Wong Nai Chung Gap trail, one of several brutal memorials to the members of the Hong Kong garrison who, alongside young Canadian farm boys, met their end here or hereabouts fighting merciless Japanese troops. The teams have only just finished playing under floodlights at the cricket club opposite and are making for the clubhouse as I'm lowering myself over a crumbling wall into the dank environs of the troops' old sleeping quarters; kicking dead leaves and crisp packets away from a rust-fringed doorway and finding an ancient iron bunk-bed frame to perch on.

"Sorry boss," says Ray, suddenly silhouetted against the entrance. He must have been hiding nearby.

"That's okay," I tell him. "Hashes don't usually have bodyguards."

I wonder if I should tell him to stop calling me boss. He can't get the intonation right. I presume he's being genuine – I'm paying him generously for his time – but the word usually arrives coated in sarcasm, despite a learned expat telling me that irony is not a luxury afforded to ordinary Hong Kongers. When it doesn't come out archly, Ray enunciates "boss" with a dunderheaded meekness – a half-burp, half-yawn of apparently unthinking obsequiousness that makes me instantly uncomfortable. Is this his way of telling me I'm only a whisker away from becoming a racist overlord or white supremacist in the North American revivalist mode? Damn my sensitivities. I get to the point.

"Did you see her?" I ask.

Ray looks down. I try again.

"Did she see me?"

Ray shrugs.

"What does that mean?" I stand unsteadily, propelled by a rising anger. "Why can't I get a straight answer out of anyone in this place?"

The blood having drained from my head, I find myself staggering forward and leaning on Ray for support. I want him to come inside and sit beside me on my bunk; to share confidences like any normal spy, but he resists my invitation.

"I stay here," he tells me. "Too many ghosts in there. All countries. Still fighting."

"Bollocks."

I get a grip on his vest and shove him towards the opposite bed-frame. Taken by surprise, he staggers backwards. In a bid to avoid parking his bony backside on a strip of unforgiving metal, he goes in too tall and hits his head on the exposed rim of the top bunk. He grunts his disapproval then settles down to simper, muttering as he rubs his injured head.

"I warn you, boss," he grouches. "Don't fuck with the spirits."

"Jesus, you're a cheery soul, aren't you? Let's have a look at your war wound."

Ray flinches as I close in on him in the darkness but doesn't resist as I touch his forehead. A sticky substance loosely tacks my fingers together.

"Rust," I explain, showing him the orange stains. "No blood."

He turns away, squinting at invisible neighbours in the next bunk along.

"She is happy," he says at last.

"Happy?"

"I hear her talking. Drinking beer. Says you had a deal."

"A deal?"

"That you won't be sorry if one dead or the other dead."

It takes me a moment to translate Ray's crudities into the more artful conversation I recognise from soon after Lennox and I had met. While sharing a bottle of red in Montmartre on a city break, we'd agreed not to mourn each other when the time came, but to simply drink a toast. That must have been what she was doing at the hash bash.

"Just be careful not to die too soon," she'd added on that balmy night in Paris. "Or I'll chase you through the bowels of hell."

It was the most romantic thing anyone had said to me at the time. And then I shouted at her on the way back to our hotel for giving twenty euros to a homeless man who'd pitched his tent on the boulevard.

"Forgive me, Ray." I rub a little rust on my own forehead in solidarity. "Seems it's almost as stressful being dead as it is being alive. Who'd have thought?"

"You stay…here?" he looks around fearfully.

"Only for one night, maybe two."

I give Ray the opportunity but no more of Lennox's words spill out of his mouth. That's my lot for the day. I don't blame him for clamming up. He's been assaulted by the living and spooked by the dead – I'd probably want to collect my money and go home too.

"Here you are," I pass Ray a grubby roll of hundred dollar notes.

"Thanks, boss."

Clearly, today hasn't marked the highpoint of our partnership. Thank God we'd been in tune last time we hashed together, or our days of running free and sleeping rough would already be at an end.

CHAPTER NINE

The twenty-or-so mourners arrived on Cheung Chau aboard three public ferries – two slow and one fast. They looked suitably sad, except for those charged with looking after young children who seemed overly distracted by the here and now. Jeanie had brought a steel thermos of steaming rice and mounds of sweet, sticky pork in polystyrene containers, of the type that washed up around the island when the tides were unfavourable. But when they had all climbed up Peak Road and found the crematorium shaded by stunted, lime-leafed trees there was no body; no ashes to be found, and Mr Yung of the local authority said he was too busy preparing for tomorrow's tomb-sweeping festival, and the arrival of many more souls – living and dead – to answer their questions about the remains of their English friend. Had they got the date wrong? Possibly. Nearly three weeks had passed since the demise of Nick Powell, the latest in a rogue's gallery of expats to die in Hong Kong through misadventure; a necessary gap existing between expiry and incineration – the coroner having his paperwork to contend with, the undertakers their ceaseless employment. A notice had appeared at the Yellow Brolly in photocopied Sharpie CAPS, pinned to the bottom of a corkboard across which regulars could splash photos of good times with transient friends:

MEMORIAL FOR NICK, 4 APRIL (PM).
CHEUNG CHAU CREMATORIUM.
ALL WELCOME.

When challenged, Jeanie assured Frank that this was none of her doing, while Frank confirmed that neither he, Paul nor Fenton were involved. Although the origin of the posters remained unclear – others were spotted around the Hong Kong University campus and at Quantum's, the famous rock 'n roll bar – I was grateful to find that my relatively few friends and acquaintances were unanimous in wanting to attend the service. Distraction arrived in the form of more unwelcome news. Ted Pepperton, the respected jazz trumpeter, who had kept the island's dance-floors swinging since arriving from Soho in the '60s, with not much more than his instrument, had died in his sleep. Despite being one of the safest cities on Earth, it seemed Death was stalking Hong Kong with an unwarranted tenacity.

"Don't these things usually come in threes?" Frank asked Kim as they lay together on the Sunday after Ted's wake.

"Only in the West," she told him. "*Four* means death in the East. Perhaps there are two more tragedies to come?"

"Look on the bright side, why don't you?"

Frank rolled over; in the same motion shoving the official letter and its crinkly envelope further under their mattress. Then he let his palm and wrist rest on their cold stone floor for a few minutes, feeling his pulse begin to slow.

"How many times have we made love today?" he asked.

"Twice," said Kim, matter-of-factly.

"Once more to avoid disaster then," said Frank, removing his hand and arcing it 180 degrees to rest on a quizzical cheek – his gift to her, his cool mistress with the hot body. What would he do without her?

Sometime after Ted's send-off, someone noticed that the posters for Nick's do had been reclaimed by unseen hands, but enough people had written the fourth in their diaries to be confident enough to dash for a ferry four days later, quickly regretting their unthinking haste; forgetting that the humidity had been creeping slowly upwards hour by hour, day by day – drawing citizens together in its stifling, overprotective bosom until one by one they cracked and ran for the ocean.

Molly Ransom, looking gaunt and listless, and her androgynous blonde twins joined Frank on the lower deck of the slow ferry. Bliss on a breezy spring or autumn day, the exposed plastic seats beside the waves were now as sticky as flytraps, fusing Frank to someone for whom he had no affection – and vice versa, presumably. Kim was suffering in a different way. She had been unable to sacrifice a guitar lesson with a new, highflying client. This latest joker thought he was going to bring the house down at his merchant bank's annual concert with only a few weeks of coaching and the most expensive guitar he could find at Tom Lee's. Frank was embarrassed for the guy, though less willing to address the embarrassment he felt about their dwindling financial resources, and his meagre contribution to them.

"You look troubled," said Molly, in that odd, flat voice she had. "Thoughts of mortality?"

"Not in front of the children."

Frank fished a copy of yesterday's *Post* from his bag and started reading, but Molly wouldn't take the hint.

"Scampi says you write poetry."

"He told me he did too," said Frank, "and then I read some of it."

"I appreciate art," said Molly.

"Really? You don't sound like you've said that word very often."

"And I'm prepared to pay," she continued.

The further Frank managed to edge himself, like an irregular chess piece, away from the family unit, the more often he found himself boxed in by one or other member of the trio. At Cheung Chau pier he spotted a familiar face – it was Fenton, fresh off his inter-island ferry. Frank was immensely relieved to see him. How often could you say that?

"Ice-cream?" asked Fenton, handing Frank a choc-ice.

"You've changed," said Frank, accepting the offering, which had the side effect of upsetting Molly's twins behind them.

"I wanna ice-cream," wailed one of the blondes.

Fenton turned and spoke in his best, clipped tones – more suited to the Riviera in the '30s than a scruffy promenade almost a century later.

"'I want' doesn't get," he said. "And 'I want' used persistently round these parts invites laceration by pirate, isn't that right, Molly?"

Molly was busy unpacking organic treats from a cool box they should have offered to help carry. Squatting to interface empathetically with her kids, the single mum shot Fenton a look which suggested that although she would be more than capable of leaping up and ripping his throat open with her small white teeth, she had more immediate concerns right now. Frank took his friend's elbow and hurried them across the public square.

"Point taken," he murmured. "Same old Fenton resides within."

Ignored by the jaywalkers and phone-checking bike riders dissecting the square with haphazard choreography, the latest hoarding designed to engage with the island community was a sight to behold for the more casual traveller. In a familiar vermillion and fringed by tiny golden stars, the foreground showed a line of smiling people holding hands in unity. The background? An imposing vista of Tiananmen Square, replete with smiling leaders waving from the royal box. Just a few short years on from Occupy, you couldn't imagine such an image lasting long in the city. It had the unintended effect of spurring the two men onwards and upwards.

"Who else is in town?" Frank asked as they scaled Peak Road.

"Jeanie's just led a pack up – Paul's here, arrived with Wei and Briggs. Looks like they've had a few en route."

"An emotional time."

"For something to be truly emotional," Fenton sighed, "you have to feel it," he punched his bird's nest ribcage through his baggy black T-shirt, "right here. Booze has a way of extricating one from any form of genuine contemplation."

"My god, can you hear yourself?" Frank stopped to catch his breath. "You're going to tell me you've found religion next."

"Don't be ridiculous. I've sobered up, that's all. You should try it some time."

"Well at the moment, you're driving me the other way," Frank binned his ice-cream then licked its residue off his fingers. "So I suggest you save your preaching until we get to the place of worship."

But the crematorium wasn't the kind of place to have a spiritual awakening. Like many Hong Kong public buildings it had been created with a clinical efficiency that no amount of instructive, cartoon-based signage – an uncontrollable passion of the municipal leaders – could save. A trilingual placard directed clients to a toilet and baby changing area but was unable to tell them how to feel. Frank and Fenton located Paul and the trio reaffirmed their collective bond through a series of nods and raised eyebrows while Jeanie continued to negotiate with Mr Yung. The cicadas began to chirrup.

"Not a bad turnout," Frank tilted his head towards the ragtag guests, some of whom had strayed from the path beside the crematorium and begun examining the tombstones surrounding them. "Considering Nick hadn't been here long."

"No sign of Jonathan," Fenton pointed out.

"No sign of Lennox," said Paul. "Or any UK family."

"Don't think he had any," Fenton told him. "Far as I can remember Nick was a grown-up orphan, like me. Parents, kids – who needs them?"

"We'll still be here tomorrow by the looks of things," said Frank, watching black smoke meandering out of the crematorium chimney. "Let's go and have a joint."

The men shuffled off to find somewhere secluded. No one seemed to notice. Wei was giving Briggs his daily Cantonese lesson, forcing him to drink Japanese whisky from his hipflask whenever he adjudged his pronunciation to be slightly off – which was most of the time. Meanwhile Molly was following the twins as they waded through the tombstones pointing at the black-and-white photos of elderly Chinese individuals or couples most incorporated.

"Who that?"

And Molly would have to read the inscription to them.

"Where they gone?"

And Molly found herself summarising the main teachings of Taoism, Buddhism and Confucianism when it came to the afterlife.

Frank led Fenton and Paul down a deserted bramble path to a semi-circle of stones. Here several generations of a wealthy Cheung Chau family were frozen in time. Once an exclusive plot, it was clear that at some point – either through personal choice or disaster, wanderlust or infertility – the descendants had stopped coming, or stopped dying here. Otherwise there would have been fresh slabs and a good view of the sea instead of an overgrown, ethereal habitat perfect for smokers.

"Places like this give me the willies," Paul confided, but he still took the pungent reefer from Frank as Fenton wafted away smoke with amused hostility.

"You don't look well, mate," Frank said, exhaling smoke into the bushes. "Terrible thing to admit, but I'd say Fenton here is looking healthiest out of the whole sorry lot of us. Been drinking more than usual?"

Paul took a deep lungful while fishing in his oversized shorts for a glasses case. He returned the joint to Frank, opened the case and fitted a pair of perfectly round sunglasses over his rheumy eyes.

"Stress," he said, barbing his voice with more Liverpool than usual.

"Fair enough," said Frank. "You get to see Poppy this week?"

"Aye," Paul admitted. "We had a good time, as it goes. Took her to Ocean Park. For once, access isn't the problem."

"Problem?" said Fenton, who was examining some wild berries like a kid on a field trip. "What problem? You're not about to pop off too are you?"

By way of answering, Paul dipped back into his shorts, this time producing an official-looking letter.

"Know what this says?" he asked them.

"I've got a rough idea," Frank admitted.

"Says my time is up," Paul continued, trying to contain his rage. "Says so long and thanks for nothing. Says all those years of teaching the next generation meant fuck all. Says collect your MPF money and use it to retire elsewhere. Says—"

"Wait, wait, wait," said Fenton, forsaking his berries. "This is a letter from whom exactly? Your wife's lawyers?"

"From the bloody government."

Fenton looked baffled, Frank intervened.

"What did they get you on?" he asked.

"That kid – May – the one I was tutoring…"

"The monster in human form," Fenton recalled. "Incorporating orally-based butter refrigeration unit?"

"That's the one. I never told you chaps how that particular assignment ended," he handed the letter to Frank, who quickly found the relevant paragraph.

"You were seen carrying Student Z to the ferry pier then taking her by the ankles and dangling her over the harbour wall for a prolonged period while screaming insults ill-befitting a child's ears. Only when several members of the public intervened did you return Student Z to safety, by which time she was thoroughly traumatised."

"Traumatised, my arse," Paul deadpanned. "She was positively glowing. Knew she'd won the war there and then, was already rehearsing how to relay all this to her mother, when to pause for tears – all that jazz."

"Still, fucking hell," Fenton sighed. "Why didn't you tell us about this?"

"What'd be the point? It was too raw to be an anecdote, too ridiculous to talk about seriously. And compared to what happened to Nick... Course I knew I'd lose that job, perhaps a few more when word got around. But there's always someone willing to give you another chance here if you're a decent teacher."

"And you are a decent teacher, from what I've heard," said Frank, whose stilted tone immediately unnerved the others.

"What's on *your* mind then, pal?" Paul asked him.

"Bastards have nailed me too," Frank produced his crinkled correspondence from the seat of his black jeans. "'From our enquiries it appears the name of Francis Leopold Taylor has become synonymous with violence in the island community of Lamma...'"

"What?" Fenton's happy mood was at an end. No longer were his clear-eyed reflections on nature sufficient to still his inner temper. "You're the least bloody violent person I know. You wouldn't harm a—"

Frank gave him a look. "I know that, you know that, but Immigration are still chucking me out of Hong Kong."

"On what basis – rumour and false accusation?"

"On anonymous testimony stating that I assaulted Kim Tang, my partner of eighteen months."

"She wouldn't say that."

"Of course not, but someone did. There's plenty of jealous, bitter, people around the islands – you should know, you used to be one of them."

Fenton was too stunned to respond to the provocation; he was busy putting two and two together when Paul decided to help him along. "Not received a letter yourself then, Fenton?"

The likely scenario was easy to work out. When drinking, Fenton had told them often enough – and with not inconsiderable glee – about the postman tasked with delivering mail to the box at the edge of his domain. "The poor bastard saw that photo of the crucified prisoner from Vietnam I'd put in the trees. Fled before he could leave me so much as a supermarket flyer." Fenton had the ultimate proof of what had happened, though he hadn't realised the implications until now. Once his lost phone had been discovered and charged there was an answer-phone message waiting for him in patient, precise English: "Please comport yourself forthwith to the Mui Wo sorting office where there is an item awaiting your collection."

"Can't we appeal?" he asked.

"There's a fee for appealing," Paul explained. "And that's before you've hired a lawyer. Got that kind of money stashed away at the compound, have you?"

"There you are," said Jeanie, peaking into their glade. "Mr Yung has located the ashes and agreed to let us take them. Whoever wishes to speak, may speak. And then we shall eat."

The men trudged out into the sunlight.

"Not feeling very hungry, Jeanie," Fenton admitted.

"Nonsense," she scolded. "You're too skinny. If you really have given up the bottle you need to get those carbs from somewhere."

Back in the crematorium gardens, it became clear to the older men that none of their young compatriots had received the same correspondence, or else how could they be larking about with such abandon? Claude had arrived and was sharing the Japanese whisky with Briggs under a tree while Wei smoked a cigar, having decided unanimously that Nick would not have wanted this to be a sombre affair. Even Molly Ransom had relaxed slightly and was running a hand through her hair, leaned up against a tree while flirting with Jasper, the silver-haired antiques dealer with the matinee idol looks.

The smokers' cannabis telepathy was unquestionably correct: they were the spare parts; their expulsion from Hong Kong would be mourned momentarily before everyone got back on with it; their photo would remain up at the Brolly until its edges curled but sooner or later the transient clientele would have no notion of who the three frowning, older people were. Still, today they had to get on with it – for me. Jeanie reclaimed the swirly-pattered urn from the foot of a tree, like a mother hen returning to her egg. She smiled beatifically at Frank, which was his cue to step forward and recite some apposite verse.

After it was all over, Frank, Paul and Fenton left the others after a quick drink and a few mouthfuls of pork outside the Praying Mantis pub. Night fell with typical Hong Kong rapidity and soon the lights of the seafront restaurants were dancing in the water between the dinghies and motorboats tied up in their protective nocturnal web. The friends sat on a metal bench on the public pier for a moment of reflection. Old men opposite smiled goofily at the upstarts while sipping at their small cans of Tsing Tao. A hospital case on compassionate leave lay beneath a blanket on the furthest bench along. Sallow-skinned and stick thin, his relatives were ensuring that the banter of his fellow islanders, the squeaking strain of ropes as boats shifted repetitiously, and the ever-present sound of overlapping water would be amongst his final worldly memories.

"Not a bad service was it, in the end?" said Paul. "Thought you injected a necessary soberness into proceedings, Frank."

"Rate they were going," Frank took a slurp of beer, "there was going to be a disco while they scattered the ashes."

"Better to chuck him around that side of the island," said Fenton. "Just the big blue South China Sea and the odd fishing boat. None of these bloody ferries."

He gestured to the latest triple-decker easing into the parallel pier.

"Got to tip the ferryman though, haven't you?" said Paul, who was still wearing his sunglasses.

"Absolutely not," Fenton protested. "Worse than the bloody postmen they are. Lazy, good for nothing—"

"He's being apocryphal, Fen," Frank intervened. "You must know the story of Charon and the journey to Hades?"

"Tell you what I do know," said Fenton, allowing his private stewing to reach the boil. "There was no way Nick was planning to top himself when I spoke to him that Friday."

"What do you mean?" asked Frank.

"It's come back to me, you see. He was rabbiting on about that silly running thing he does...did."

"Hashing?"

"That's the one. And how he was excited about the weekend because he was bringing along a new friend who'd give the others a bloody nose."

"I guess the friend let him down," said Paul.

"Or else he decided that in the bigger scheme of things, life was still pretty shit," Frank added.

"Very odd, that's all," Fenton mused. "He just didn't seem the type. And I'm not completely sure he'd given up on Lennox."

"Well it seems she's given up on him," said Frank. "If he knew she hadn't bothered to turn up to his memorial service—"

"—he'd top himself," Paul finished the thought and the friends exchanged morbid glances.

"Sampan for me," Fenton got to his feet. "Missed the last inter-island ferry. Don't drink too much, there's a suspected link between alcohol and depression."

"And a proven link between your company and suicide," Frank told him.

"Think on, anyway," Fenton advised them. "If someone like Nick can—"

"Christ, Fenton!" Paul removed his sunglasses, revealing eyes red raw with tears. "Nick's dead. He's gone – he doesn't have to deal with this shit, the jammy sod. The one thing we should be thinking about is how the fuck we all avoid being deported."

Fenton was about to respond when Frank caught his eye, urging him non-verbally to sling his hook.

"Very well," Fenton saluted sarcastically. "Until next time."

"Until next time," said Frank, his gaze settling on the black water beyond the railings.

CHAPTER TEN

I can't resist returning to Cheung Chau the next day to sweep my grave; or rather, dust my plaque. On the fast ferry I meet a middle-aged expat, though not of the hairy British variety, and deeming his polite enquiries innocuous I decide to drop my guard for the course of a ten-minute chat. Like many educated Hong Kongers, his English is impeccable and his name – Winston – more anglophile than a departing royal yacht stuffed with outdated dignities. I improvise a barely feasible alias that my new friend calmly accepts.

"You must be rather hot in that Mackintosh, Mr Letterby," Winston tells me, his well-preserved face shining with mischief.

"Not really," I pant, smoothing down the ends of my moustache. "I heard there might be rain."

"No, I don't think so," Winston says, looking out of the tinted window at the approaching harbour. "The air is extremely still out there. I may not have been back here for twenty years but I still remember the basics of island meteorology, as taught to me by my father."

"That's who you're here to…see?"

I apply some spittle to a forefinger then dab it under the curling tips of my facial hair in an effort to revive its crispy adhesive mooring.

"That is indeed my duty, Mr Letterby," Winston concedes. "Sadly, I was unable to leave Canada for my dear old dad's funeral, but I can at least pay my respects at his place of rest on this auspicious day."

"Quite."

"And you yourself are on a daytrip?" Winston asks.

"Yes," I admit. "It's not an island I can keep away from for very long."

"You have good taste. And Cheung Chau women are the kindest in all the world. Perhaps you mean to attract a suitable mate with your magnificent moustache?"

"Something like that," I nod, my self-consciousness adding another coat of red to my features. I tug my PINK DOLPHIN TOURS cap further over my eyes.

The lull in our conversation lets me appreciate the full extent of the crowds on the harbour-front for the Ching Ming festival and the implications for my narcissistic mission. It seems I've wildly underestimated the mass of people intent on offering incense, fruit and grave-based housework to their ancestors by a factor at least as high as the sun cream required on a broiling hot day like this. It's only 10.30am but people are already visor'd-up; their handheld electric fans hovering millimetres from foreheads sheened with sweat. The less prepared use impenetrable local newspapers as hats or fans; the expert majority heft camping chairs and cool boxes full of goodies towards Peak Road.

"Excuse me," I ask Winston to let me by so I can be among the first to depart.

"No problem," he bunches his legs to one side. "Have a great day, Mr Letterby."

"You too."

I find my sea legs and wait by the downstairs door, which doubles as a gangplank, for the ferry to be drawn into its berth. The captain will want a quick turnaround. The crewmember charged with operating the door is similarly wired. Passengers fan themselves impatiently or remain perfectly still, like penguins on a hop on/hop off iceberg. No one seems to notice the young boy kicking at the door then threading his fingers dangerously through the rope mechanism that will lower it on arrival.

He's a wild-looking white kid of eight or nine in grey vest, pink shorts and blue Crocs. The singsong muttering he produces while interacting with the boat is either of his own invented lexicon or a European language I'm yet to encounter. I look round for his parents. Finding no sign, I try to get his attention while drawing as little as possible to me.

"Dangerous," I hiss, wagging a finger. "No do that."

The kid squints up at me, tilting his head to one side. His dirty blonde hair is matted in places. He puts his hands on his hips, deciding if I'm worth engaging with.

"That's right," I say. "You just stand there and relax."

But then his sharp little ears pick up the squelching of the ferry's hull against the car tyres that insulate the piers from their bulk, and soon after the tell-tale buzz of the door release. Before the gangplank is three-quarters down, he's pushed past the crewman and leapt out onto the pier, causing me to garble something concerned yet angry in my own secret language. I rush out after him as he scuttles towards the prom.

But he's not playing ball. At the last possible second he dives to his left and pushes open a small metal gate only a little taller than himself. This private entrance allows the shore crew access to the moorings that secure the heaving hulks to their berths. There is a low, whitewashed wall between us – and no protection from the agitated water on his side.

"Stop that," I call over the wall, but he ignores me again. His intention is clearly to creep back towards the ferry and give either the crew or his absent parents a huge fright.

Sweat has now enveloped me to the extent that my moustache simply slides off and takes flight like a hairy butterfly. I turn to intercept the kid back at the ferry door, determined to admonish him in some way – but to no avail. A zombie army of tomb-sweepers is almost upon me. Were I to fire off a barrage of apologies I could only hope to stall a quarter of them. But what if the boy were to fall between the ferry and the harbour wall and be crushed? You hear whispers of this happening more than it's ever reported. Too late, too late…I must be gone.

I allow myself to be carried from the ferry terminal by the undead then steady myself against an emaciated bicycle. The boy will be okay, I tell myself – boys will be boys will be boys.

Up at the crematorium a lizard is chewing on a cube of sticky pork someone has left beneath my plaque as an offering, or dropped through drunken fumbling. None of the usual shadow-fearing cowardice pulses through the animal and it takes two claps before he decides to lick his lizard lips and scurry away. The small plaque, set amongst many on the green-tiled wall, looks too new to be true; reminding me of a demonstration model you might find displayed at an engraver's in an English market town, alongside pewter hipflasks and silver-plated sports trophies.

NICK POWELL
"As long as there shall be stones, the seeds of fire will not die."
(Lu Xun)

Not a bad quote for my friends to choose, though it brings to mind the author's unmarried anti-hero Ah Q and his less assured, if not downright panicky, thoughts on life and love. Despite his reckless independence, Ah Q struggles to contain the age-old belief that the worst form of filial conduct is to leave no descendants; married to this fear, the fact that spirits without descendants are destined to go forever hungry.

I should be more grateful. The mourners have done their best to give succour to my woe-begotten soul. It's just that their best isn't very good. I promise the real victim of recent tragic events that I will commemorate them in a more permanent way. By living for them as well as me? Going to places they never saw? No, that's too easy – I will find and claim a virgin patch of earth somewhere in Hong Kong and plant a tree where private services will be available to a highly select audience.

My pledge made, there's no point hanging around in the heat. I head back down to the ferry pier where I'm dealt another blow. A queue snakes from the ticket office, past the seafood restaurants with their depressed groupers suspended in mildewed tanks, and on to the pungent wet market beside the cargo dock where boxes of IKEA furniture and other exotic imports are slung onto electric-powered wagons before their grizzled drivers do battle with the bikes.

How is this possible? What time did these people come to sweep up? Either they are spreading themselves thin – the victims of large families; and having done a little sweeping here are off to find more ancestors on other islands – or have given the merest nod to their duties and are departing to enjoy the rest of the bank holiday at a theme park or banqueting hall. Either way, after being accused of pushing in by two smiling police officers in sky-blue shirts, I find myself at the back of the queue.

For a while I think I'm going to make it. A couple of enormous slow ferries arrive consecutively, consuming around a quarter of our number. As the rest of us shuffle forward obediently, I spy a longhaired western couple working the crowds methodically but with a nervous electricity underpinning their movements. They ask the same two or three questions to everyone they meet. They are looking for someone. A child. Long hair. Naughty. But nice. Eventually they reach me. Have I seen a little boy? "No," I tell them. "Sorry." They leave me swaying like a decommissioned flagpole, but not before the mother – my age, nose ring – has shot me a concerned look, oddly devoid of compassion.

It's strange what the imagination is capable of when seasoned with paranoia and left to simmer in sunshine. I think of the slow-cooked turtles they serve in some parts of China, who don't realise they're dinner until the water temperature goes from tropical to boiling. Just before fainting I convince myself I can see a whiplash of red hair weaving through the clusters of souls ahead of me.

"It can't be…"

Someone is trying to hold me upright. Too late, too late – I'm going, going, gone and the unfortunate Chinese family beside me, perhaps aware of Cheung Chau's starring role in a soap opera back home, find themselves calling for help as I slip into unconsciousness and they wonder if this is real or an exclusive preview of the new series.

By the end of Jeanie's day, she had experienced a couple of surprises seemingly designed to reassure her that there were still new things under the sun. After opening up the bar just after 11am and saying goodbye to a couple of departing backpackers, she sensed the opportunity for a mid-morning meditate, but transcendence was denied by the package addressed to COLIN SWOON-PATS that continued to loll diagonally across the lowermost pigeonhole beneath the check-in desk and still snagged her attention at inopportune moments like this.

"Okay, Colin," she addressed the undelivered item. "Let's get this over with."

She took the package and weighed it in her hand while snipping at its edges with her nail scissors. The contents weighed as much as one of the steins she kept refrigerated behind the bar, and might also be prone to break if tackled too vigorously. Peering through the small dark hole she had created revealed nothing to the eye, though an odd, familiar smell – musty and metallic – found its way to her quizzical features.

She snipped some more. Nothing spilled out as a result. She was dealing with a single solid object. Finally, she cut straight across one end and upended the parcel to relieve her impatience once and for all. Then wished she hadn't.

The package contained a grey-black stone of many irregular sides. Beyond its unique but unspectacular shape it had no special features. It was of the earth – a chunk of what is underfoot, ripped up and presented to humanity without display case by way of geological fault-lines and the chaos they inspire in tides and weather. Although the rock looked damp and shiny in places, this was simply a trick of the eye. It was bone dry. Even the bloodstain that covered a quarter of its exterior was completely matt; the faded thumbprint within it could have belonged to a caveman. Only the human hair – black and shiny and not unlike the ones her mother used to unpick from her bone-handled brush – looked like it had a trace of fluid within it. Otherwise how would it be stuck to the face of the rock like that?

Jeanie vacated the space behind the check-in desk, which had begun to feel confining, but she couldn't leave the stone there, manning the fort with its witless innocence; a curiosity piece without a plaque to add context. Nor was it right to throw the thing away, were it even possible to throw something away of which the earth is made. She circled the desk, watching Swoon-Pats' property do precisely nothing as she stroked her chin. Then she walked over to the bar, returning with a huge, crystal-cut ashtray. With pincer-like fingers she lifted the stone an inch or two off the desk and transferred it to the ashtray. With two hands she returned the ashtray to its home in a cupboard beneath the bar.

The shower helped her come to terms with the discovery. It had been a prank of some kind. That famously impenetrable British humour – friends sending each other odd things through the mail. The staining had been caused by fake blood, the type they used in TV shows; the hair was an accidental addition provided by a passing mother, sister or girlfriend – for only men could be the instigators of such stupidity.

She closed her eyes and let the water pepper her changing body. Here, where her breasts had been, was an alcove like a ledge behind a waterfall around which warm, watery mist danced. Her long hair had been replaced by an elfin cut; the strong roots inherited from her mother supporting slivers of silver more than one man had found attractive. Her body may have reverted to its childhood form, but it remained ready for whatever life threw at her. She was still well-proportioned, energetic, "full of beans", as her father put it; hence the need to meditate, hence the need to be a water-baby for five more minutes…

"Can I help?" Jeanie asked the well-dressed couple waiting downstairs at the Brolly.

Damn, was her hair still wet?

"Ms Lau?" asked the woman, her accent American.

"Yes. And you are…?"

"We are Mr and Mrs Falk," said the man. Like his wife he was tanned and slim and dressed in beige designer-wear. While she carried a small, brown handbag of honeyed leather on a gold chain, he held a diminutive brown attaché case of similar quality. They looked more European than American, though his accent matched hers.

"More precisely," Mrs Falk was involved in an elegant tussle with her own tongue, "we are the parents of Jonathan Falk. We have been told that Jonathan regularly frequented your saloon."

Saloon? Jeanie smiled at the word but her face was quickly neutralised by the blank expressions of the Americans. They were tired. Tired and hungry – for news.

"Yes, I know Jonathan," she told them. "What a handsome boy you have. A student, I think? Of engineering, maybe?"

"We don't know where he is," Mrs Falk interjected. "We haven't heard from Jonathan in weeks."

"Since we video-called him on March twelfth, to be precise," Mr Falk said. "We wonder if you may have seen our son in the meantime?"

Jeanie did the maths. "Within the last month?"

They nodded.

"Perhaps not," Jeanie confessed. "But then it's not unusual for the youngsters to go travelling in spring, while flights are cheap and the weather is still...reasonable."

"This is reasonable, is it?" Mr Falk grimaced, running a hand through his dark blonde hair.

"First time in Asia?" Jeanie guessed.

"Ms Lau, forgive us," Mrs Falk took over. "We wouldn't be here if we hadn't exhausted all other possibilities – Jonathan has not exited Hong Kong during the last month, nor had he spoken to us, or any of his colleagues, about travel plans. His university are as astonished by his disappearance as we are. As you might imagine, he was an extremely conscientious researcher. They're keeping as many assignments open for him as possible, meaning he's still on course to gain his doctorate this year."

"If he checks in soon," Mr Falk added.

Jeanie nodded, looking them both in the eye.

"Forgive me," she said. "I've had an emotional twenty-four hours myself, though it's as nothing compared to your suffering. Let me check with Jonathan's friends for you. Most will be in here later. Take my card." She picked up a Yellow Brolly business card from a Perspex container on the bar and passed it to Mrs Falk using both hands. "And leave your number with me so I can call you the second I hear anything about where he might be."

Mrs Falk used a slim-line, hotel-branded pen to write her number on the edge of a beer mat.

"Thank you so much, Ms Lau."

"Jeanie."

"Thank you, Jeanie. We're staying at the Mandarin Oriental. It's –"

"Don't worry," she reassured her. "I know where that is."

"Much obliged," said Mr Falk, leading his wife towards the noisy street.

"Can I find you a taxi?" Jeanie asked.

"We have a car waiting," he said. "Speak to you soon."

And they were gone.

Meanwhile, I come round on a different island – the one I share with Frank, Kim and a thousand other expats. I'm lying in bed in my shack in the jungly backwater of Pak Kok, the least salubrious part of Lamma. In the '80s and '90s this was where the soaks and the skagheads who'd overstepped the mark sat around smoking joints while waiting to be deported back to their anonymous British towns. Back then it was the colonial government who rounded up undesirables, now it was the turn of the Hong Kong authorities. People like me, who refuse to work hard or play by the rules, have never been popular in this part of the world.

Several scenarios spring to mind to explain my blink-and-you've-missed-it journey. What seems most likely is that I revived myself after my near-collapse in the ferry queue and got back here on autopilot. I was in a bad way – that much was clear. It isn't beyond the realms of possibility that the reserve willpower required to propel me homewards was only available at the expense of my short-term memory. I had been operating at full capacity, and in doing so may have short-circuited my consciousness. What does it matter? I've made it back safely. I'm not in a police cell or handcuffed to a grunt on a plane bound for Blighty.

Yet something's bugging me, and I don't mean the mosquitos dancing through the net curtains to have a nibble on my veiny limbs. The shack looks as banged up and damp-mapped as ever – the lopsided painting of an unidentifiable landscape remains lopsided and unidentifiable – but the constitution of my surroundings seems to have changed in subtle ways.

There's the glass of water on the upturned orange cart beside my mattress, for example. I have no fridge here; without electricity there's little point, nor am I used to drinking water out of anything except a plastic bottle. Yet here is a cool and soothing beverage served up in a civilised way. Can I really have stopped off for fresh water, lining up and paying like an ordinary consumer as I staggered home in a catatonic state, then found a clean glass in my bombshell kitchen?

Only one person is sufficiently indebted to me, and concerned for my welfare, to trail me, observe my distress and then mount a rescue operation that must have taken strength and guile. Only one person holds me in high enough esteem to provide a proper receptacle for me to drink out of – Ray. Is he here now or has he gone out for supplies? Where's my phone? I need to ask him exactly how he got me home and who saw us en route.

My clothes are folded neatly on the floor beside the bed. I stretch over and feel for my smartphone. Then I hear a noise. Someone is entering the room.

"Hello Nicolas," says Lennox. "Who's been in the wars then?"

CHAPTER ELEVEN

Fenton addressed his dog, Hunter, as he pottered around the garden.

"Do you know what the three indicators of real generosity are, according to Sufism?"

Hunter was truffling for bugs in a tangle of roots and chalky earth. He paused to look up at his master.

"First, to remain steadfast without resisting." He kicked a crab apple into the long grass a terrace below them. "Second, to praise without the emotion of generosity."

Hunter sneezed.

"And finally, to give before being asked."

He led them up to the bench in the pockmarked concrete yard beside the lawn. The garden hadn't looked this good since the peak of Miriam's horticultural ambitions but prettifying the yard was a job he intended to leave for the next residents, should any be forthcoming.

"I mean look at the wording," he sighed, producing the letter from a side pocket of his overalls. "'Your track record suggests an appetite for destruction ill-befitting of a mature resident of Asia's World City...'"

Fenton shifted his skinny buttocks from side to side on the ironwork in an attempt to gain relief. None seemed likely. Hunter lay at his feet, snapping at invisible mosquitos.

"After everything I've done for this place. The woodworking workshops, the tree houses for the neighbourhood brats. I even helped make the grandstands for the locals' pagan parades – risking the wrath of my own lord and master. If all that wasn't generous then maybe I *am* bleeding Axl Rose."

Hunter looked up at him blankly. These things had happened before Miriam left – before everything changed. By the time he met his master, he may as well have had a barrel full of brandy sloshing around his neck, like a skinny St Bernard's.

"I mean, I know what you're thinking," Fenton continued. "That the charges levied against me, while not pretty to read – disturbing the peace, verbal abuse of a tax inspector, ordering municipal workers off public land – are missing their trump card. That Miriam remained steadfast without resisting the time I..."

A sudden soupy dampness coated his lashes, blurred his vision. The side effects of his sobriety continued to surprise him. First, a revived sense of smell – enabled by the lack of cigarettes – had allowed him to bask in the sheer bloody awfulness of durian flesh when he stooped to study a fallen fruit at the market, now a revival in his dried up tear ducts was threatening to wash away his credibility in the eyes of his long-term companion.

"I only hit her once. Not hard," he sniffed. "Do I regret it? Of course I bloody do. I let her see my father in me. I let her see what I was capable of and what I would become. She stormed out of here like a banshee. When she came back for her things, I accused her of reporting me to the police. Smart move, Fenton, smart move," he rolled his eyes. "All this time, I wondered if they had me fingered for assault – were waiting for their chance to haul me in. No, Miriam didn't let me down. Turns out she never let me down."

Fenton checked his watch. 4.15pm on a Friday – Paul would have finished work and made it to the Brolly. He was probably about to take his first sip of beer. He fished out his supermarket specs from a breast pocket, located Paul's number on his mobile and hit 'call'. Just because he'd given up drinking didn't mean he had to stop annoying people.

"Hello Fenton," Paul rumbled down the line in his deep, primordial scouse. "What do you want?"

"I've only got the blasted letter, as per you reprobates."

"Congratulations. IKEA do some reasonably priced frames if you want to stick it on the wall."

"Damn it, Paul. It's alright for you, you can preserve yourself in alcoholic amber until they ship you to the British museum, what about the rest of us?"

"If you've just called up to insult me, you can fuck right off."

"Sorry," Fenton backtracked. "My concern was...given the timing."

"They want us out of here by the end of May," said Paul grimly.

"Exactly. Given that, what's our plan?"

"Plan?

"How do we fight this?"

"Fight it?" There was a long pause. He wondered if Paul had hung up, or laid his phone down in surrender. "How can we fight shadows, Fenton? We're a dozen Robinson Crusoes against a billion Man Fridays."

"Well, listen, you may be interested to learn that even Chinese bureaucracy has a human face from time to time. Remember that Friday?"

"Seems unlikely."

"You do. The Friday before Nick died."

Paul grunted.

"Something else came to me, just yesterday – no, not religion – in a pre-morning dream – no, not one of those dreams, not at my age."

"My beer's getting warm, Fenton. Please get on with it."

"We were being watched that night."

"So what? We make a lot of noise. We're handsome bastards. What's your point?"

"This was someone altogether different from the usual type. Official, but dressed casual. Like the undercover cops you used to get at Glastonbury, looking for hippy dealers. Must admit, I used to point them in the right direction from time to time. But I wouldn't be keen on helping this individual."

"What's any of this got to do with the price of eggs?"

"I'm going to find this bastard. Work out who he is, then track him down. I've got a sketchbook somewhere round here. Maybe I'll try to recreate a mug-shot in pen and ink. Hawkish appearance, bony beak."

"And should you find this bird man, in a city of seven million people?"

"Get him on a harassment charge. Prove we're being unfairly treated."

"Dream on, boyfriend."

"So what are you going to do?" Fenton demanded. "Just give up?"

"Maybe the British government will do something. Lodge a complaint at the UN. China isn't meant to do anything like this until 2047 at least, by which time…"

"You think those dysfunctional hypocrites will go to the UN for *us*? Washed out reminders of a forgotten empire? Now you're being ridiculous."

"Well call me back when you've got it sussed," Paul signed off unceremoniously.

There seemed little point in continuing their conversation, but while Paul would soon have anaesthetised himself for another night, Fenton was destined to remain fraught and fidgety until he found release of his own. His thoughts returned to Miriam. How old would she be now? Ten years younger than him, so that would make her – forty-five, give or take. Surely married, kids maybe, but perhaps still hanging around her beloved Taiwan. Hanging around! That was his style, not hers. She'd been a lecturer in film – she might be a professor by now. A letter could appear overblown, intimidating even, given recent experience. But a postcard of thanks…of overdue gratitude might be in order, if he could find her address.

"Check our floppy discs, shall we?" he asked Hunter, standing up and stretching.

Inside the house he found a sketchpad in a dusty drawer, once the property of you-know-who. He hacked a pencil to a point with his penknife and as the computer throbbed into life, going through its various interminable updates, he began to sketch their unlikely stalker from a six-week-old memory.

I don't have the opportunity to fret and fuss like Fenton; to luxuriate in a world of cause and effect within which I can still pretend I have a role, because it appears I'm being held captive by my wife.

"Where's my phone?" I ask Lennox, as she stands watching me, one forearm tilted forty-five degrees from the other.

"What about *my* phone?" she asks, removing a ball of fingers from her lips.

"What about it?"

"Honestly, Nick. Your determination to turn this marriage into a B-movie, casting me as the super bitch you tell your friends in the pub I've become. I don't mind any of that on paper...but once you start putting your silly ideas into practice."

I wonder how her hysteria will manifest itself this time. Shouldn't I have planned an escape route? Wasn't that on page one of the Fugitive Handbook?

"I don't know what you mean," I tell her.

"I mean that once I'd found the bug, I was able to turn it back onto the bugger who bugged me. Hence, Exhibit A. Late husband."

"You're telling me you're a tech expert now?"

"The midget who owns the phone shop on Tung Street?"

I turn to study the dirty net curtains, as close to embarrassed as I get.

"Seems he doesn't work only for husbands," Lennox continues. "But is quite willing to reverse the tracking process so that wives may find their errant spouses using the same technology implanted in their phones."

"Implanted? You make it sound sexual."

"Don't go there, Nick. If I don't sound sufficiently angry, it's because I'm still stunned you'd do this."

"What was I supposed to do? Return to the UK with my tail between my legs? You know what I have going for me there – precisely sod all."

"We could have talked about it," Lennox softens her tone. "Made a plan, like we used to."

"But I'd lost you," I explain. "Sometimes it feels like I lost you the minute we stepped off the plane. Perhaps if you'd shared the news with me...?"

"It was highly confidential. A leak could have brought down the firm. If I'd warned you—"

"You'd have lost your status. I understand how important that is to you."

"Christ," she snaps at last. "You think I have any status at the firm with a fantasist for a husband?"

Lennox produces a cigarette from a slim packet in her purse. She lights it without offering me one.

"Anyway, I knew you weren't dead," she exhales. "You're too greedy to die."

"Greedy?"

"Not for material things – greedy for facts and figures, for information you might use to your advantage later."

"You make me sound like a blackmailer."

"Don't play the innocent. This isn't the work of any innocent. Tell me how you did it – faked your own death, I mean."

"Tell me how much you know already. How long have you been following me?"

"Believe it or not, I've been unable to devote as much attention to your silly games as you may have liked. The midget and I established you were living here on Lamma. Nothing more dramatic than that appeared to be happening for a while. I went away on another trip. When I saw you were heading for Cheung Chau and it coincided with a public holiday I decided to see what you were up to. Seems I caught up with you just in time."

"I got a bit overheated, that's all."

I'm not sure whether to be relieved that Lennox has made so little fuss about my disappearance or offended by her lack of curiosity. Neither do I know why I'm obliged to answer her questions all of sudden.

"We had some visitors at our firm this week," she continues, toeing out her smoke on a flimsy floorboard. "Perhaps you've met them before? The Falks. Parents of your old friend, Jonathan."

"I haven't had the pleasure."

I begin to look around for my phone with greater purpose while hiding my intentions from Lennox.

"It seems Jonathan disappeared around the same time you did, only he's enjoyed a little more success in keeping his whereabouts secret. I might have known this escapade was connected to another of your bromances. What happened? Did you fall out with him? Over a woman perhaps?"

"Jesus, Lex – when did you get so cynical? I mean, honestly, can you pinpoint the exact time it happened? We were happy, you and I. You remember that, don't you?"

An open cardboard box, full of wires belonging to old phone chargers, computers and God knows what else, has changed position from below the window to a corner of the room. Despite her above-average height, Lennox is surprisingly dainty on her feet. If she hadn't kicked it scudding across the floor, then she might have investigated the contents; perhaps she'd already plopped something new into it – like my phone – before tidying it to one side.

"You're right," my wife says, unexpectedly, gazing into the gently bobbing fronds outside. "We were happy. I mean, we weren't perfect, but we managed to forgive each other our minor indiscretions. Until one day. Poof! The spell was broken. We stopped talking, and then we stopped having sex."

"Lex…"

"Well we did, didn't we? Any normal husband encountering his wife after returning from the dead…"

I begin to choke convincingly. My water is gone. I am a husk. Lennox gives me a look, the one that says, "If you're faking this, I'm going to make you wish you weren't." Never has it been more appropriate.

"You get a top-up," she says, taking my glass. "I get some more information before I leave you here rotting in your own filth. Deal?"

I nod, my face a healthy red by now. Perhaps I can even get her on a passive smoking guilt trip. It's a crying shame when marriages come down to such petty point scoring, but it takes two to tango – two to fuck things up this badly. As soon as Lennox is out of the room, I scramble out of bed and start rooting around in the box of tricks. Soon enough I identify the cool, slim body of my phone. I smear my thumb across it and call Ray. He answers immediately.

"Plan B," I tell him. "I'm here, at home. I need Plan B – now."

Lennox re-enters the room with a full glass of water. I've already hung up and plunged my phone under grey sheets.

"A rapid recovery," she smiles. "In case you decide to scarper just as quickly, let me tell you what I need you to do for me in return for my silence."

"Who's the blackmailer now?" I ask, trying to remain casual.

"I am," she says breezily. "And so as not to upset your little band of friends – not to mention the authorities – you probably prefer to be dead for now. All I need you to do is meet this man in Soho next Wednesday evening. That shouldn't be too difficult should it?"

"What man?" I ask, taking the business card she passes me with my free hand.

"Not too much to ask, is it? In exchange for your wife's discretion."

Lennox puts the water beside me and scans me up and down. It occurs to me that having my right hand thrust under my bedding isn't a great look.

"I'm going now, Nick. You won't need your Plan B. I've taken the tracker out of my phone but it still operates as a normal means of communication if you decide you want to tell me more."

"To confess, you mean?"

"I suppose I do," she is tying her hair up, a precaution against the creepy-crawlies that may try to hitch a ride from the trees overhanging the path outside. "Though to what I'm not sure."

"Tell me," I ask, trying to sit up and look half-dignified. "Am I dead to you too?"

"Life support," she shoots back. "You're on life support, Nick."

And she is gone.

CHAPTER TWELVE

Leaving and disappearing are two different things. I had it in mind to leave and ended up disappearing instead. Hong Kong is like that. You visit somewhere else and complain about the city's climate or the pollution or the crowds of tourists until you're blue in the face. Then it sucks you back in. Before you know it you're clinging to its teat, hooked on those sweet and sickly experience cocktails once again. You feel revitalised at first but then the old suspicion returns: that you're rotting. You reach for a drink and wonder whether, zombie-like, your arm might snap and crumble, releasing a cascade of maggots onto your marble-effect flooring. And then the realisation returns: by the time you decide to get away it might be too late.

The leaving thing was thundering through my head when we began that fateful hash. Lennox and I had turned our home-from-home into a peculiarly British kind of hell. The sex strike I conducted to draw attention to her lack of respect had failed to make an impact, serving mainly as a grim reminder that she had plenty of admirers elsewhere. In Wan Chai I waited for Lennox to tell me about the changing rules for expats I'd chanced upon, but received only platitudes – when we spoke at all. Our relationship was shipwrecked. We'd reached a depth of misunderstanding and mistrust from which no recovery – however expert the salvage job – seemed possible.

Ray had a way of taking my mind off things. On a good day, with the wind behind him, he could carry it up dale and down valley with ease. From such unlikely vantage points I began to imagine I could see things through his eyes: a skitting lizard frozen to a rock far below the trail; insects communing joyously around the rancid spatter-filth of wild boar faeces; a distant border over which paternal Mainland guardians peeked. It might look like I was running beside him but in this alternate reality my body had been left far behind at base camp, necking protein drinks and belching like a baby until his return.

When we started training together I thought I might be humiliated again. That Ray, like Lennox, would overtake me and never look back. Instead he helped me develop my core strengths and circumvent my weaknesses. It turned out my legs were far from useless. He directed me to the necessary gym equipment. Fat became muscle. My lungs were another story. In an effort to become one of those manly boys, whose accelerated life pattern has doubtless culminated in death or children by now, I had started smoking as soon as I could find a few quid, a quiet lane and some fire. Twenty-five years later, my lower limbs were powering my whistling air sacks towards infinity. There was no going back. Smoke-logged into stasis from the waist up, I was a jerky automaton below the pant-line. It was a necessary compromise; one more sign of mortality to be trampled upon as I flat-footed my way along life's unrelenting trail.

"Faster," Ray yelled over his shoulder. "Pretend I'm pretty girl. HBO dragon fuck lady."

"Your English," I inhaled, "is disgraceful," I exhaled. "Your English…"

And this became my chant until we separated two miles later. Our plan was very simple. We would set a fiendishly difficult trail for both Wimps and Rambos on the Pure Hash I was masterminding. Or rather, we would set the first few clues together and then I would veer off to collect cold pilsners and champagne, pre-ordered on Lennox's credit card from a high-end merchant prepared to meet me in the scrub, and then take a shortcut towards the finish up on Lion Rock. Secreting the stash at a suitably panoramic location for the post-race knees-up, I would then double back to the start, get changed into fresh gear, and prepare to begin this perfect hash anew. All went well, so much so that it was almost a pleasure to converse with my fellow hashers as we limbered up.

"Your man's pretty good then is he? Going to give us something to get our teeth into?" asked Leonard, a member of Hong Kong's banking aristocracy whose boarding school education had made him at least as English as his colleagues.

"Yes, it's all in hand, Len," I replied, noting the varicose veins cruelly parodying the blue Nike flash on his shorts. "All you have to do is decide if you're feeling like a Wimp or a Rambo today."

"Rambo, of course." Leonard looked offended. "Do I look like a puff?"

"That's the spirit," I smiled sweetly. "Go with the winning side. Just like your granddad when the Japs invaded."

"Beer better be cold this time, Powell," smirked Patterson, a South African lawyer with an undersized head, over which a halo of blonde hair seemed to hover of its own volition.

They were all at least ten years older than me, these men, which added to the joke. When they were my age they were probably aiming for a top fifty spot in the Hong Kong marathon, armed with the same wincingly unfunny humour and grimacing winks. I think of the young cop in *Chungking Express* telling the woman in the wig that when he's heartbroken he goes running to work up a sweat, so there's no water left for tears. I don't believe any of these men have ever allowed themselves to be heartbroken; whether knowingly or not they run to escape such mortal foibles.

At least Jonathan was of a similar vintage to myself. We warmed up together. I noticed that our bodies reflected one another too, and not just because of their pinky-pale pigskin complexions and faint tang of deep heat muscle rub. Both of us had been kids at a time when it was fashionable to be skinny, only to find ourselves outmuscled further down the line by youngsters who appeared to have been raised in the gym. Yet despite our former waif-like status, we had both grown fatter than we looked – especially around the middle. Perhaps our uneven bodies were another reason why neither of us wore the tattoos beloved by those five or ten years our junior.

"My first hash," Jonathan told me, tugging at his designer leggings. "Found it online. No idea you were involved, Nick."

"You chose wisely," I said, mirroring his final adjustments. "Pure Hash has none of the typhoon-chasing lunatics you find elsewhere. It's basically a stroll in the park set up to give the wives and kids of these old cunts a break."

"Yeah, it's really fucking *mellow*," snorted Patterson. "You two girls want to hold hands on your way round, we won't bat an eyelid."

"Ignore them," I told him. "Concentrate on your own race."

"Don't mind if I start off as a Wimp, do you?" Jonathan chewed his lip.

"Buy me a pint at the Brolly and I won't tell anyone."

It was unusual for a hare to double-back and run with the hounds. I suppose I wanted to check that the course we'd set was as flawless as possible and I wasn't destined to receive any vitriol in person, or from critics with disgusting pseudonyms on the web. Ray was to keep out of sight, content to watch the rewards of his good work with typical humbleness and a bellyful of gourmet food on my ticket. Once a dozen Pure Hash devotees had assembled, scraping their hooves and sniffing the moist air for blood, I felt it wise to contain them no more.

"Hashers," I paused for effect. "Begin!"

"On, on, on," cried Leonard, spotting the first clue squiggled on the trail up ahead.

"Now what?" Jonathan asked.

"Follow those arseholes," I told him, pointing at the shrink-wrapped bottoms disappearing into the bush.

Once I'd ensured my North American friend was following the wimpy trail – the others all deciding they were Rambos that day – I eased up. My hamstrings were beginning to tighten. There was no point ruining myself on this day of relative triumph. Inevitably, as I took a shortcut up towards the finish, watching the bobbing heads of yapping yuppies scale boulders and navigate dry riverbeds, a hollow feeling gradually replaced the thrill of directing my fellow athletes across painful terrain. So what if they liked the course and the champagne and I got moved up a notch or two in their estimations? Who was I trying to impress? Who was I trying to kid?

My thoughts were interrupted by a sharp cry of pain, followed by curses and communal laughter. The Rambos had their work cut out, but I wasn't worried about them. They were psychologically incapable of registering fear in the presence of other high-achievers. Even if they found themselves skidding along a shale path above a precipice – which was more-or-less what they would be facing before the summit – they would keep on keeping on; goading and shaming one another towards their goal. To me it seemed a strange way for human beings to behave. They would argue it was a longstanding and effective one. As I prepared to climb the steep stone steps to Lion Rock, the groans of the Rambos were replaced by the sound of agitated voices to my right. It was too early for tourists. Even the quickest Rambo would be a quarter of an hour away. Was I imagining things?

An American accent made up half the dialogue. That discounted the ghosts of the precious few prisoners of war who had escaped to China this way. It must be Jonathan, finished early and chatting with an egg stealer or furtive fungi snatcher – ne'er-do-wells beloved by local reporters desperate for a story. I abandoned the steps, following the conversational to and fro along a dirt path fringed with flattened grass. Soon a homemade wooden sign offered lame discouragement. "Danger: no access to Lion Rock from here." I was surprised these warning words hadn't been picked up and flung into the bushes by previous hash-heads. Still, I proceeded cautiously, possessing none of the true hasher's foolhardiness.

The path narrowed and crept around a corner from which a smog-smeared slice of Hong Kong's famous skyline could be seen. Damn. Here was the flaw in my perfect plan. The booze might be flowing but all it took to obscure the billion dollar view from the city's highest point was a rolling bank of a trillion miniscule particles – the closest we got to a whiteout in East Asia.

"Jonathan?" I struggled to find my footing while navigating a more precarious bend. "You made it up here mate? Well done!"

Could the voices be echoing down or around to me from elsewhere? Their volume had increased. Was that because I was edging closer to them, or had an argument begun? I started to doubt my own senses, perhaps inevitably given the amount of exercise undertaken that morning. What I was sure of was that neither the Wimp nor Rambo routes should have delivered Jonathan to such a precarious viewpoint. Don't look down, I told myself. Fortunately the pollution was softening the outlines of the outcrops below. The exact gradient was unclear, though to fall now would be suicidal. I stopped in my tracks halfway round the next bend. The voices had stilled too. It was time to turn around and return to the public steps, as any normal person would.

"This is Nick," I delivered some parting words – just in case. "I'm going back. See you at the top."

I expected more silence. What I received was a bloodcurdling scream and then an even deeper silence. Was my body playing tricks on my mind? I replayed the scream in my head. It was vicious. Animal. Real or not, it was over now. Time to go home. And then I saw a silhouette taking on the impassable corner ahead of me, deftly palming aside a sheer wall of rock before scuttling towards me; ignoring the shards of shale that slid willingly towards the eternal graveyard below. In seconds the figure was upon me – yellow vest and blue shorts billowing around a bloodless form, like sails clinging to a steel mast.

"Jonathan?"

But it wasn't Jonathan. It was Ray. And I was blocking his intended route. Rather than waiting for me to back up along the slender path, Ray hitched a lift on my shoulders, endangering us both, and then catapulted himself away, soft-toeing back towards the safety of the steps.

"What the fuck are you doing?" I yelled, righting myself and staggering after him. "You could have killed us both."

Ray turned and looked at me. His face was grey, his chest rising and falling like a set of industrial bellows. The soundlessness surrounding us seemed to emanate from him as much as the landscape.

"Well?"

"Your friend," he said at last. "He fall down. He dead now."

The next thirty minutes or so – the time it took the Rambos to reach the picnic I'd laid out at the summit – are still unclear to me. To put it bluntly, I'm not sure who was in charge. Looking back on it now, I think Ray and I must have taken turns deciding what to do next. I suppose that's what they call teamwork. I don't remember us talking very much. Instead we staggered downwards through ever-decreasing swirls of undergrowth using grunts and gestures, much as our ancestors would have done. Ray knew roughly where Jonathan would have landed, but it seemed unlikely he had been alone in seeing him fall fifty metres or more from the summit. Hong Kong isn't the kind of place where things happen unnoticed.

I recalled a friend at the Brolly telling me how he had been bitten by a snake while hiking solo in a remote part of Lantau. The son of a Ghurkha, he quickly found the culprit, snapped its neck, and flung it into the bush before continuing on his merry way. He was a big guy but nothing was going to stop the venom doing its work. He became sluggish, woozy. He had no phone. No one knew where he was. He would walk it off. And then – from nowhere – two medical orderlies appeared, like angels, and insisted he accompany them to the nearest hospital by chopper. He fought them every step of the way, he told us proudly. They had to strap him down in the helicopter but still he wouldn't stop screaming at them to let him go. After two days in hospital the medics had had enough and threw him out. My point being: they won't let you die here without someone causing a stink.

Until I saw the body I suppose I thought Ray might have been mistaken – that Jonathan had fallen only part of the way down, then picked himself up, cursed the hash and all who hash in it, and limped to the nearest MTR station with no more than cuts and bruises. But in a small clearing we found him laid out on a slab, looking skyward with open eyes – from here he'd watched his life force ascend to a higher place. Now he looked peaceful, if you discounted a couple of bones sticking up and out of his pinky-pale skin the wrong way.

Ray circled the body while my heart thudded and schlepped within my tightening chest. I wondered if I was about to join my friend on his journey. Perhaps this rock was destined to become a sacrificial altar for the white man. What do they say about heart attacks and how to survive them? Deep breath and then cough everything out. Deep breath and then... Ray stopped me. "No noise." A cardiac arrest was a luxury we couldn't afford at this stage. We had to hide him. We could bury him later, but in the meantime we had both accepted that the ever-helpful authorities were likely to misunderstand our inherent innocence, and that a pair of officious angels could appear from behind a bush at any moment.

"Yeeee-haaaa!"

The voice came down from on high. Was this an American god, celebrating the capture of another soul? No, it was Patterson. He'd finished his race and needed to let everyone know about it. We looked up to see him standing legs apart up on the mighty Lion Rock, looking as skinny and insignificant as he felt immense and omniscient. A dozen more pumped-up hashers, equally exhilarated, would be right behind him, ready to reward their efforts with some Bacchanalian excess. There was no time to mourn the one who hadn't made it. But just for a moment, with Jonathan's corkscrewed legs still refusing to tuck themselves neatly below a row of ferns, we let our gaze linger on the enormous banner unfurled from the summit. Yellow, of course; an umbrella, naturally, and those Chinese characters which demanded nothing less than universal suffrage for the Hong Kong people.

"Fuck," I said. "I didn't realise they'd done it again."

"Big march today," said Ray, wiping his brow. "Whole city come out for it."

"You should have gone," I said, without thinking.

"Yes," Ray caught me with a stone-cold glare. "I should have gone."

CHAPTER THIRTEEN

You never know what people get up to when you're not around. Perfectly good friends from different parts of your life – calm, reasonable people – meet one another and develop a venomous hatred within the time it takes you to zip up and return from the bathroom. Meanwhile long-term confidantes make advances on your wife the second they're left alone together. It happens. What's your excuse? I blame my laidback nature – a bigger and less complicated lie than that behind my occasional flashes of temper, and thus one most acquaintances are willing to accept. Laziness plays its part as well, though contrary to appearances I'm no advocate of laissez-faire relationships. If necessary, friends must be forced to get along together, while partners who suggest swinging are to be viewed as party poopers, trying to extract the fun from the exquisite pain that comes with lifelong commitment.

Happily, now and then we find ourselves and the people in our lives behaving with life-affirming predictability. Before taking evasive action on the ferry, much as the ferry itself is forced to deviate from its course as we rock into Pier 4, I'm able to see that – if only for this moment – Frank and I are perfectly aligned: me bobbing along in a selfish haze, consoling myself with the thought of a compensatory pint after meeting Lennox's contact in Lan Kwai Fong; he somewhere perfectly suited to his spontaneous, vulnerable, tragi-heroic nature – the front line; or in this case, the bow.

A few weeks ago, the Macau hydrofoil struck something large and mysterious as it sped out of Hong Kong harbour with its quota of gamblers, two of whom sustained serious injuries in the collision. Some say they hit a barnacle-encrusted whale, lured into the shipping lanes by improved fish stocks – or else seeking revenge on the fucker-uppers of the sea in a passive-aggressive way. Others claim they hit a Chinese sub, bang within its rights to be patrolling here. Either way, the speed limit has since been lowered and ferries advised to take extra precautions, something that is surely helping to keep the *Christina*, a thin sliver of yacht manned by Frank, Paul, Fenton and an unidentified local sailor, afloat.

"Stand up for expat rights," Frank yells towards the vast blue-and-yellow hull of the Lamma ferry. "Deputations not deportations!"

I lower the bill of my HSBC-branded baseball cap and peek out of the nearest window; taking a mental snapshot before the captain swings us round again in an ongoing attempt to circumnavigate the *Christina* and reach our allotted berth.

"Hong Kong, not China! Hong Kong, not China!"

Paul and Fenton are huddled together looking sheepish, or seasick, but Frank is standing firm on the churning water – blue-green today with wave tips paint-flecked with effulgent emulsion. The sailor manning the tiller I now recognise as Kim. While Frank, Paul and Fenton wear white T-shirts daubed with slogans reflecting the homemade banners tied to the mast – WE WD DIE 4 HK TOO; UNITE; SUFFRAGE 4 ALL – Kim opts for navy-blue slacks and a figure-obscuring orange lifejacket. I wonder if discretion is the best part of valour for her. Perhaps her uncle has insisted on her anonymity, because having recognised Kim, I'm now remembering that this is his boat, and was last boarded by *gweilos* – to the best of my knowledge – during an infamous junk trip off Sai Kung at which a pilling partygoer shat in his trunks and puked in his mask (in which order I can't be sure).

As the ferry turns noisily, I can't stop myself from rushing over to the opposite row of windows to see more. I'm not alone in being curious. The crewmembers – a mix of wiry matures and overweight youths – are chatting and pointing animatedly, in no way concerned about their delayed arrival in port. Likewise the curious passengers – mainly western and from the same vaguely artistic subset as those on board the *Christina* – are in no hurry to dock. A middle-aged woman with a whipped-cream haircut is cooing delightedly. "Oh Frank," she murmurs. "You bad, bad boy." My friend needs no encouragement, unfurling another banner, on which are scrawled three names in block capitals, along with "B" and "D" dates.

"These poor bastards lived and died here," he shouts up at us, shaking his bed sheet. "Don't we have the right to tend their bones and leave our own here too?"

"Oh fuck," I sigh.

The first dead expat on Frank's roll of honour is our predecessor Ernest Goucher (1894–1915) who, as we know, was killed by a tiger when they still roamed the Chinese border, and whose bones lie in Happy Valley Cemetery; the second is an Australian called Justin Green (b. 1991 d. 2017), a teacher of English who drowned off Cheung Chau in the early hours of a clammy weekend last summer. Despite the island's morbid reputation, as reflected in my own fate, it appears Justin had no intention of ending it all. A few empty beer cans were discovered on the pier, near the greasy steps down which he had been seen descending into the night water with his surfboard.

Sadly, what was most notable about this young man's death was the coverage it received in some sections of the Chinese media. Online, Green was portrayed as a drunken womanising fool; a perfect example of what Hong Kong could do without. His family back in Oz must have been mortified at the blatant racism.

The third name – almost inevitably – is my own. NICK POWELL (b. 1979 d. 2018). Not much more I can tell you about him.

"These men – and plenty of women too – will not be forgotten," Frank continues. "Cannot be dismissed as parasites. Yes, they may have sought adventure here. Yes, they may have drunk a beer or two. But they also gave back to the community. The so-called communist government up north has no right to—"

My blushes are spared thanks to a radical decision by our skipper who, through his own volition or radioed advice, gives up on Pier 4 and heads towards the Star Ferry terminal, in the hope of snaring a free space off 5, 6 or 7. The last I see of the *Christina* is the Union Jack fluttering at its rear – no doubt attached at Fenton's insistence. I also note that their audience of sympathetic riff-raff on our weatherworn Lamma ferry is about to be replaced by an altogether different type of Hong Konger aboard a super-slick new arrival.

Taken to and from their private playground on the tip of Lantau Island in an air-conditioned cabin resembling that of the Cathay jets to which they are accustomed, one imagines most occupants of the Discovery Bay ferry would have a low threshold for screaming kids and drunken hippies. Eye-watering income levels are indicated through unflashy designer clothes, a dash of jewellery; an understated wristwatch. It is they, the authorities would argue, who are the real expat contributors to Hong Kong's progress. So in a few months the rock bands they take their more daring clients to see at Quantum's might be missing their pale-faced members, but otherwise what does this jolly roger of a protest have to do with them? Time is money. A line of identical red taxis wait at the harbour front to take them to important meetings. Their crisply uniformed skipper with the gold braid trim guides the commuters into Pier 3, leaving the *Christina* in its gently mocking wake.

"You getting off, mate?"

It's Scampi, the crusty bookseller. I've bought a volume or two from him on more than one occasion but he doesn't appear to recognise me. Perhaps it's difficult for Scampi, who favours long floral dresses, a bleached topknot, and purple Doc Marten's, to distinguish one workaday punter from another. Add to that a prodigious weed habit, and it's safe to assume his Rolodex of customers is somewhat frayed around the edges. Still, there's no excuse for complacency. I apologise for dawdling in a broad West Country accent and continue along the gangplank. I could duck back along the harbour wall to see more of the *Christina*'s valiant efforts, but deem the chances of being recognised too high. Besides, I have business to attend to.

The card Lennox gave me is heavy, like a handshake. I study the embossed gold letters as I make my way up the steps and escalators and along the narrowing walkways that will take me over six decisive lanes of traffic and a dozen meandering market streets to Soho.

MARTIN CHAN, LLB, LLM

This upstairs world grants the pedestrian direct access to the foyers of world-leading banks and law firms; but cast your eyes to the butt-peppered sidewalk and you'll find a shifty arrival from the DRC demonstrating the latest must-have toy; on Sundays a female army of South Asian live-in helpers camped out in cardboard and having more fun singing and laughing on the street than the highflyers achieve in a lifetime of corporate karaoke. Umbrella sellers appear out of nowhere on rainy days, charging exorbitant rates for designer brollies with leaky logos. That's the Hong Kong spirit, we're told; its innocence maintained by oddities like the kilt, sporran and imitation sword shop outside which I stop to read more about Mr Chan.

Gold Member: Law Society of Hong Kong
Secretary: Hong Kong Literary Circle

Big shot, by the sound of it. As a friend, colleague and/or lover of Lennox's I'd expected nothing less. Clearly the backstreet Lan Kwai Fong setting is for anonymity, for him as much as me perhaps. Popular with expat teens whose idea of rebellion is linked to shots of fluorescent spirits and casual sex, a hedonism carefully arranged around exam times and lifts in daddy's car, the congested nightlife district still hosts enough of their age-denying parents for men in their 40s and beyond to join what passes for fun without facing approbation.

Via an unclogged Soho artery, over cobbles that have seen too much, I approach the black spiral staircase that will take us up to the pub Lennox has chosen for this meeting of mutuals – Putin's Proxy, the only Russian bar in the area, and one of the least popular drinking holes in the city. It's mid-afternoon. Last night's casualties have been swept away, but new ones are already in the making – drawn here by the promise of sex, sanctuary or oblivion.

"Do you know who I am?" asks a frazzle-haired septuagenarian, blindsiding me.

"What?"

"I said, 'Do you know who I am?'" he repeats, managing to relay an air of menace, despite the pyjamas.

"Yes," I sigh. "I do."

Harpo Brills, aged Australian photographer, rocks from side to side, anticipating my answer with a crooked smile. He's carrying a half-empty wine bottle with a loose fluidity. Now he grasps the neck and taps it against the almost transparent material covering his ghostly legs. Maroon liquid sloshes about, impatient to escape – eager to sacrifice itself to its master's cause.

"Well?" he croaks.

"You're Harpo Brills, portraitist to the stars, you sometimes drink at the—"

"Fuzz sake," Harpo snaps. "Just needed my name. Don't need to know my cocking life story."

He's up the road before I can establish whether he's recognised me. Probably not. A toilet roll streamer, stuck to the underside of a flip-flop, dragon dances behind him as he scales the sticky cobbles towards home. I do a quick audit of my senses. Make sure I'm fully scanning the pavement in anticipation of further surprises. Next time I might meet someone more sober and less wrapped up in themselves – someone I have to bribe or kill to prevent my cover from evaporating in the fuggy heat.

Three cigarettes later and there's still no sign of Chan. 3pm is now 3.22pm. Twice I've mounted the staircase – jet black like it's been dipped in tar – and peeked into the bar, but it's deserted beyond a young waist-coated waiter mournfully drying glasses. Then eventually I spot a diminutive figure in a smart black suit and skinny black tie coming towards me, deep in thought. Here's the first hint of class since I entered the neighbourhood. I wait until he's twenty feet away.

"Mr Chan?"

The figure looks up from the stones and I see below his dark wedge of hair the neatly creased features belying a man five or ten years my senior. He arches an eyebrow.

"That's me."

"Thank God, I was getting worried," I admit. "You had to go somewhere else first?"

"I did, to be perfectly honest." His English is faultless, but with an accent I can't place. "Needed to reacclimatise."

"Just back from business?"

"Something like that…"

We shake hands warmly, Chan holding onto my hand a little longer than might be expected in an Asian context. Once I've rescued my digits I ask the inevitable.

"Drink?"

"Thought you'd never ask."

Chan takes the spiral stairs like a cat; I get wedged halfway up while trying to let the dishwasher out for his break.

"You've put on weight," Chan giggles, which I might consider a bit of a liberty, if I weren't in such a rush to get this over and done with.

We find a table a discreet distance away from the barman. The sun is permanently barred from the place so I'm forced to fumble for a seat under the dim supervision of electric candlelight. The waiter brings us a bottle of chilled white wine in a silver bucket wrapped in a tea towel, then two wine glasses and two shots of vodka on a matching tray. I haven't ordered anything – presumably this is Chan's regular tipple. From his first sip of wine I notice that Chan is looking giddy, rocking up and down in his seat like an excitable schoolboy.

"Celebrating something?" I ask.

"Being alive," he smiles.

Ah, there's the rub. No doubt Lennox has told him that her husband occupies the realm of the undead.

"Perhaps you could tell me what she wants?"

"That's the million dollar question, isn't it?" Chan taps the side of his glass with a perfectly chewed fingernail.

"Hard to put a price on it," I reply, wondering how Chan is being rewarded for his errand.

"Your first love, was she?" There's that accent again.

"No," I admit, "that was—"

Too slow. Chan raises his shot glass.

"To first love!"

And his vodka is gone. I feel compelled to follow his lead, though I'm keen to modify my toast.

"To first wives."

Another slurp of wine, to wash down the vodka, and the next thing I know, Chan's ordering oysters.

"So what's your place like?" he asks while we wait.

"My place?"

"Tried to check into a hotel across the way, but they wanted thirteen hundred a night. Thirteen hundred! Fuck! When you work out what that is in drinks…"

I try to work it out then stop myself. We're not here to talk about Chan's desire to nail a city centre *pied-à-terre*. Then he's suddenly coy.

"Couldn't stay at yours, could I?"

"It's miles away," I remind him, taken aback. "And not up to your standards."

For some reason Chan finds this funny. Colour floods his face and he unleashes an unexpectedly powerful laugh; its abrasive edge quickly prompting a rip-roaring coughing fit. He holds his chest and I begin to worry, but he's just retrieving a Marlboro Red from a dented pack in an inside pocket, before indicating that he's off for a smoke, all the while continuing to laugh and cough and laugh some more. My companion exits as our plate of oysters is delivered.

"Everything all right, sir?" the waiter asks.

"Perfect."

We both know it isn't. Perhaps they're used to Chan's ways in here, but confusion is writ large across my clammy forehead. I need some answers, fast. It's more difficult to stand up than it should be. The tables are undersized, the light insufficient for me to watch my limbs into their optimum positions, but soon I'm also making for the door. The waiter looks concerned before his attention is engulfed by a sombre-looking pair who have just doubled his number of clients, the man middle-aged, Chinese, prominent nose supporting John Lennon specs; the woman younger, a pale European with lank brown hair.

"Back shortly," I tell the waiter, smiling in that self-loathing English way which foreigners seem to accept as common currency.

I'm not overly surprised to see Chan heading down the street towards Queen's Road, singing softly to himself; bent cigarette unlit by his side. Despite his meandering gait it takes me a while to catch up with him. I'm out of condition – my running days have become lying and waiting days; I will get fit in prison, I promise myself, if it comes to that. In the meantime: damn this man and his happy-go-lucky nature.

"Excuse me," I call out, prompting him to turn. "Aren't you forgetting something?"

"I'm so sorry," Chan smiles sweetly while retrieving his wallet. "Here," he passes me a credit card with BANK OF IRELAND stamped across it.

"What's this?"

"Tell them to keep the change, it's honestly no problem," and Chan turns to walk away again.

"What about Lennox?"

"The Lennox? Sounds expensive. I adore The Hilton but it's beyond my means just now. Terrible cliché, but I happen to have lost a lot of money on a certain horse at Happy Valley yesterday."

"Your accent…?"

"Irish."

Oh shit. A creeping realisation is busy colonising the extremities of my optimism.

"And the Hong Kong Literary Circle?"

Chan's face is blank for a millisecond, then the warmness returns.

"Circles within circles," he says. "So many circles in this world. Never very far from anyone, are we, when you think about it?"

I pause, reluctant to be wrong but faced with no alternative.

"You're not Martin Chan, are you?"

"No," Chan beams. "I'm Ewan Chan – of the Galway Chans."

I slap my face, shake his hand and then allow my new friend to continue on his merry way. Meanwhile, I'm left to stare down the angry waiter – already at the foot of the oily staircase – and the two silent punters who are following him down while sharing a filterless cigarette. Do I face the music or run? Has Lennox done this to me, or have I done it to myself? My phone begins to vibrate. It's Paul.

"How are you?" I ask.

"Wet."

"Saw you on the water today."

"Not going to work, is it?" Paul tells me flatly. "So I need to know when we start the next stage, Nick. And I need to know fast, because I've got a feeling that my mad ex-wife is about to take Poppy on a one-way trip to the Mainland."

"Look," I try the authoritative tone I've been practising on Ray. "Do you trust me or not?"

"Nicky…" Paul squirms.

"You have a choice," I explain, "either give me some more time to sort this out, or go rogue and end up in an elderly father's institute."

"It's just, you know. I was on that yacht, imagining Poppy and me sailing off into—"

"Mate, I don't have time for this – are you going to give me the chance to make it up to you?"

Paul reluctantly agrees. I gesture amicably to the waiter then turn and flee towards the Central-Mid-Levels escalators.

CHAPTER FOURTEEN

The next day Jeanie found herself in the blinding expanse of Hong Kong International airport beside an American consular official and a scruffy police inspector, saying goodbye to Bob and Barbara Falk. They'd found no trace of their boy in the city, leaving only because Bob had urgent business in New York and the trio of helpers seeing them off had promised to do all they could to continue the hunt. The couple gave a sad salute then trundled their cases towards the departure gates.

"I have to go," the young American sighed. "Car's waiting. Duty calls."

The policeman, Lam – middle-aged with pockmarked skin – prepared to follow, but Jeanie stopped him.

"What exactly are you doing to help find this young man?" she asked.

"We're following a missing person procedure, as we would for anyone."

"Is that it?'

The policeman smiled. He was coated in a viscous layer of sweat. For defence maybe, like those Amazonian frogs that snakes are forced to regurgitate.

"Some higher-ups would prefer we didn't waste five minutes on wilful foreigners."

"He's a nice man, Jonathan. Clever and responsible, so far as I can remember."

"They don't all look the same to you?" Lam smirked.

Jeanie hesitated. Didn't rise to the bait. Sometimes the rudest ones were also the fairest. Possibly he'd told his superiors to get lost when they told him not to bother going to the airport. The police she hated most were those who faked friendliness when they called in at the Brolly; accepted drinks and gossip, and then wrote reports claiming she was running a house of ill repute populated by the same aging agitators as Think Tank. Many complaints from your neighbours, the official letters said.

One more complaint and we close you down. Yet most of her neighbours were friends. Often elderly, they signed the petitions Jeanie organised against gentrification; against the closure of cheap local restaurants; against the landlords who wanted to exploit their tenants or make them leave so they could sell family homes to Chinese or western moneymen.

"No, they don't all look the same to me," Jeanie answered, "any more than policemen do. What do you think happened to him?"

"Two possibilities," said Lam, as he walked Jeanie towards the Airport Express. "He wanted to disappear. Didn't want the career. Didn't want to be like Bob and Barbara. Wanted to go live in Thailand. Or Vietnam. Or Myanmar. Spent the last of his money on fake documents and a 'Fuck You' tattoo."

Jeanie wasn't amused.

"Or...?"

"Maybe he was like the American just now."

"Meaning?"

"Too clever for his own good. Mandarin at Harvard. Cantonese at weekends. Shopping trips to Shenzhen. A tourist in Tiananmen. Chinese girlfriends. More trips. Asks too many questions. Gets greedy. Gets careless. Gets taken over the border. No holiday this time."

"You think he's a spy?"

"You don't think you've met any spies, Jeanie Lau, during all your years serving drinks to expatriates?"

"I suppose..."

Lam took a silver card case out of his pocket and attached some incongruously fashionable horn-rimmed glasses to his face while examining its contents.

"Here's my card," he said. "And there's your train. Keep your eyes and ears open Ms Lau and call me if I can be of assistance."

"You mean if I can be of assistance?" Jeanie slapped her Octopus card down on the automatic barriers.

"It works both ways," Lam flashed his yellow teeth at her. "Don't worry. If the boy's still in Hong Kong we'll find him."

Back at the Brolly for the late afternoon shift, Jeanie found her patrons behaving more cryptically than ever. She had expected to find the back table in good spirits following the previous day's waterborne protest, which had made it into the *South China Morning Post*. On her way in she noticed that Beryl – secretly proud of the gruff clientele – had affixed the relevant clipping to the notice-board, between a recruitment ad for an LGBT dragon boat team and an invitation to workshop your nascent fiction with the Hong Kong Literary Circle. But instead of celebrating, the boys were arguing.

"You're an idiot!" Paul – usually so quiet – was standing up, gesturing towards Brills.

"Steady on old chap," said Frank, using his comedy posh tones to try and diffuse the situation.

"I tell you I saw him," Harpo drawled. "Clear as fucking day. That fat skinny waste of space that used to come in here."

"Nick," said Fenton quietly. "He's called Nick."

"And he's been dead for almost a month," Paul reminded them.

"Period of mourning officially over then," said Harpo, unperturbed by Paul's upset. "That's if the bastard's actually snuffed it. Dead or alive, can't say I'm a great fan of old Nicky. Bit of a snob. Not as funny as he thinks he is."

"Like your ghostwriter?"

Frank admired Brills' work, but that didn't mean he was obliged to worship everything he put his name to.

"Tell us what happened in Chile again," Frank's counterattack against the Beckett-haired image-maker enabled Paul to retake his seat and have a slurp of beer. "Your photoshoot with the sex midgets?"

"Not quite as interesting as seeing Nick's ghost," Fenton muttered.

"Horny little bastards," Harpo roared, "Had them chasing each other up and down the mountains. And when they caught up with one another…"

Harpo stood, his skinny thighs butting the table with enough force to topple his wine.

"Harpo!" Ditzy shouted from the bar, rushing over with a tea towel, but the Australian was not to be deterred, miming copulation with his short red fingers while rasping laughter over his unsmiling companions.

"Getting handy in the Andes," he offered in summary. "Reminds me of getting rock-hard in the Rockies. Did I tell you that one?"

Ditzy timed her run without due care and attention, but that did not excuse Harpo encircling her slim waist, then trying to caress the contours lurking beneath her tight red sweater. It was a fine line, Jeanie reflected – and a fine waistline; one thing to have the boys fantasising about Ditzy, another to have them crossing the border into no man's land. She sprang into action.

"How many has he had?" she asked Beryl, pulling Harpo away from Ditzy's stiffened body.

Beryl held up four fingers, a thumb; another thumb. Harpo had stopped struggling, was a dead weight; seemed to be channelling all the darkness in his photokinetic brain to make himself even heavier. Jeanie heaved him back into his chair; amazed the cheap wood could take the strain. And relax? Not quite. Paul was taking the flowers out of a vase Ditzy had foolishly left on their table. With a flick of the wrist he flung the tepid vase water into Harpo's goofy face. It might as well have been urine, or acid – Harpo's expression changed to one of unmitigated rage.

"You stuck-up, Beatles-loving, cock-sucking Pommy arsehole."

Smash. Harpo's wine glass became a weapon. He lurched forward, fixing its jagged crown millimetres from Paul's reverberating jowls. Too late the Brit realised he'd messed with the wrong artiste. But Jeanie was quicker than both of them. Instead of re-entering their testosterone-tagged territory she was standing behind her check-in desk at the front of the pub, a circular ashtray spinning at her feet and a bloodied rock in her throwing arm aimed squarely at them.

"Harpo Brills – here's a new development for you," she said. "You're going to put down that glass. You're going to go to the bar and pay Beryl your tab. Then you're going to go home for a long cold shower. The next time I see you will be in a month's time when you're going to come in here sober and order a lime soda. If you behave that night then you *might* get a glass of wine the next. Understood?"

Jeanie's lucky. The more quietly she speaks, the more people listen. Brills lowered the broken glass to the table, then quietly licked the nicks he'd self-inflicted on a couple of fingers. Frank and Fenton looked solemn and respectful. Paul looked…white. Harpo slowly hauled himself to his feet, but Paul was up first, skirting round the table in an agitated state. His eyes hadn't left the rock in Jeanie's hand.

"You're all fucking crazy," he said. "If I don't get out of here soon, I'll go crazy too."

Now he was edging along the wall towards the door, keeping a safe distance between him and Jeanie.

"Don't touch that thing again," he instructed her through trembling lips. "You don't know where it's been."

And then the mad old scouser was gone and Harpo was requesting another drink before being roughly escorted outside by Frank and Jeanie.

Poor Paul. This is where he needs a kind word from someone with secrets of their own, but I'm too busy replaying a scene from the previous afternoon guest-starring Martin Chan, who proves to be a lot less fun than Ewan.

"I trust the terms of the agreement are acceptable to you?" Martin looks up from his copy of the document he has passed me to sign.

"Not really," I tell him.

Playing for time I scan our surroundings for distractions but they are few and far between. A snotty child launches a broccoli spear at his mother. A cutesy European couple practise their chopstick skills by feeding each other sweetcorn kernels. Putin's Proxy is closed for renovations, according to the sign outside, which has forced the unimaginative suit before me to suggest we talk in an open-plan vegetarian restaurant within a nearby mall. He's paying; I'm acquiescing – but not when it comes to the small print.

"No booze?"

Martin Chan adjusts his spectacles. He has a face both innocent and hard, like a young prince born into a turbulent historical period. He doesn't blink, doesn't flinch when I stab a baby potato and rip its skin off with my wonky British teeth.

"As it states here – no alcohol of any kind, Mr Powell. And no trips to the licensed establishment known as the Yellow Brolly."

"Why would I want to go somewhere everyone thinks I'm dead?"

"As is made clear in Paragraph 2A, this agreement will be initiated by you reporting yourself alive to the British Consulate and selecting a reason for your absence from a dropdown menu of excuses provided by me and my colleague."

"My wife?"

"Exactly. Soon after you will be free to show your face again – anywhere bar this particular drinking establishment."

"And we'd stay married?"

"Yes…"

Martin Chan hesitates. I wonder if he's under Lennox's spell, as I used to be, and is holding out hope of replacing my surname with his own at the end of her moniker.

"Is that a big yes or a small yes?" I ask. "Because to me it sounded like—"

"You would stay married for a three-month trial period," Martin Chan explains. "During which time you would be expected to comply with the conditions laid down above, in addition to finding appropriate employment."

"Meaning?"

"A role within the legal or financial sector that—"

"—stops me being ejected from the country as a bum, I see."

I order a lemongrass and Cornish new potato smoothie from a passing waiter. I have no intention of drinking it, nor do I have any intention of splitting the bill. I take pleasure in Martin Chan's discomfort, even if we both know he's still winning the long game.

"Do you need a pen?" Martin Chan asks.

"No," I tell him. "I need a proper drink, but that can wait. Would I be able to take this document away with me?"

Martin Chan looks at me like I'm mad or stupid or both.

"This is a one-off opportunity, Mr Powell. There is no time for further consideration. You sign this now or walk away from your marriage."

"Martin Chan, may I ask you a personal question?"

I take a sip of lemongrass and spud to affirm my fears. It is disgusting.

"Well I'm going to anyway. Do you think it's possible for both partners to accept compromise in a marriage or do you think one partner has to submit to the demands of another?"

"In my professional experience—"

"I'm not talking about the legality of the thing. I might even be suggesting that marriage certificates and documents such as this – with their disregard for the subtleties of human nature, and the cornucopia of circumstances we might find ourselves within – are not worth the paper they're printed on."

"So you're not going to sign it?"

"Is there a Mrs Martin Chan?"

"If you're asking if I'm married then no, Mr Powell, I'm not."

"Come back when you are," I stand up, scraping my wooden chair against the reverent hush of the mall. "And I might reconsider."

I feel a bit giddy. I hadn't imagined refusing to do something would be so liberating. My strength worries me. I wonder if in fact my heart was broken many months ago, and rejecting this last chance for reconciliation has merely hardened it; sealed it into its lead-lined coffin, as it were. Still, I seem to be pissing enough adrenaline to paraphrase Fenton while taking a last look at the mall.

"Don't stay in here too long, Martin Chan," I advise him. "It's hard to get the smell off your skin after a while."

"There's no danger of me lingering," he snaps back, returning the juice-stained documents to his briefcase. "I have an occupation, Mr Powell. I have prospects. I have a future."

It's only when I get back to Lamma that the trite wisdom instilled in Martin Chan's words hits home. Whoever's broken into my shack is keen to let me know that I'm not important enough to inspire subtlety. The orange carts are upturned; the hairy wood splintered. The unidentifiable landscape that hung from a spore-ridden wall will be forever mysterious thanks to the hole someone has punched through it. Already unfit for human habitation, the intrusion has confirmed my temporary home's temporariness. There's no way I'm staying here tonight. Yet even in its current condition, my former sanctuary is still offering shelter to one biped of my acquaintance.

"Ray," I spot him hunched in a corner – a dim human fire deterring the inevitable animal invasion. "What happened?"

He looks up; the brightness in his eyes increasing, like a prodded laptop coming back to life.

"I was...hiding outside. Big Chinese dude come with skinny white chick. Dress in black. Maybe communists."

"Sure, I know who they are, but I meant what happened to you."

Ray puts his hands over his face and starts to massage his jawbones. The bags under the eyes I can accept as a by-product of Hong Kong life, but he is unable to erase the facial bruising with his small grey fists.

"Did they do this to you? Those two spooks?"

"No," he insists.

"Then who, the triads?"

"Doesn't matter."

Stubborn bastard. Sometimes I think he's worse than me.

"Well look, it's not safe for either of us to stay here," I tell him, peering into the jungle with some pretence of expertise. "You need to lose yourself in the kitchens of Wan Chai for a while, as we discussed. Kitchen porters won't be on the radar of anyone who saw you up to no good."

"*Me* no good? *You* no good," Ray laughs, his English as tattered as his T-shirt. "I hide myself easy. You need idea."

"You need to..." I bite my tongue. "Okay, you're right – I need an idea. How much?"

It's an act of charity. I refuse to have an employee of mine wearing rag shop clothes.

"500."

Which leaves me 500. And in return Ray passes me a well-thumbed Tourist Board map with some circles scrawled on it in biro. I groan as I unfold it.

"Cheung Chau? You must be kidding."

"Listen," Ray becomes animated. "You hide on Cheung Chau, no problem. Stay there. Wait for them to forget about you."

"Have you been to Cheung Chau?" I'm feeling less sympathetic, increasingly bankrupt. "It's full of tourists at weekends and locals during the week. Besides, what if I meet someone who saw me dragging Jonathan up the hill towards that bloody hotel?"

"Here," Ray points at the map, undeterred. "This part Cheung Chau very peaceful. No tourists. Locals here old, crazy or stupid. Near the pig killing workshop."

"Near the what?"

"Best plan for you," he gets up unsteadily. I worry about his blood sugar levels, but in seconds he has shaken off his fatigue.

"I must go. You safe there in Cheung Chau, Mr Powell – promise."

Not the most convincing of promises but here I am, having rejected Martin Chan's beautifully punctuated offer of truth and reconciliation in favour of a tatty map proffered by the owner of the bony runner's bottom fast receding into the jungle.

CHAPTER FIFTEEN

Paul is not a shapely individual, nor could he be described as fitting in well with any of the myriad social groupings that come as part and parcel of modern life, but to me he was the final piece of the jigsaw. Yes, most of us suspected that Paul had been an exuberant young man, fully participating in Liverpool's '80s – perhaps even '90s – art-pop subculture, but these days he was known for his taciturn nature, which – along with the acting skills he kept stashed deep in his box of tricks – made him the perfect person to testify to my demise, so long as he could be steered away from too much self-reflection.

"I got the wife I thought I deserved," he told me one time, as he prepared to undertake a solo snake-spotting trip to the dehumanised Grass Island.

"What does that mean?" I asked.

"How well do you know yourself, Nick?"

"We're on reasonable terms. More work to be done perhaps."

"Well as you get older you'll get to know yourself a whole lot better. And before you accept yourself – warts and all – there's sometimes a period of self-loathing."

"Which is when you married Ling?"

"Exactly."

"And now that you know yourself fully?"

"I'm off to hunt snakes on a deserted island."

Of course you don't know your friends fully until you call on them to do something remarkable for you. When I spoke to Paul under cover of darkness in the Wan Chai park where months before we had first encountered Ray, he could have easily bolted for the nearest police station using reserves of hitherto untapped energy. Instead, he chewed my words over slowly and deliberately, occasionally regurgitating some of my lexical choices for further examination.

"So this 'fatal accident', Nick. You didn't kill Jonathan…murder him, I mean?"

"God no. Why would I want to kill Jonathan?"

"What about Ray?"

"You've met Ray, you know he wouldn't hurt a fly."

"And I'm to pretend you're dead?"

"You have to *believe* that I'm dead, Paul. You have to let me disappear for a while. It's the only chance I have of getting Lennox back."

"What about Jonathan? What about what he would have wanted?"

I pass him my hipflask.

"Jonathan's dead," I remind him. "And you don't need me to tell you what he'd think about that."

"Classic atheist," Paul recalled, as I knew he would, "in the Woody Allen mould. Intellectual family. Insufficient time to fully develop his neuroses."

"A blessing, if you believe in that kind of thing – which he didn't."

"So from this moment on, and I'm paraphrasing Ling here, you're dead to me?"

"Until the heat dies down. Then we'll work out how to fix things with Poppy. Promise. One grisly, criminally deceptive good turn deserves another."

"Okay," Paul sighs and nods. "But why grisly?"

I look away, towards the forest of night-time traffic.

"Someone has to identify the body…"

A month on and I've grown my first beard and bought my first bike. It's unreliable, an indeterminate shade of brown, and needs constant oiling – and the bike isn't much better. Yet despite the lack of a stand-up career, or any of the associated trappings, I'm beginning to enjoy life in my neglected chunk of Cheung Chau. Not that it's remotely remote; it's simply off the tourist trail and, as Ray promised, closer to a pig slaughterhouse than all but the most fervent sausage fanatic would desire.

From my home, which can be reached by skirting the north-westerly rim of the island, past a succession of small beaches for which I already have self-explanatory nicknames – Dog Beach, Driftwood Beach, Washed-up Plastic Faceless Figurine Beach – the nocturnal lapping of the waves fails to merge with the sound of porcine screeches on murder night at the slaughterhouse. The pigs are brought in by boat so you never see them on the island's narrow highways; neither bicycles nor the buzzy utility vehicles that, aside from the electric cop cars and fire engines, make up the only four-wheelers permitted on Cheung Chau, are deemed suitable transport for our temporary guests. Sometimes I glimpse a rotund form being herded ashore through binoculars from my rooftop and emit a shudder. It comes to us all, one way or another. And with my money almost gone who's to say I won't be next?

I wheel my bike down from palm-fringed Block 20, past beautifully tended tropical flora in coral-coloured concrete basins, towards the turquoise gates of Fragrant Villas. Built a couple of decades ago on the back of a housing bubble, the original investors behind this scarcely inhabited estate must have failed to smell their own fragrant effluent. The apartments within the off-white, three-storey blocks boast big windows, terracotta trim and sea views, but even those unoccupied from birth – the aging virgins of the estate – show signs of disrepair. External tiles come loose and fall from the clammy skin of the buildings, exposing grey patches of the type that did for a space shuttle. Front gardens left to their own devices have sprouted chest-high snake grass that strains to obscure gummed-shut patio doors and the ghostly interiors beyond.

Venture to the central courtyard to find *Apocalypse Now* dragonflies making gung-ho sweeps over the unruffled surface and chipped mosaic of the cold-water pool; check out the tennis court with the sagging, see-through smile being slowly encroached upon by the surrounding green. The estate has long since proved itself too lowbrow for investors, too highbrow for locals; too far from Cheung Chau's ferry port for either demographic. The artificially cheery ethos its marketers used to launch Fragrant Villas beside a beach where once the bones of the dead were washed before burial has been legitimised by the crack team of genuinely lovely geriatric security guards and gardeners who man the place, one of whom approaches me now, his two-tone blue uniform billowing about his diminutive frame.

"*Jo san*," I offer up, expecting nothing more than a tonally accurate echo in return.

A "*Jo san*" is duly delivered, but this morning it's followed by a pause and then a "How you do?"

My favourite enforcer is paying me special attention today – and in the process risks exhausting our tiny collection of shared words. Like many in this ancient fishing community, his skin has been burnished by the elements in a way that Hong Kong Islanders, overshadowed by skyscrapers and held captive by long working hours, can only dream of. But whilst in most Cheung Chau men this characteristic is accompanied by Alpaca-thick black hair that would be the envy of any gaucho, my protector has a perfectly smooth, hairless head; his skin stretched economically over a well-defined skull.

"How am I? Not too bad, Ken," I reassure him. "Not too bad at all."

Ken's delicate facial features form an incurious mask of friendly integrity. He could be anywhere between sixty and eighty years old, though the way he helped haul me back onto my bike when I toppled off it just before the gates last night suggests an ageless physiology.

Preparing to remount my steed, apparently with Ken's blessing, my progress is next delayed by Archie – a rotund, smiley, and exhaustively helpful young man in his late fifties. It was Archie who offered a second shoulder to lean on when I came a cropper mere hours ago. The fundamental decency of the guards at Fragrant Villas is just one reason I feel terrible for giving them all invented names – and myself a false one when asked to submit the essentials to my overly trusting landlord. Which is not to say she or the guards are softheaded, or – as Paul so often calls me – 'daft'. To prove the point, Archie is in the process of removing a juvenile snake from the grounds using what appears to be a pair of oversized wooden tweezers. He cuts things short by slinging the reptile into the perpetually rustling mangrove that borders the coastal road and partially obscures our view of the beach.

"Morning, Archie."

But Archie won't let me make a quick getaway either.

"One minute," he smiles, dashing into the tiny guardhouse and emerging with a bundle of mail. I groan internally, nod politely as he passes the post to me – I know what's coming. Here's my personal roll call of western residents past and present; a duty I'm obliged to perform every few days. The guards can't differentiate between Romanised names any more than I can differentiate between Chinese letters, their consciences thus dictating that they have to run every piece of junk mail by me. I should be more relieved that no one's tracked me down as I flick through the starchy envelopes with their neatly printed names – RA ADAMSON, F CRICK, TT O'GRADY, WILL PATTERSON, ER REDMOND. Only the latter rings a bell. Wasn't Redmond the name of the journalist I'd met last night at the island's single ex-pat drinking hole? Had he let on where he lived? Of course not, he was a journalist. He asked all the questions.

"Nothing for me," I tell Archie, aware that I've been standing directly in the sun while doing my admin. "Hot today, eh?"

"Very hot," says Archie, fanning his round face with the letters. "Go swim?"

"Maybe later."

The sea had been stormy last night and my stabs at conversation giddy and misguided. I'd drunk too much. I was only out because I'd told myself I needed to socialise, or else go mad through lack of human contact and expose myself that way.

As far as I can remember, the conversation at The Moon mainly swirled around the implementation of the Undesirable Expats Act, now less then a month away. Those in receipt of the "thanks but no thanks" paperwork had until the fourth of June to sling their collective hooks. Someone wondered if the date had been chosen to lend some perspective to our fate. It was a tasteless choice in any case.

We were sitting outside the pub on tiny plastic chairs around a low, black lacquered table. Cheung Chau's expat heavyweights were few in number, which as far as they were concerned only added to their gravitas.

"So, Vivian," a man who'd been introduced as Cameron Silverback addressed me. "Are you on your way out too?"

I scanned my companions. Most of us were in shorts and polo shirts. Must be that time of year already. Redmond was frowning into space, the handkerchief he used to counter forehead stickiness clenched in a pale, freckled fist. Fung, a middle-aged playboy with a receding hairline, had an undistinguished top half, but from the waist down his tiny denim shorts revealed the tanned, hairless and curvaceous legs of a San Tropez sun queen. He was prodding the ice in his Japanese whisky. Neither of them seemed interested in the fate of this newbie.

"Guess I'll be given the heave-ho," I told Silverback. "Unless anyone wants to hide me in their cellar?"

Silverback had the habit of reclining in his miniature seat in what I imagined he thought was an impressively cool and casual manner; unaware or unconcerned that halfway through the motion his shirt rode up his midriff to reveal a smooth, babyish belly and thumb-sized stump of fifty-odd-year-old umbilical cord. I turned my attention to his wide, grey-green moustache, which twitched provocatively before each proclamation.

"No cellars round here, Vivian," he huffed.

"I guess I better make plans then. Are you—?"

But at that point we were disturbed by a very drunk man whom I'd been dimly aware of as he staggered from lamppost to lamppost on his way up from the ferry pier. Skinny as a rake with chunky glasses that failed to mask his mischievous leer, he made for our table with a final surge; the lack of reaction from my fellow drinkers suggesting they knew him and his behaviour quite well. The stranger put a hand on Redmond's shoulder. Redmond shrugged it off, so he transferred it to Silverback's back.

"Oo ees dees?" he pointed at me with a long, bony finger.

"Vivian," I smiled, "Vivian Letterby. I saw this rabble and figured I'd found the artists' corner."

The Francophone laughed silently, mouth agape, cigarette tomb-stoning to the sandy grime.

"Dees ees not the artists' corner," he clarified, arms spread to embrace the small concrete garden. "Dees ees the wankers' corner!"

Laurent was not unfriendly after this initial piece of theatre. In fact he was in the process of telling me that on Cheung Chau it was important to pay close attention to innocuous things – sticks, leaves, the silhouettes of tall grasses – because things that weren't so innocuous – snakes, spiders, and worse – were often designed to look like innocuous things, when Redmond shot out a warning.

"There!"

"Where?"

"By your bag, Cam."

Silverback turned crimson. Even his moustache seemed to darken. He transferred his weight from one broad butt cheek to the other and back again.

"Fuck's sake – where exactly, Red?"

"It's hiding behind it."

All our legs – the majority of which were bare bar a gauzy, middle-aged fur – instinctively right-angled away from the dark underneath of the table. Then we all lowered our necks to lock eyes with Silverback's innocuous-looking backpack. New to the island, I wondered what the hell had given my grizzled companions this overdose of the willies. Land shark? Spider crab? Sabre-toothed vole? Silverback slowly reached for his bag. I swear those hairy hands were trembling as he gripped the top handle as if it were the cerebral part of an insolent snake. Then he jerked the bag up and towards him. Something long and armour-plated shot out from under it.

"There it is!" I yelped.

It was making for a drainage grid beyond our table at significant speed, scuttling along on its countless yellowy legs in the manner of a fleshy radio wave. Its fortified exoskeleton glistened in the moonlight; sometimes light grey or brown; transforming from a dark green to an almost jade-like hue. The rhythm of its movement thrummed hypnotically like the engine-room of a ship, but Redmond was not to be transfixed, let alone seduced by the monster.

"Bastard!"

The journo employed a Cuban heel to squash the fanged head of the giant centipede; then struck twice more to make sure the job was done before toe-ending the corpse into the sewers. Thank God one of us had spurned sandals and flip-flops. I thought of the much smaller bug I'd sprayed to death in my Wan Chai flat, but there was no sign of any sympathy as we returned to our drinks and cigarettes.

"Don't tell me," I turned to Redmond. "A gang of them killed your family?"

He wasn't amused.

"I wouldn't hurt a fly normally," he confessed, "a mosquito, maybe. But those bastards! You're lucky you don't have a ground floor apartment, Vivian. They come in during the night and—"

"—chew your balls off!" Laurent interrupted, breaking the spell.

We laughed, though I noticed the fastidious Redmond didn't feel the need to clarify his friend's comment, leaving me with the impression – cross-referenced later – that the damn things really did draw blood. Now hip to the presence of vampires, and conscious that my humour wasn't cutting it, I decided to down my seventh pint and head for home, blissfully unaware that my bike and me would become separated as I drew alongside Fragrant Gardens.

And now I'm off again. I wave goodbye to Ken and Archie and huff and puff until my bike pedals have summoned the oomph required to circulate the rust-heavy chain. By the time I see the water to my right I'm soaked in sweat. Typical. I try to relax, reminding myself that in less than twenty minutes I will be enjoying the gusty air-conditioning that makes my local Wellcome supermarket so welcoming. Off Dog Beach, old women wearing wide-brimmed straw hats have waded into the water to detach mussels from the rocky outcrops. Some are waist-high in the swell caused by the fast ferry as it heads to the city. They bear it no mind.

Fuck. I forgot to text Paul last night. He was having some last gasp meeting with his lawyer yesterday, over his right to see Poppy. I curse myself for being such a bad friend. I wonder if he'll kill himself, for real I mean. How would I feel then? I curse myself for bringing everything back to my own, selfish feelings. A stray dog looks at me with vague disgust then raises himself from the asphalt and lopes out of the path of my bike. He'd chew my face off if I came off at this corner and broke my neck. Slowly but surely I remember why I decided to stop drinking so much.

I lock my bike up under a banyan tree once the promenade becomes clogged with day-trippers and I can cycle no more. The baseball cap goes on and a Paisley neckerchief is positioned to obscure the rest of my features. I look at the fishing boats in the harbour with their brightly coloured cabins vivid against the gaping hills beyond; the shore-hugging craft piled with lobster cages and polystyrene tubs ready to ice up the next catch. A wan sun offers enough kindling to make the water glisten and I almost feel glad to be alive.

"Crap."

I'm halfway into Wellcome when I realise I haven't texted Paul as I intended to on dismounting. Short-term memory loss – another of drink's mixed blessings delivered unto me.

"*M'goi, m'goi,*" I tell the distracted shoppers in my wake, "reversing here. Sorry."

The public pier is only yards away. I'll find a bench and text Paul then grab some essentials and get the hell out of here. The next slow ferry is being loaded with its cargo of four hundred-odd souls. Best I sit on the other side of the pier, away from the public gaze. And then I see her, changing lenses on the SLR cradled in her lap. Lost in her own world; eyes narrowed, eyebrows stooped but otherwise content.

She's about my age but half my size. She'll tell me later that Asian women are fascinated by her appearance; that they can see her ancient family origins. In my ignorance I see only an attractive, athletic woman with tangled black hair, in jeans and a sleeveless T-shirt with a faded skull logo. The tattoo that covers one arm appears to be barbed wire on first sight, but the pattern in fact replicates the thorns of a rambling rose.

"What are you shooting?" I ask, sitting down next to her. The bench is formed from metal tubes. It's not uncomfortable. She glares at me, but decides to answer the question anyway.

"Wildlife."

"I see. You'll never guess what I saw last—"

"Yes, I will," she sighs, "a giant centipede. News travels fast around here."

"So you know who I am?"

"You must be the new one. Vic?"

"Vivien. Viv for short."

I'm simultaneously offended that my pseudonym has been so readily forgotten and relieved that no one seems interested in who I am or where I'm from.

"What's your name?" I ask, continuing the theme.

"Sky. Sky Burgess," she flicks hair out of her face. A vein pulses neatly in the muscle that underpins her dramatic jawbones.

"You're kidding?"

She isn't. I fumble for something to say, grab the nearest cliché.

"And what do you do, Sky?"

I hate myself all over again. She seems to sense my vulnerability, agrees to humour me anyway.

"This," she holds up the camera. "I photograph animals. People too, if I'm in the mood."

"It's a shame about the pink dolphins…"

"I've just seen a pod of porpoises," she surfs my negativity with ease, "off Pak Kok Tsui."

"Porpoi?"

"What?"

"Wouldn't it be porpoi, rather than porpoises, grammatically I mean?"

Sky looks at me for the longest time. Her eyes are blue-green, flecked with gold. There are dark crescents beneath them – bruises caused by insomnia or addiction that only serve to highlight her unusually soft and creamy skin. I dare not raise a finger to divert the sweat from my eyes.

"Are you always like this?" she asks, at last.

"No."

"Good," she smiles, getting up from the bench and disappearing into the throng. I stroke my chin; decide to shave off my beard the moment I'm back from the shops.

CHAPTER SIXTEEN

Kim slipped from under the sheets in one fluid motion. She would let Frank sleep it off and try not to think about how this was the third time this week and it was only Thursday. She walked the crooked Main Street, past the bottle shops and vegetarian bookshops of Yung Shue Wan; noted some new anti-government graffiti at the harbour-front – expat brats probably, though some of the local kids could sling English phrases around as effortlessly – then caught a mid-morning ferry into the city.

Her first port of call was the Man Mo temple in Sheung Wan where she burnt incense to honour her grandmother, Lily; the family's last all-powerful matriarch. This neighbourhood had been ravaged by plague two centuries ago, her descendants dropping like flies. Depending on your point of view, the British had either condemned the local population by corralling them in unsanitary conditions, or saved them with their western medicine and fancy sewerage system. As if in recognition of this dichotomy of views, roughly half of Kim's family continued to pine for the days of the protectorate while the rest cautiously welcomed the advent of Chinese governorship.

Whatever their political leanings, no one could disagree that the descendants of the plague survivors were being forced out of Sheung Wan by rabid gentrification. Not a single member of Kim's extended family could afford today's inflated rents. Her uncle's noodle shop had been wildly popular right up until its closure in 2014. Once he stopped increasing his prices at the same rate the landlord increased his, he was screwed. Kim had tried to talk him into trying his hand at selling something else, but noodles were all he knew. His sons had already left to pursue careers in Canada and the States, said they were too busy to help her change his mind.

Now that Granny was dead there was nothing to stop Kim's brother and remaining cousins from swallowing their pride and applying for public housing, but the waiting list was long, and they probably shared Kim's suspicion that Granny was watching for any shameful acts from behind a half-closed curtain. Yes, Kim had successfully hidden her pole-dancing days from Granny, but that didn't mean she was positive Granny would never find out about them.

"Rest in peace," she whispered, before abandoning her mixed emotions. "Wish you were here, Granny."

Next she faced the prospect of giving a guitar lesson to a highflying, high-rise-dwelling creep in Kennedy Town. Typically, this paunchy paleface in ill-fitting designer jeans already thought he was twice as good as he would ever become on his Les Paul copy. Worse, his confidence extended to fantasies of seducing his long-suffering tutor. She groaned at the prospect of him using the heat as an excuse to unbutton his shirt, or the aircon as a reason for them to get cosy on his couch. Men. She'd had enough of their reptile brains. Only Frank gave her hope for the species, and soon he'd be gone.

"People are taken away all the time," said Jeanie, pouring her another Jack Daniels. "I had a couple from the US in here. They've lost their son. Not dead necessarily – they just don't know where he is. At least you and Frank can keep in contact until things are sorted out."

"You mean Jonathan's parents, don't you?" Kim took a slug. "Frank talks about him sometimes. Not much, but I know he likes the boy."

"Yes, he's still their little boy too. Parents worry. Imagine finding out your son or daughter was one of the kids leading the protests."

"Are you closing up today?" Kim glanced at the clock above the bar.

"Not today," Jeanie picked up her mop and resumed damping the terracotta tiles. "They need somewhere to come and talk after the marching's done. Somewhere to relax."

"How are the police these days?"

"Wrapped around my finger," Jeanie smiled, admiring an imaginary wedding ring. "What about you, Kim Tang? Are you taking care of yourself?"

"I'm okay. It's Frank," Kim sighed. "Maybe I've been too hard on him. I said he had grown numb."

"It's hard for them, these restless men – the artists especially," Jeanie told her. "If they achieve their dreams young, they go crazy and drink or drug themselves to death. If they don't make it, they get depressed, go underwater – leave you snatching at the bubbles. But eventually, if they meet the right partner, they learn to accept their fate. He won't stay numb forever. Not Frank. Not with you to love him."

"I know he reads his poetry in here sometimes," Kim noticed the crack in her voice. "I know other times he sings and dances on the table. Why can't he do that with me?"

"He's shy," Jeanie stopped mopping and came over. "He's a shy extrovert. They all are – the British especially. That's why they created such a messed up Empire."

"Except in Hong Kong," Kim said quietly. "They did okay here."

Jeanie put an arm around her.

"You've asked your parents about that, have you?"

"What do you mean?"

"Never mind. There's enough politics happening now to keep us busy. Another drink?"

"One more," Kim looked back up at the clock. "I haven't eaten yet."

Jeanie grabbed a menu after splashing some more amber into Kim's glass.

"I'll order you a takeaway. The sushi up the road is pretty good."

"It's okay," she grimaced. "My client gets me lunch. It's part of the deal."

"Before you go," Jeanie took the barstool next to Kim. "I need to ask you something. Promise not to get mad?"

"With you?" Kim laughed. "No one gets mad with you Jeanie."

"If you say so," Jeanie cleared her throat. "Tell me. There's nothing in these accusations, is there?"

"Accusations?"

"Against Frank. How he beats people up. How he gave you a black eye. Rumours the government tried to firm up in his exit letter."

"Total bullshit," Kim choked back bitterness. "Frank's a puppy dog, always has been. Everyone knows they make up things in those letters."

Jeanie let her calm down, went to fetch something from a low shelf near the door.

"Why do you ask, Jeanie?" Kim said, biting her nails. "You know Frank isn't violent."

"This…"

Jeanie put the stone down on the bar between them.

"Is that blood?" Kim asked, shocked.

"I think so."

"Why do you have this?"

"Someone sent it here," Jeanie scratched her buzz cut. "I could be wrong, but I think they sent it here as a warning. About one of the regulars."

"The bloodstains – can you have them tested?"

"I asked a friend in the police," Jeanie grinned. "Yes, a friend! They said the stains were too old, the blood no good to test."

Kim looked at the stone and then at Jeanie and back again, wondering if this was one of the landlady's crazy jokes. Since Jeanie went into remission, friends and customers alike had noticed a playful, mischievous charisma had outflanked the serious, political side of her character that didn't suffer fools, or Chinese apologists, gladly. She was prone to seizing the day, with all its wonderful absurdities, and this sometimes translated into unexpected pranks.

"I don't know what to say," said Kim. "Isn't it just a creepy old piece of rock?"

"Maybe," said Jeanie, going round the bar to rinse Kim's glass. "Or maybe it's the first part of a mountain hiding just out of view."

"Now you sound like Granny," Kim smiled, sliding off her stool. "Thanks for the drinks."

The women embraced. Kim wobbled a little as they unclenched.

"Get some food," said Jeanie. "Promise?"

"Promise," Kim set her face for Kennedy Town. The door to the Brolly shuddered open and shut and Jeanie was left alone with her stone again.

CHAPTER SEVENTEEN

"How did you find me?"

My first visitor to my new home is in all-black running Lycra. Her upper arms are more muscular than they appear when clad in her usual vests and T-shirts. The stretched fabric is defining her, or redefining her. She looks like a pocket-sized superhero.

"You told me the other night, when you were drunk."

"Did I?" I circumvent her to close the flat door. "What else did I say?"

Does she want to sit down? Do I want her to sit down? The cream leatherette couch stretches out beside us. Together with my overly elaborate dark wood table and chairs; the oversized TV that my landlady refuses to remove, it appears I have an embarrassment of riches. Am I going to share them?

"You said you were celibate," I sense Sky is trying not to enjoy my embarrassment too much, "and that you preferred it that way. And that women were too much trouble for you."

"I came out, basically?"

She laughs. Thank God. When she looks defiant – if only at a stallholder who's trying to charge her too much for a fistful of chillies – it takes my breath away, but she looks even more beautiful when she laughs. Whenever we've bumped into each other on the island since first meeting it has been my sole aim to make her laugh. I remind myself that she is gay; that nothing is ever going to happen between us, and this seems to relax me sufficiently to resume normal human functions.

"Sit down," I point at the couch. "Want a drink?"

"Water."

"Of course."

I go into my tiny kitchen, take a jug of filtered water out of the fridge and hold it to my head before pouring us both a glass. I've been home with the fan on; she's been doing laps of the island. How can I be sweating more than her? Then I remember – Sky Burgess doesn't sweat. She told me that when we met outside the café. Is she following me? No, we just stand out here; strangers obliged to stop and distract one another from their otherness. We're different. Ultimately, that means I can't stay here long. For now, I should try and enjoy it.

"Nice view," Sky hasn't sat down – she's looking out at the pool, dimly lit in the dusk. "Do you get in there often?"

"I try to swim every other day," I pass her a glass; she takes a small sip then places it on my grandiose coffee table.

"You work from home?" Sky takes a seat at last.

"I'm not working at the moment," I tell her. "Living off my savings."

"Not working, not dating," Sky smiles. "What do you do, Vivian Letterby?"

"Drink," I raise my glass. "Cheers."

She clinks her glass against mine, remains unsatisfied.

"I told you about my past, didn't I?" she reminds me.

I scramble for the scraps she's fed me over the last fortnight.

"Your dad was English, but you never knew him. He was a…thingy…an engineer. Helped build skyscrapers in the Mid-Levels. Met your mum when she was working as a helper. You think he probably had a family back home. When you were a kid, your mum took you to the UK to find him. You didn't. She ended up marrying someone else but you don't like your stepdad."

"Impressive," Sky deadpans. "Almost stalker-grade. But I meant my more recent past. My marriage…"

"You only said she was…" I hesitate.

"A she?"

"Well, yeah."

"We fucked each other up," she looks back at the pool and for a second I think she's going to suggest we go skinny-dipping. From what I know of Sky, she's not one to dwell. Is she doing this for me?

"In the end, anyway," she continues. "The usual problems – sex, lies, jealousy – but we had an amazing few years. It's sometimes hard to remember that, isn't it?"

I nod, wondering whether I should suggest skinny-dipping. Her scent has pervaded the living room. It's not sweat, obviously; it's not exactly animal – possessing more of a mineral tang. Eventually I realise she's stolen the last rays of the sun and they are clinging to her body with the same determination that I might in a parallel universe. Cosmic, man – I'd almost choked on a mouthful of sausage when she'd used the word to describe human fates over breakfast at the café. Only Sky could get away with talking horoscopes to me.

"Your wife," Sky offers up her green, green eyes as bait. "You said she was dead. She's not dead, is she?"

"No."

"You seem very keen to kill things off. Any particular reason?"

"I guess I need a fresh start," I answer; then try to make light of my lack of insight. "Haven't killed you yet, have I?"

"No," she laughs – a little generously in the circumstances. "Not yet."

I can't find another joke to follow up with. We lapse into silence. The sound of the waves reaches us from the other side of the building. The distant thrum and bounce of a speedboat returning to port. There's no sea view here, but there's no mistaking where we are. I wonder, absently, how many more meals I can eke out of my sack of rice and budget bag of frozen seafood. Sky detects my shift in focus.

"Okay," she springs up. "I best skedaddle. Just wanted to see what a man cave looked like."

"Impressed?"

"Better than I thought," she cups a foot in one palm, then the other in another, warming up for the run home.

"How did you get past security?" I ask.

"I seduced them," she tells me breezily, reattaching her featherweight runners. "You should try it sometime."

"Not my type," I hold open the door. "Thanks for calling round. Safe journey."

"And you," she takes the internal stairs two at a time. Given the insect life that congregates on them, it's not a bad idea.

I spend the next half-hour doing little more than staring into space. Sky would suggest I've sensed something is going to happen and know deep down I've little option but to sit and wait for it. My phone vibrates on the coffee table and I lean over to check it. It's a text, from her. One line: "Why didn't you kiss me?"

Five minutes later I'm on my bike, trying to negotiate my way out of Fragrant Villas with the same guards who should have prevented Sky's arrival in noirish Nike less than an hour before.

"You drink?" asks Archie.

"Only water," I promise.

Ken is manning the gate, his hand on the latch.

"Please," I beg them, "before I change my mind."

Archie nods at Ken, who opens the gate for me. I arc through the gap before it's fully formed and start peddling along the deserted coastal path. I don't have lights but the orange glow cast by tree-shrouded streetlamps should prevent me from hitting any of the wild dogs that slouch between bush and shore this time of night. Bats boomerang about in the low-hanging branches above my head.

My erection adds an unwelcome extra spoke to my bicycling enterprises. I have to stop every hundred yards to tuck it back under the beltline of my shorts. Thank fuck it's dark. Did I ever feel this delicious, electric, skin-tingling, giddy-making, almost nauseating sense of anticipation when rushing to meet Lennox? Of course I did. Can the stomach-churning lust continue indefinitely, in any human relationship? Seems unlikely. Even as I rush to meet Sky I'm aware of this, but far from slowing me down it adds pace to my pedalling, as do the warning wails of the pigs as I pass the slaughterhouse. "Life is short," they tell me. "Go get her."

"Christ in a bag," I swerve away from the ghostly figure who's loomed up out of the murk, bashing my thigh against the metal railings that have prevented me from freestyling onto the rocky shoreline of Washed-up Plastic Faceless Figurine Beach.

"You trying to kill me?" I ask the stumbling phantom.

Perhaps it's the unexpected sight of a deflating boner, but he seems genuinely scared.

"Sorry, sorry," he mumbles.

Time to stop being such a dick. From his clothes and blackened feet, it's clear this nightwalker is down on his luck.

"You okay?" I ask.

"Tourist," he says, refusing to emerge from behind his fringe. "Lost."

"Where do you need to go?"

"Tourist," he repeats, at a slightly lower volume. "Lost."

Well that makes life easier. Directions have never been my strong point.

"This path," I point up and down, "only path here. This way," I point in the direction he's walking, "only snakes, pigs, and crazy people. That way," I point over the brow of the hill, "civilisation".

"That way," he nods and smiles; still none the wiser but – I tell myself – appreciating my friendly tone and feeling far from patronised.

"Tourists that way," I emphasise. "Bun festival, expat pub, old men drinking on the pier, souvenirs made from shells, fishing boats leaking diesel."

"That way," he looks over his shoulder. I've almost convinced him.

"This way," I nod and smile, remounting my bike and feeling the pain in my dead leg recede as I freewheel down the hill towards the promenade. Soon my thoughts have returned to Sky, but any hope of reaching her quickly dissipates once I reach the seafood restaurants, whose tables overlooking the inky blackness attract queues of tourists blinking in the bulb-light. Sagging canopies extend almost to the water's edge and accommodate a glut of hungry souls, all primed to attack clams, prawns and lobsters with a variety of tools before resorting to their bare hands.

The women whose job it is to entice customers into these establishments, by brandishing oversized menus rich with alluring images, regard cyclists as their natural enemy. As a regular nuisance – and someone who had the nerve to present himself as a tourist before turning resident – I get a special kind of status. *M'goi* doesn't cut it round here. Instead I need to bump rubber against a few shins, run over the odd toe – I try to spare the children.

"Emergency," I tell a family of gawping guppies, transfixed by the dancing lights of the trawlers. "My wife is pregnant."

A skinny front-of-house comes at me with a laminated menu. I feel the breeze it creates as I veer beyond the blow, pedal on fearlessly to face the next maître d'. A bunch of expat brats in skimpy beachwear loiter and flirt while deciding in which of the almost-identical eateries they should park their spoilt arses.

I ride directly at them. They scatter, but not before I've snagged a flip-flop.

"Bon appétit," I shout back at them, by way of compensation.

The tourist shops on the front have closed up for the night. If my lost friend wants a shell necklace or giant conch centrepiece he's destined to be disappointed. For me, this equates to a smooth ride up to the start of Peak Road. I dismount and push my bike past The Moon, relieved that none of the regulars rush out to demand more scintillating anecdotes, and then extend my arms to scale the steepest part of the journey, trying not to sweat too much tropical cologne.

The last time I scaled this traffic-free road... I try not to think about it, but it's hard to completely cleanse my mind. Here's the marker beyond which no native Chinese could live. Here's the place I cursed Jonathan's corpse for its dead weight.

Where does Sky live again? I mean, I know the number – that wasn't going to leave my brain however many beers I sunk once she'd surrendered it. It's just that the numbers on Peak Road don't count for much. 21. Anyone seen 21? Oh, to be 21 again. No thanks. You'd have to do this kind of thing all the time. I try to work out how old her place would have to be to be number 21. Pretty old. The twenty-first house to be built up here might be as old as Hong Kong itself. 48. 16. 109. 32. I'm getting nowhere. I'm getting some funny looks.

I check my phone, only it's not a phone anymore – it's a lump of plastic. Sky's surprise visit stopped me remembering to charge it. Thanks a lot, lover. Retracing my steps I come across a whitewashed building. A balcony crammed with pot plants sags above a metal door. There's no number but it matches the brief description Sky has given me. Renewed hope; the ghost of something mechanical, with the potential to blossom into something sensual later on, is stirring in my loins.

But this proves to be one more mistimed erection in a long line shaped by the body of this lapsed celibate. Peering in at a downstairs window I find myself immediately turned upon by a middle-aged couple sitting on a sofa in their underwear. Able to afford a giant TV, on which they're watching a game show in gruesome HD, their budget clearly doesn't stretch to air-con. I wave, indicating that they don't need to get up, back away, and then let myself glide down to the sanctuary of the local sports ground.

The floodlights are on, just for me. I sit on a bench, trying not to smoke a cigarette in such close vicinity to an athletics track and expansive soccer pitch. No night-time runners here. No players on show. After a while, feeling alone and abandoned, I begin to walk around the track in a kind of trance. Only when I hear her calling do I realise I've been walking with my hands over my face. I've no idea how long she's been watching me.

"Up here."

I look up, shielding my eyes against the floodlight nearest Peak Road. There she is, on a cluttered balcony – the only one facing this way. Perhaps she likes to watch the guys playing football or the girls playing basketball, or vice versa. I can't keep track; I can barely remember my name – she's going to have to help me out.

"This way, Viv," she points out some steep metal steps that scale the backs of the buildings I've been inspecting. When I notice all she's wearing is a white towel wrapped tightly around her, I decide my bike will be safe where I left it. Even more delicious is her teasing expression when she meets me moments later at her front door and leads me to the upstairs bedroom of her small but perfectly formed house.

"Long journey?"

"I don't want to talk about it."

Sky opens her towel and I fall into her body. Her skin is cool and soft and covered in goose bumps. The smell of day has been washed away. Now she smells of the night. Soon I will too.

CHAPTER EIGHTEEN

The next fortnight passes in a giddy whirl of intimacy when we are together, hope and longing when circumstances keep us apart. We are strapped into a vertiginous fairground ride which thrusts and spins our hapless bodies into submission on a daily basis, but which we tolerate because every now and then the cranks and gears fling us close enough together to see one another's pale faces and bright eyes. It is then we appreciate that both of us are holding on for dear life – that we are in this thing together and there is to be no easy way out.

"Let me put some more cream on you," I say, trying to sit up on my deckchair on Kwun Yum beach.

I like this beach because on their way here most visitors expose themselves on the rocky outcrop by the Windsurfing Club. By the time they've passed the gated-up watercraft and beach-bound catamaran, I've been able to have a good look at them. What I like less is the HK$50 charge for deckchair hire that the Beach Bar levies, something we've rationalised by taking turns to lie on the hot sand and topping up our single soft drink with supermarket gin. We're broke, but happy. Sky doesn't believe in keeping hold of money, any more than she believes in rationing the passion that propels her through life. She's spent the bulk of her remaining cash on a new tattoo, which I'm keen to attend to.

"S'okay," she murmurs, turning a cheek to the sand, but still resembling a semi-naked human whose head has been engulfed by a hairy octopus.

"It looks a bit red."

"They always look red at first," she explains. "That's just the way it goes."

When she went into the city to get it done, I was gripped by a feeling that I would never see her again; that she would disappear into the urban jungle and emerge transformed, or fully reconciled with her old life. But she isn't like that. Sky doesn't share my chameleon-like properties. She does what she says she's going to do. If she tells you there's no future for her and her estranged wife, and she never expects to speak to her again, then that's almost certainly what's going to happen. Having accepted this unusual clarity of thought and transparency of action, I naturally want more. I reach over and remove her sunglasses. Her eyes are closed. She's dozing again. I reappraise the Buddhist symbolism that has been painfully created, through a hundred-odd bamboo pinpricks, on her lower back. A lotus flower from which emerge receding squiggles of ancient script. Does it look impressive? It's part of her now, so I'm already biased. Was I secretly hoping that her new tattoo might pay tribute to me, in some small way? No comment.

Skinny teens are busy trying to drown inflatable animals in the sea, safe within the confines of the shark net; extra safe considering Hong Kong's last shark attack was in the early '90s. But how safe are we? Whilst almost all the tourists, including any that might have known me in my former life, are stationed on the much larger Tung Wan beach, below the modern gothic of the Gloucester Hotel, it's still a risk to be here on a weekend, even partially obscured by a parasol.

"What are you getting stressed about?" Sky asks, her eyelids flickering. "I can feel it, honey."

"Oh, you know…"

I reach for our drink.

"Worried about being too happy?"

"Maybe."

"Shit happens, Viv," she turns over and sits up, flicking sand from her lips and readjusting her bikini. "The key is to enjoy the moment."

"I just wish we'd met a little earlier."

"Wouldn't be the same people then, would we?"

"I guess not."

"If it makes you feel any better," she's up on her knees, kissing me. "We could call it a day, go back to mine and get a shower?"

"Sounds good," I smile, trying to believe my luck; trying to accept that she's mine to enjoy, would give herself as naturally as the sun or…

"Oh no," I say, barely aware that I'd fished my crappy phone out of our beach bag and turned it on. Seven missed calls from Paul. One text: "FFS call me now – EMERGENCY."

"What is it?" Sky asks.

"Got to make a call," I try to sound as relaxed as possible. "You head back. I'll sort my shit out here, then join you."

"You could always talk to me about it."

"It's just some…admin, baby."

Sky smiles weakly. It's amazing how much lovers will forgive in the first days and weeks of romance. Before you know it, you're fused together; and while you might know each other's hopes and dreams by then, you probably don't know the dirty secrets that will tear you apart later. I watch as she rewraps her womanly gifts, digs out her flip-flops and departs with a wave, after which there's no putting off the grim task at hand.

"Paul?"

"Nick, you cunt, where have you been?"

"What's wrong with you?" I hiss, taking a walk to the far end of the beach, hoping to scale down the confrontation in the manner of the Mini Great Wall that meanders through the rocks above. "How would you like it if I called you a—"

"—cunt? I wouldn't give a flying fuck. Your friends are up shit creek and you decide to go AWOL."

"I'm in hiding," I remind him. "Remember?"

"You don't turn your phone off, ever – that's what we agreed."

"I'm sorry, Paul. Now tell me what's got your knickers in a twist."

"It's Fenton."

"Fenton?"

"He's done something extremely fucking stupid."

"He's fallen off the wagon? That's to be expected—"

"No, he's not fallen off the bloody wagon." Paul despairs at my naivety. "He's kidnapped that pair of snoops."

"What pair of snoops?"

"I don't know who the fuck they are. Commies, he calls them, though I doubt we've had a proper communist set foot 'ere since the '80s."

"More reds in Liverpool?"

"No time for gags, Nick. We've got to do something before he gets himself into even more trouble."

"How could he possibly do that?"

Paul's incoherent answer is interrupted by a brief, apologetic exchange with someone on his end of the line. My Sky obsession means it takes me longer to work out their identity than it should.

"Are you with someone, Paul?"

"What do you mean?"

"I just heard you talking to someone. Who are you with?"

A pause. "Does it matter?"

"Apparently so."

It's Paul's turn to be defensive.

"Look, I needed some advice. On the Poppy situation."

"So you thought you'd go and see Lennox?"

"Nicky, I was desperate. You said you were going to help and then—"

"I don't need this, mate," my thumb itches for the red button. "Give me one good reason why I shouldn't just leave you all to it."

"Because I know you're still alive...and Fenton does too."

Twenty minutes later I'm at the back of the rickety inter-island ferry to Mui Wo, watching Kwun Yum beach recede into the distance. I haven't told Sky where I'm going. No point making a whale out of a porpoise. Said I had a bit of business to take care of on Lantau; included just enough of a hint that close at its heels would be a gift or treat I was organising in exchange for my secrecy. Paul is taking a bus from Sheung Wan, where he may or may not have slept with my wife. She wouldn't, would she? He wouldn't, would he? Have I let them down that badly? Failed to connect at such a basic, human level that they would disregard my feelings to that extent? I recall the last time Lennox and I spoke – by phone the morning after I'd met Sky for the first time. I'd tried to explain that I still loved her, despite my unwillingness to agree to the terms set out by Martin Chan.

"A tribe in Colombia – the Nukak – use suicide as a way of expressing their love for someone," I told her.

"But you didn't take your own life, did you?" Lennox sighed. "You faked your own death. Which is something completely different."

"Even better, if it means we can stay together – isn't it? I mean, until my career takes off, it's best for me to keep a low profile, given what's happening."

"I have to go to work, Nick. Can I ask you to do one thing?"

"Of course."

"When you get a spare moment and an Internet connection, look up 'Falk Family Appeal' and have a read."

"Lennox—"

"Bye, Nick – look after yourself."

It's true I've visited Fenton's jungle encampment once before, but on that occasion – over a year ago – he drove down in his latest clapped out car to fetch me from the seafront. I remember being struck not only by the physical manifestations of his self-imposed exile from civilisation – the barbed wire, the signs, the CCTV cameras – but also an absence about the place that despite the meagre mouthful of words Fenton dedicated to her, I became convinced was Miriam-shaped. Did anyone know where she was? She'd surely have a better chance of persuading Fenton to step back from the brink than his friends. I put the question to Paul as we slid into the backseat of a taxi.

"Trying to pass the buck again?"

"Come on Paul," I implore him. "Throw me a bone."

My friend's face is red and blotchy, his eyes hidden by new, blue-lensed sunglasses. He's chewing methodically on a wodge of gum. It doesn't take a genius to work out that he's drunk himself sober, just someone who's known him for years and not bothered to question why he might do this so regularly, let alone stage an intervention. There would be time for that later, I told myself.

"What do we know so far?" I ask as the taxi shoots off.

"He rang me in a right state. Said he'd caught a couple of trespassers on video and was detaining them 'at her majesty's pleasure'"

"Oh no…"

"Told him where I was and he said that they'd been asking after you. That they confirmed what he'd already suspected – that you were alive."

"How did he take the news?"

Paul looks across at me, dips his shades, and manages a rueful smile.

"Insert foul language here...then a bit more...then add another sprinkle and a final flourish. The upshot was that he doesn't trust anyone anymore and that he'll be making a last stand up at his place until he's left in peace."

"Kind of a mixed message," I chew my lip. "But he called you. So he must want help. He reached out for it."

"Not really," Paul explains. "He wanted me to contact the media, tell them that the Chinese had pushed one Englishman too far. Get as much publicity as possible."

"You didn't—?"

"Fuck no. I called you. Thought about calling Frank too but assumed you'd want to do that yourself, given the circumstances."

"Bloody hell... I mean, thanks."

The taxi driver stops abruptly, turns around and holds out his hand.

"Alright, mate," Paul says testily. "Wish we could all get out of here as quickly as you want to."

We walk along the drainage canal towards Fenton's place in near-silence. It's sunny and warm. Unseen birdlife occasionally offers up a squawk.

"This is where he fell, isn't it?" I ask Paul.

"Apparently."

Another hundred yards, I try again.

"Was she any help? Lennox, I mean."

"She did her best, but the implication was clear."

"Which was?"

"It's no longer our time here. No judge or jury is going to order the deportation of a Hong Kong-born child to the UK, however psycho the mother is."

"What are you going to do?"

Paul points to a skull and crossbones hanging limply from a nearby coconut tree.

"One thing at a time, eh?"

I'm mumbling fresh promises about reuniting father and daughter as Paul uncovers an intercom and gives it a buzz.

The homeowner's crunched-up voice greets us almost immediately.

"Yes?"

"It's me, Paul."

"Have you brought the media?"

"No, I've brought Nick."

"Hello," I say.

A pause.

"Fenton," Paul clears his throat. He's practically croaking. Funny how we get increasingly dehydrated as we age – as if the juice were being slowly sucked out of us; the same rationing of liquid assets applying to eyeballs and testicles, I've been told. I wonder why there isn't more middle-aged rage.

"Fenton, lad," Paul softens his tone. "We want you to let your two…guests…leave in peace."

"The British government doesn't negotiate with terrorists."

"What makes you think they're terrorists?"

"Because they tried to terrify me – and failed, I might add."

"Have you been drinking?" I ask, as delicately as possible.

"If you're suggesting a lack of judgement, Nick, I recommend taking a look in the mirror."

I rub my arm where Paul has punched me. He resumes his softly-softly approach to negotiating.

"Let us in mate, then we can all sit down and have a cuppa and talk about it."

Fenton's replies are veering towards the unfathomable, so riled is he becoming, and so close is he to his end of the intercom. However, there's no mistaking his sign off.

"Bugger off!"

"Come on," Paul indicates the faint, unwelcoming path to Fenton's house. "Worse things happen at sea."

I remember failing to convince myself that the TRESPASSERS WILL BE SHOT sign was loaded with irony when I was last here. I keep an eye out for snakes in the long grass beside the trail as Paul repeatedly tries Fenton's mobile. What I hadn't expected was the galumphing of a quadruped, from straight ahead.

"Paul!"

I alert him to the black and white blur heading at us. It's up and at Paul before I can do anything to defend him. Hunter – Fenton's faithful dog. Doesn't he know he could be shot for desertion?

"Hey, boy," I hold out my fingers for him to sniff. "Where's your master?"

Dogs don't tend to trust me and Hunter is no exception, or maybe Paul's crotch is too irresistible to part ways with prematurely. Paul himself is distracted.

"Cheese wire," he's running a hand along an invisible line between two trees. "The mad fucker."

We duck under the wire, Hunter wagging his tail beside us – keen to lead us to our fate. Soon we are approaching the clearing Fenton long ago carved out for himself in the pristine jungle. No sign of anyone. We edge towards the house. The vegetable garden has been overhauled. Runners wind around beanpoles; rows of pak choi, squash and garlic are neatly labelled. I guess that's what happens when you give up booze. The fastidious detail contrasts with the expansive peaks of Lantau that now come into view beneath a cloudless sky.

I'm drawn to the outhouse that Fenton uses as a workshop. I remember there being something reassuring about the way his woodworking tools were all laid out neatly, like the veggies. Here was an organised artisan, in full control of his faculties, not the car-destroying dervish he was rumoured, and occasionally proved, to be. The remembrance slows my breathing, preventing a heart attack when I'm addressed from the bushes.

"Nick, how nice of you to call by."

Like his crops and his tools, the figure emerging from the trees on my blind side is immaculately turned out – especially if you have a thing about camouflage jumpsuits, ink-black face paint and khaki sunhats with ferns sticking out of them. And crossbows. Let's not forget the crossbow he's pointing at me with professional efficiency. I remind myself that Fenton's story about having trained with the French Foreign Legion was nothing more than an acceptable way of testing the gullibility of a new arrival.

"Do you know what's the best thing to do if you're feeling seasick, Nick?" Fenton asks me.

"No," I tell him, determined to hide my queasiness.

"Rock the boat yourself. It's what you did Nick. And it's what I'm doing too. It's what our forebears used to do, before everyone got too bloody nice."

"Too…nice?" I query.

Fenton swings around in a smooth arc and fires a bolt into a tree a few feet from Paul, who freezes like a cop-show body outline – a silhouette of intent caught sneaking towards the house while me and Fenton got reacquainted.

"Too nice," Fenton grins, the oily substance covering his face making his averagely white teeth sparkle almost as much as his revivified eyes. He's having a ball. The question is whether killing us would add to his excitement or diminish it.

CHAPTER NINETEEN

It's always amused me – if that's the right word – to observe other people being shocked by the fragility of human life. But then I had my parents wrenched away from me, barely extractable from a heap of twisted metal, when I was twelve. I have previous, as they say. For as long as I can remember, my philosophy has been thus: each generation, with or without their family beside them, sets off on a perpetually challenging hike together. Inevitably, somewhere down the line, one of us will be struck by lightning, another taken by a tiger, and one poor sod shot by a madman in the jungle.

Unfortunately, when we find ourselves falling in love anew, or perhaps more accurately, when we become the subject of renewed affection, and witness a wide-eyed someone finding value in all we have thought valueless for so long, it becomes harder to die than might normally be the case. Damned if you do, damned if you don't...

As Fenton draws back his bow in order to reload, I try again with the dog, waggling the dusty tube of mints I've found in a forgotten pocket.

"Here boy..."

Paul looks across at me as if I've lost my mind. He's made the mistake of having a child, making it even more difficult for him to accept a premature death.

"Blasted buggery." Fenton has got himself flustered and forgotten his crossbow basics, allowing me to stoop down and scoop up the hesitant Hunter. A whine alerts his master to his fate.

"Put him down, Nick," pinpricks of fire appear beneath Fenton's wiry brows. "Put my baby down – now."

The crossbow is aimed at me again, but now only my head is a clear target, my torso covered by the black-and-white curls of the aged hound, who – now he's formed an essential part of me

– I see could do with a good brush down, and a little more modesty in the furry penis department.

"Show me where they are," I tell Fenton.

"You're a monster," he bites back.

"No one needs to get hurt," I tell him. "And I include Hunter in that—"

"—promise?" he helps me finish my sentence. "You're so blasted naive, Nick. Do you really think these Maoists play by the same rules we do?"

"You mean the rules that involve threatening people with a medieval weapon?"

"Nick…" Paul pleads. He's talked Fenton down from countless peaks of fury in the past. Time to whisper some sweet practicalities to his old pal.

"'Don't let me do anything I'll regret.' Isn't that what you used to tell me, Fen?"

Fenton lowers his bow, the red mist subsiding. "Come along then," he refuses to drop his military tone. "They're just here."

"No shooting?" I readjust my grip on Hunter, all the while trying to avoid contact with his dick and arsehole.

"If I'd wanted to kill you I could have picked you off in the jungle. Did you know the Viet Cong used to hide spikes in—?"

"Jesus Christ, Fen," says Paul. "Will you give it a fucking rest?"

"What's up with the scouser?" Fenton asks me as we approach the outhouse.

"Parental issues."

I allow Hunter to slowly body surf down me into the mulch. Fenton unlocks the door to the outhouse with an oversized key, kicks it open then immediately steps back to offer cover. Paul holds the door open for me while I peer into the gloom. I spy little wooden Santas, goblins, boats and racing cars on shelves among old pots of paint, varnish and glue.

"Hello?"

"May we come out now?"

The male voice, mildly accented, carries a trace of amusement.

"Yes," I tell him. "You're safe to come out."

He lets his companion test the water – the Eastern European woman from Putin's Proxy comes blinking and scowling into the light, closely followed by her Chinese companion who unfolds his large and distinguished frame before resting his eyes on the three of us with a mixture of curiosity and pity. He dips into his lightweight hiking trousers and produces a pair of John Lennon glasses. They're missing a lens.

"This one," he looks at me while pointing at Fenton. "Broke my spectacles. I'll let it go. But I want the money for a replacement lens dropped off at an address to be provided via email once we're released."

"Do you see what I mean?" Fenton points at the trespasser while looking at me. "Threats! We can't let these turncoats go. There'll be no end to their demands."

"So you're going to kill them, are you?"

"Well…that is to say…"

"No," I turn back to the prisoners. "He's not going to kill you. I think you probably knew that anyway. So the question is how do we extract ourselves from this awkward situation while causing one another the minimum amount of pain?"

"Rip the bloody plaster off," suggests Paul, "always the best way."

"What do you mean?"

"Chuck 'em out of 'ere. If they go crying to their overlords, so what? We're all fucked anyway."

"And have them report Fenton for being armed and dangerous? See him dragged off to jail and deported before he can say his goodbyes? No way."

"What then?" asks Paul, eyeing up our charges.

"If it's me you're after," I address the snoops, "then I'm happy to come quietly – so long as you can guarantee my friends won't be arrested."

Specs puts his one-eyed glasses back on and consults with his stern accomplice. It's she who turns to me within seconds.

"We agree," she says. "Our transport is nearby," she points back down the path. "These two…men…and the hund are to stay here until one hour after we leave."

"The hund?"

"The dog."

"We also need the film," Specs adds, pointing to the trees around us. "We want you to destroy any CCTV images you have of us."

Fenton becomes agitated. Counts to ten; allows the craving for a cigarette to pass and then admits, "The cameras are empty. Fake. No film."

"Sorry?"

"No movies. No recordings. No smile for the bloody camera, understand?"

"Prove it," Specs insists. Fenton is still seething but allows Specs to guide him towards the house.

There follows five minutes of feet shuffling and unfocused bird watching as the three of us wait for Fenton to demonstrate his antiquated computer system inside. Paul mentions that he likes the woman's hair. She does not respond.

At least, once I'm in the back of the SUV, sweeping past water buffalo on the sleepy roads between the prison and Mui Wo, we're free to speak bluntly.

"Are you agents?"

"We prefer to think of ourselves as deniable assets," says the woman, who's driving.

"You're in denial? That makes sense."

"Don't try to be clever. You've tried that before and it hasn't worked."

I appeal to Specs, "You can at least give me your names?"

"Panda," he pats his chest. "And that's Salamander."

I watch an aging buffalo tottering along the roadside towards the sea. It's not a useful image when you're trying to suppress laughter. Panda detects my mirth.

"You can laugh. Believe me, we love the British sense of humour. Looking for the fun in everything, especially in your language – the language of Shakespeare, no less. The language you've used so eloquently to justify your wars through the centuries. But sooner or later – beyond the satire – I recommend you visit the plain and simple facts. You live on Cheung Chau?"

Christ. Did the interrogation start here?

"Yes," I tell him. "That's no secret – not any more."

"Have you spoken to anyone on Cheung Chau about the future of Hong Kong, or indeed its past? Anyone from the local population, I mean?"

"Haven't had the chance. If you drop me off at the ferry pier I could happily—"

"Perhaps you don't realise that the community there – the ancient Chinese fishing community – is much older than Hong Kong itself. That the ancestors of your friendly locals were forced to watch the colony grow – had to accept the ships that clogged up the harbour, the plundering of their natural resources. Had to give up their migratory way of life, living on the water and following the fish stocks from island to island, in return for colonial housing designed to keep them in one place, so they could be taxed by the British more easily."

"That wasn't me," I remind him. "Any more than you're responsible for the famines under Mao."

"And you British expect to live here without contributing to the culture, when immigrants moving to the UK are expected to earn – what was it again? Thirty-five thousand pounds a year?"

Salamander nods.

"And learn English, or else risk expulsion? You think it's fair that because your descendants colonised this small part of Southern China, you can live here, get drunk here, have your junk parties here, treat our women like whores, and seek your fortune, while learning fewer words of Cantonese or Mandarin than a Chinese toddler knows of English?"

Rant over, Panda turns back towards the windscreen. I don't disagree with him – how can I? What I can and will object to is being fed rhetoric while child-locked into the back of a fun-sized SUV and heading for…where, exactly? Surely a *gweilo* faking his own death is worthy of no more than a slap on the wrists and one-way ticket to London? Nothing in my résumé would appear to justify deportation to the Mainland. But in these troubled times, who knows?

Just before the Lantau Bridge we pull over onto a slipway and Panda gets out. He clicks open my door and gestures towards the boot of the vehicle. Cars swish by oblivious to my fate.

"You've got to be kidding me."

"How many people know you in Kowloon?" he asks.

"A few."

"How many of them know you're alive?"

"Okay," I scratch my head. "I take your point. But we're only going to Kowloon, right? Not across the border?"

Panda spreads his arms. He's a big man, but his glasses are out of shape.

"Would I lie to you?"

Disappointingly for fans of action movies, I fall asleep in the boot of the SUV. Perhaps it's the overpowering smell of the hiking gear belonging to my captors, perhaps I've been exhausted by Paul, Fenton, Frank, Lennox – the whole lot of them; perhaps I should curl up in a confined space more often. No blindfold when I'm extracted from the boot and hauled out into an alleyway of pirouetted bins and strewn packaging – Panda must assume my ignorance extends beyond local languages – but once I've been guided down some concrete steps and shoved inside a basement it's pretty clear which side of the border I'm on. No bookshop in the PRC would have a cartoon of any famous Chinese person doing *that* on the wall.

"Please sit down," says Panda, pointing to a solitary chair in the centre of the room.

Whoever operated from here left – or was taken – in a hurry. Shelves have fallen nose-first. Small slicks of books and magazines fan the grimy concrete floor. Supermarket flyers and junk mail encroach on the subversive air provided by the faded posters and caricatures that reach the low ceiling, only some of which have been torn down or defaced. I plop myself on the rickety seat. Panda and Salamander seem content to stand.

"So my first question," I reveal, "is why are you so interested in my love life?"

"We ask the questions," says Salamander, who has changed from hiking apparel into black leather jacket and jeans.

"If I were to answer it," Panda is standing a little closer to me than I'd like. "I'd suggest your love life is less interesting than the death of your compatriot, Jonathan Falk."

"Not my compatriot," I clarify. "He's from the USA, specifically New England."

"We're not interested in him either," Salamander clarifies.

"Congratulations," I raise my hands. "You've cleaned me out. Aside from my untidy love life and the accidental death of my friend, I have literally nothing to offer you. So if I could be on my way?"

"It's a third orbiter we wish to discuss," Panda says, beginning to circle me, hands behind his back.

"A third…what?"

"The trois in your ménage," Salamander offers grudgingly.

"No, sorry," I frown up at them. "None the wiser."

"Young radicals are often drawn to older men," Panda informs me. "Their crackpot ideas can evaporate into the ether if not legitimised by a more superficially mature individual."

"Usually a male," Salamander adds.

"I've literally no idea what you're talking about."

"There's no need to feel embarrassed," Panda coos. "Role models are important, however dangerous they may be. Given your own family situation – lack of parents, lack of kids – you may have been working on impulses beyond your immediate control."

"Which is why we're giving you the benefit of the doubt."

"Which is why I haven't been sent to China?"

"Exactly."

I take a deep breath. This is going to take longer than I imagined.

"You have me mixed up with someone else. In case you haven't noticed, I'm not young and I'm certainly no radical. Yes, I have some older friends but they're hardly role models. Or if they are, hanging around with them hasn't radically altered my fortunes. If you want a summary of my disastrous temping stints in insurance, finance and PR you can ring Dirk at the agency."

"They'll be no need," Panda assures me. "We know how tough you've found it to adapt to a country where hard work comes before hedonism. But that doesn't mean you haven't got any interesting entries in your contacts book."

"Okay, I've had just about enough of this bollocks," I try to stand up, but Panda's behind me, a strong hand on my shoulder.

"Funny," he says. "I imagine that's exactly what the inspector in charge of investigating Jonathan Falk's disappearance is thinking."

"Imagine his relief," Salamander chips in, "were he to find out that his key witness, someone who was with Jonathan just before he disappeared, was still very much alive, despite evidence to the contrary."

"Okay, okay," I concede. "If you want information about any of my acquaintances, I can provide you with an honest account. What I *can't* do is—"

"We're going to leave you now, Nick," Panda interrupts. "Give you some time to get your thoughts in order. But when we return tomorrow, we must insist you reveal everything you know about your special friend." Salamander takes a bottle of water and some pre-packed 7-Eleven sandwiches from her bag and places them at my feet.

"Think he's in love with the guy?" she asks Panda.

"Not Nick," Panda smiles. "He's a one-woman man. Or a one-woman-at-a-time man, anyway."

Fuck. Does that mean they know about Sky? They must. Lennox will be okay – insulated by power and money – but Sky is exposed out there. I need to give my gaolers something but my mind is as empty as my pockets. I can barely muster a cursory curse as they lock the door of the bookshop behind them, leaving me fully in the dark.

CHAPTER TWENTY

The night of my imprisonment, I was later to learn, most of my remaining friends were having a lock-in at the Brolly. Normally a treat provided by Jeanie on celebratory occasions, in this instance it had been prompted by the tardy arrival of a deeply flustered Fenton.

"What is it?" Jeanie asked, ushering him towards the back table. "You're white as a Scotsman. Whisky?"

"Coke. I'll have a Coke, my dear. I'd kill for a cigarette but I think we're in enough trouble already."

"What's up with you?" asked Frank, spiky as his wide-boy collars. Jeanie had remarked how he and Kim looked like a pair of Elvises when they rocked up but Frank wasn't in the mood for compliments.

"Where to start...where to start..."

"Try sitting down and having a swig of burnt sugar shit."

"Yes, you're right, Frank. Of course you are. Where've you been anyway, '50s night?"

"It's not important."

"Corporate gig at Quantum's," Kim explained through thin lips. "One of my students wanted me there. Ex-student, I think we can safely say."

"I'm shutting up shop," Jeanie announced. "You three finish your drinks. Take as long as you like. Two Colombians and my first Papua New Guinean are still unaccounted for. Expect I'll be up 'til they crawl home from LKF."

"Out with it then," Frank demanded.

"It's Nick. You remember we said our goodbyes, cast him into the waves?"

"Like it was yesterday."

"Resurrected."

"What?" Kim's quiff trembled as she reached for her drink.

"And?" asked Frank.

"Couple of people were after him, man and a woman. Sinister pair," Fenton took a slug of Coke. "Had to hold them off at the ridge, for as long as humanly possible."

"Meaning?"

"They have him now."

"The authorities?" Kim blanched. "What did he do to deserve that?"

"Maybe they want to question him about Jonathan's disappearance," said Jeanie, collecting empties. "If Nick's alive...well, somebody got cremated that day."

"I can't believe you're all taking this so calmly," Kim banged down her glass. "I mean, Nick – he's not fucking dead!"

"We're living through strange times, babe," Frank told her, "perhaps the strangest any of us can remember."

"Well, did they?" Kim turned back to Fenton. "Want to know about Jonathan?"

"Seems unlikely," he replied. "One of those creeps – both of whom I waylaid single-handedly—"

"Get to the point, Rambo."

"—I'd seen before. Sat here at the bar the night Nick disappeared. Watching Nick like a hawk – or kite, perhaps."

"So?"

"So this was before anyone disappeared. Nick seems to have been on their radar for a while. Perhaps there's stuff about him we don't know. Not sure if you've noticed, but there's a lot of chitter-chatter and a dearth of curiosity in society these days. For example, no one ever asks me about my time spent flying low level sorties in The Falklands."

"That's because it didn't happen," Frank broke it to him. "Whereas you're implying Nick might have been doing all manner of things we don't know about?"

"Are there really still spies in Hong Kong?" Kim asked. "Western ones I mean?"

"Apparently so," Jeanie sighed.

"So what do we do?"

Frank and Fenton regarded one another warily; each suspecting the other might pounce on their words as soon as they were released.

"Rescue him," they said together, though Frank's sour mood saw him discarding the pronoun in favour of 'the fucker'.

Jeanie returned to the bar but continued listening carefully.

"Where is he then?" Frank asked Fenton.

"No idea."

"Great."

"Anyone else see him being taken?"

"Paul."

"And where's Paul?"

"No idea. He legged it after their car. Phone's off. Likely he had a massive cardiac while in pursuit. We could try the hospital, or the morgue?"

"So you're the warrior king," Frank asked, "while Paul's incapable of running out of your sight without keeling over?"

"I'm just telling you what happened," Fenton insisted.

"Seems a bit rich to me."

"So do we ask the police to help?" Kim was trying to hurry things along.

"I have a number if you need one," said Jeanie.

"Let's wait until we hear from Paul," Frank suggested.

"Yes, and after that you can dig out your Napoleonic uniform and lead us into battle," Fenton grinned; then dodged a half-hearted haymaker from the ancestral war chest.

For some reason, Paul waits until morning to rescue me. I never receive a satisfactory explanation for this. Was he tempted to leave me to my fate? Had Lennox tried to dissuade him from helping? I don't suppose it matters. There's no sense dwelling on ifs and buts, nor any chance of me overcoming the joy I feel on seeing his chubby face distorted by the thick glass of the bookshop door at dawn.

"Paul...thank God."

And then there's the unexpected genius of his plan to free me from my cell. Sensing that the door is firmly locked he begins lighting pieces of the old packaging and flattened cardboard boxes that litter the alleyway and shoving them through the letterbox. It doesn't take me long to realise what he's up to. I pin myself to the furthest wall and wait for the alarms to sound, the sprinklers to go off, and the emergency services to arrive. Sadly, not all old buildings in Kowloon meet the rigorous safety standards imposed by law; otherwise subdivided flats would have to be fit for habitation – something their landlords aren't too keen on.

"It's getting hot in here, Paul... Paul?"

The oily smoke from burning plastic and card has already obscured my view of the door. From actively stoking the fire, I am now using the last of my bottled water to try to keep it away from my toes. In retrospect, Paul should have phoned the fire brigade at this stage, but fortunately he doesn't need to. Shouts begin resounding around the upper floors of the building. Someone has sensed a much drier heat than Hong Kongers are accustomed to. Within moments sirens are sounding outside, and the next thing I know a gang of rubberised axemen wearing phantasmal breathing apparatus are hacking their way in. I cover my mouth and run past them as they get to work quenching the fire.

Once I've finished coughing my guts up, I'm able to provide the police with a false name and address, and assure the medics I need no further treatment. No sign of Paul, but I figure Panda and Salamander won't be too far away. A wizened centenarian is pushing a trolley stacked with unspoiled cardboard to safety. I stick close to him and we leave the backstreet plot together. Perhaps he's expecting me to offer to help carry his load, but I've always been too respectful of crotchety old-timers to risk hurting their pride by lending them any assistance. With more emergency vehicles arriving all the time, I seize my chance and dart off down a side road towards the nearest MTR stop.

On the Cheung Chau ferry two things occur to me. Firstly, that the so-called "deniable assets" won't take long to find out about the conflagration, nor my survival. My only hope is that Paul might have somehow sacrificed himself in the blaze. If he has been burnt beyond recognition, I might get a second chance to fake my own demise, this time fooling Lennox and prompting genuine remorse concerning her previous hard-line stance. I have to accept that this is a long shot. More happily, I also realise that my pursuers are unlikely to be in a hurry to contact the police with regard to my suspected indiscretions – if they're misguided enough to think I'm withholding information from them, will they really expect me to spill the beans at the start of a long sentence behind bars?

What I understand most pressingly is that I need to get to Sky before Panda gets his claws and Salamander her suckers on my new love. The look on Sky's face when I reach her flat tells me

I'm already too late. Even the way she lets me kiss her long and hard, prising open her full lips and letting my tongue impose its will on hers, is a sign that everything has changed. We go inside. I tell her I like her new perfume. She says I smell like burnt toast and asks me what's happened.

"It doesn't matter. All that matters is we get out of here," I explain.

"You want to go and eat?"

"I want to marry you and—"

"We're both married already."

"Okay," I take a deep breath, "I get it. One step at a time – first we need to get off this island, find another one."

"No," she says, a little sadly. "I can't do that."

"Pack your rucksack. We'll hire a boat and head for one of those uninhabited islands you hear about. Grass Island or Shark Island or Mosquito Island, or whatever they're called in Chinese."

I've assumed that Sky will respond to my panic with her own nervous energy, but she's too weighed down by unmentionable burdens to get anywhere near the level of anxiety I need to persuade her away.

"Has something happened?" I ask, feigning naivety. "I've only been gone one night."

"Why should I tell you? You won't tell me what's happened to you."

"Because it's one and the same thing and we'll have plenty of time to discuss it later on. In the meantime…"

She closes the familiar, shiny metal door behind me but doesn't offer me a seat on the sofa on which we've made love so recently.

"Nick, we shouldn't be seen together."

"My point exactly – we lie low until nightfall. Then we get a slow boat to somewhere rocky and barren near the border. Don't they say the best hiding places are right under their noses?"

"Whose noses?"

I notice she's swapped her island garb for a charcoal trouser suit.

"Were you going somewhere?"

"I have an appointment," she looks at her stocking feet. "It's a private matter."

I try to glean more information from the flat from which I am about to be ejected. To these jaded eyes our former love nest looks more like a doctor's waiting room. The tie-dye throws and dream catchers are gone; the Buddha replaced by a vase of fresh flowers. What have they done to her? Pride of place on the dust-free coffee table is a smiling photo in an ornate frame.

"Is that her?" I ask, frowning at the slim brunette. "Is that Harriet?"

"I think you should leave now, Viv."

"Funny how sane they look when they're not speaking."

"I could say the same about you, dear."

This term of affection seems to be no more than a tool designed to lever me back towards the smudged metal of the doorframe. Likewise I take the kiss on the cheek and pat on the bum as part of the same passive-aggressive arsenal.

"We'll meet up when things settle down," she says.

"Promise?"

There might have been an affirmative emitted from behind the closing door, it could have been an untended hinge; either way it has been made crystal clear to me that the sooner I get Panda and Salamander the information they need, the quicker they will release Sky from the hypnotic hold they have over her, and the less chance there is of her returning to the open arms and fractured charms of her ex.

Back at the Brolly, the night appeared to be winding down inconclusively until a phone call breached the communal silence.

"Can't you change that ring tone?" Frank asked, as Fenton's brick vibrated across the table-top chiming God Save the—

"Yes?" Fenton answered the phone suspiciously. "Right... Yes... I see... Understood... Indeed... Agreed... Real shame, yes... Will do."

He hung up then began rubbing his forehead rapidly, as if encouraging a parasitic genie to leave the shady enclaves of his furrowed brow.

"What is it?" asked Jeanie, whose guests were now accounted for.

"That was Paul," Fenton sighed. "He's been arrested for arson."

CHAPTER TWENTY-ONE

How could I have been so stupid? Don't answer that – just consider the stress I'm under. If I only had to think of myself that would be one thing but juggling so many different fates in your hands isn't easy. Fatalism can kill and on my way to retrieve my bike I narrowly avoid a potentially lethal overdose. The broiling injustice of being denied Sky's counsel combines with unwelcome midday temperatures and before I know it I'm flicking head sweat at innocent gardeners while stomping down Peak Road from the only proper sanctuary I've known these last few months.

There's only one way I can think of to escape the glare of the sun and the sea and the elderly plant-botherers. The island's police station sits off a shady pathway close to a quiet square where birdmen come to compare caged avian. It's an old-fashioned kind of place with a veranda and small ceremonial cannon perked outside it. What's to stop me throwing myself at the mercy of some bored island cops? What do I have to hide beyond a tragic accident and post-traumatic body swap that failed to pay off?

I have to remind myself that any confession would almost certainly implicate one or more of my companions, something I continue to brood on as I slog along the busy prom, sunglasses sliding down my moist nose at regular intervals. My bike is chained to a steel balustrade, pointing out to sea. Leaning over the water's edge to fiddle with the lock, I catch sight of a less-fortunate two-wheeler destined to end its days half-sunk in greenish water too shallow to host the crabbers and motorboats beyond it, too deep to permit easy retrieval.

The island's so-called bicycle graveyard, stretching for around a third of the promenade, is rumoured to have been created solely by "Hunger" Pang, an enormous but little-seen kitchen porter who offers his services to several of the seafood restaurants along the front. If a sufficiently important or high-spending customer finds their view of the twinkling harbour obscured by an unlocked bicycle, they only have to say the word and Pang will emerge from whichever steamy kitchen he is encased in to hurl the offending bicycle into the water.

I shudder at the prospect of the man, but find unexpected solace in the dormant bicycle. Yes, it has fallen – like Jonathan – but that doesn't make it, or the situation, completely unsalvageable. If I was cunning enough, I could easily co-opt a crabber into some midnight haulage work, and wind up with enough money from scrap – from re-cycling, as it were – to keep me fed and watered for a month. I'm not going to do that, but the point remains that only death is truly an ending, and Ray and me still have a good chunk of our lives ahead of us. Good old Ray. Where the hell is that crazy kid now?

The question is asked idly, but there's nothing idle about the way I cycle back to my flat at Fragrant Gardens, nor how I punch his number into my phone repeatedly in a fruitless attempt to reach his mobile, nor the map I download with gritted teeth and saintly patience from the tourist board website, which claims to show each of the multifarious islands stillborn into Hong Kong waters many thousands of years ago.

"Where the fuck are you, Ray?" I ask the screen as the map jigsaws itself together. "And why didn't I realise you were the orbiter they're after?"

I'm trying so hard to make sense of the fragments of Ray's character I've managed to absorb that when there's a knock on the front door I wonder if I've somehow summoned him psychokinetically, an illusion ruined by the appearance of a tall, gaunt figure in shorts and polo shirt, distinguishable by his sandy hair and large freckled hands.

"An unlocked door," says Redmond. "You mustn't have any enemies, Viv."

"That's what you think."

After this initial display of confidence, Redmond hovers awkwardly above parquet flooring reminiscent of school assemblies, trying not to upset any of the weirdly ornate furniture crammed into the place by my landlady. Only Sky has visited me here before, and she must be around half Redmond's size. Fitting two gangling men into an apartment this small will be a challenge – as if I'm not busy enough.

"What can I do for you?" I ask, still sitting at my dining table – the computer screen angled away from my guest.

"Nice place," he smiles. "Excellent view of the pool."

Redmond is jolting his head between the few tangible features of my bolthole with a kind of journalistic Tourette's. Yet despite his apparent nosiness, something tells me my neighbour is less interested in digging the dirt than chewing the fat. Fragrant Gardens must be a lonely place in which to sit and write all day.

"Hear the pigs last night?" he asks, once he's taken a chance on my cream, faux-leather sofa.

"I was out last night," I tell him, closing my laptop and heading for the tiny kitchen to brew up. "Were they bad?"

"Screeching like banshees," he grins, "made me feel glad to be veggie all over again."

"I'm only making tea," I pop my head out of the kitchen. "No sausages in here, your honour."

"Good to know."

Where's he from? I can't remember asking. I know he quit his posh public school and then worked on local newspapers across the UK; that would explain his neutral tones. If he wasn't so twitchy I could see him reading the news.

"What's going on in the world?" I ask, putting a cup of tea in front of him.

"Aha," elbows on knees, Redmond steeples his fingers thoughtfully. "Pains me to tell you, what with you busy planning your trips, getting to know your surroundings, but on the other hand forewarned is forearmed and in these uncertain times—"

"I don't mean to be rude," I interrupt, "but I need to get ready for another trip soon. Insatiable wanderlust I guess you'd call it."

Redmond shuts up, whips out his smartphone.

"Don't always follow the news," I admit, now feeling bad about cutting him off. "Too many amateurs involved these days. What happened to the old pros we grew up with? What happened to proper grammar and syntax, copy-proofing and all that jazz?"

"Indeed," Redmond frowns into his screen, scrolls down a bit, then holds it at eye level for me. I recognise the green and black

livery of an online news source, *Hong Kong Uncensored.*
LARGEST PRO-EXPAT MARCH YET – SUPPORT
OFFERED BY DOMESTIC HELPERS; STUDENTS

The by-line suggests a certain Ed Redmond has written the piece.

"Congratulations," I say, wondering if he's popped round for a cup of self-affirmation.

"We're screwed," he says glumly.

"Yes," I remember, "there is that. But it's good you're making a stand."

"I'm not having to spin things too much," Redmond takes a slurp of tea. "There really is support out there for everyone due to be expelled. Trouble is, it's coming from sections of the community that have always been ignored by the government."

"And you yourself, are you staying on here?"

"Lost my accreditation when my coverage of Occupy was deemed too partisan. Bullshit, of course. Plus I barely make enough money to keep me in beer. No surprise to find my name on the list of malingerers. How about you, Viv? Don't recall you telling me what you do professionally?"

"Male escort," I deadpan, now actively seeking a way out of this neighbourly embrace.

"Aren't you a little old for that?"

"I was a kept man," I confide. "Wife had a good job, five-year plan, prospect of kids, managed to fuck it up."

"You're not the first, won't be the last."

"There's a bit more to it than that, but…"

I've been slow to sense the serendipity of this visit from the momentarily bored, perpetually frustrated brain-on-stilts next door. Time to make up for it.

"But…?" he follows up, out of politeness.

"I wonder, Mr Redmond, if I could interest you in a proposition?"

"Not if it involves male escorts or giant centipedes."

"I have a particular task at hand that may require more backing – by which I mean financial backing – than I have at my disposal just now."

"You want a loan?"

"I want a loan."

Redmond shifts uncomfortably in his seat.

"To be fair, Viv, we barely know each other."

I wonder how big a portion of each day Redmond dedicates to being fair. A lot more than me I suspect.

"It wouldn't be a personal loan, Red – can I call you Red, or is Ed better? – in fact, I think an advance from *Hong Kong Uncensored* in return for the scoop of the decade would be much more appropriate."

"Scoop of the...?"

Redmond's concern is replaced by silent, rocking laughter.

"I know," I persist. "You've heard it all before. But let me show you a story from a few months ago you may have missed."

I hold my hand out for his phone and Redmond obliges. It only takes me a few seconds to find what I need. The translation isn't perfect, but the thrust of the story is clear.

AGING EXPAT BRAT SUICIDE
WHY CAN'T THEY DIE AT HOME?

"Yes," Redmond thins his lips, "I saw this in a few of the Chinese tabloids. Disgraceful coverage. Sadly not without precedent."

"Ignore the text and take a closer look at the photo beside it."

Redmond enlarges the grainy image, zooming in on my shrunken head. It's an old photo taken on our honeymoon in New York. Lennox's face has been pixelated beyond recognition; mine superficially bloated by puppy fat and cheeseburgers.

"Jesus," Redmond finds and unfolds his specs, but doesn't need them to confirm his suspicions. "It's you."

"I can't tell you everything now," I warn him. "But it's fair to say a lot of strange shit has happened to me recently. What you need to know – and what I'll relay to you in graphic detail as soon as it happens – is that I anticipate meeting one or both of the following parties within the next twenty-four hours: a young man I've been mentoring who could play a key part in Hong Kong's future, if he's given the chance, and two spooks of uncertain provenance who've already imprisoned me once, and seem very keen to extract any information I have on said youngster, then kick my battered husk back to Blighty – via the PRC if I'm particularly unlucky."

"Seriously?"

"Seriously."

Redmond stands up and looks out at the pool.

"You know there's a lot of bullshitters in the expat community," he says, "That's one thing the Chinese dailies are right about. Even that bunch at The Moon. I wouldn't trust them to—"

"I'm no fantasist," I tell him. "Believe me, I wish I was."

"Where are you planning to go?"

"I can't tell you, because I haven't worked it out yet. If you could get me three thousand dollars that would give me enough scope to do what I need to do. It's only the cost of entertaining a few contacts at the Correspondents' Club. Not much of a gamble is it?"

Redmond turns back to me.

"I'll have to think about it. Talk to my editor."

"Understood. Look, I've taken a huge chance revealing my true identity. Don't let me down, Red."

He smiles weakly, his hand on the door handle.

"Tell you what," I toss him my bonus ball. "When all this is over – when I'm in the clear and you've got your story, I'll take you out round the island. We'll have a session like no session you've ever had. Japanese whisky, karaoke, dressed crab – you name it."

"Sounds dangerous."

"It's all dangerous," I tell him. "Get back to me soon – later this afternoon?"

"Okay."

"Deal," I get up and shake his hand, a little prematurely, but confident I've finally found an ally to replace those who've gone before.

My research over the next couple of hours doesn't get me anywhere, but I stick to my virtual scouring of the islands, unable to visualise Ray back in Wan Chai despite my suggestion that he haunt its restaurants as a pot washer. Of course he may still have decided that safety in numbers was the best option, and with Kowloon being amongst the most densely populated places on Earth, where better to test the theory? Yet when I think of Ray on the hashing trails, standing tall and aloof in virgin grasses like a young prince overlooking his fiefdom, I decide he has to be taking refuge in bucolic surroundings, where – as well as benefitting from the fresh air – he will be less likely to encounter any of his old triad acquaintances.

The Internet only gets me so far. I rule out Peng Chau after reading of its annexation by French expats determined to transform the sleepy island into a gastronomic destination; Tai O is too touristy – like Cheung Chau but without the useful hinterland; in fact much of Sai Kung and the New Territories seem to have been colonised by cyclists, yoga louts and extreme runners. Ray can run with the best of them but I have a feeling he'll be in hiding until I can flush him out.

"Hello?"

The number isn't logged in the memory of my latest cheap mobile and it takes me a while to recognise the aspirational Received Pronunciation coming down the line.

"Know where you're going yet?"

It's Redmond, checking in.

"I've got a pretty good idea."

"Okay," he doesn't sound convinced. "Well, on the off-chance that doesn't reap dividends, I thought I'd pass on some information the significance of which isn't completely clear to me yet."

"That's kind of you."

"It's just that a colleague of mine recently travelled to the Po Toi islands. Heard of them?"

"No," I bring up my map and begin a new search.

"My colleague's someone you might call a temple spotter. Trains, birds, women – none of them do anything for him, but give him a new temple to add to his collection..."

"Got it," I tell him. "Wow, all the way down here off Stanley."

"They call it Hong Kong's South Pole. Ferry leaves from Aberdeen at weekends and on days beginning with a 'T'. Place isn't on many tourist itineraries – everyone heads north as a rule. But while he was walking round the main island, colleague notices something incongruous."

"A shoreline free of plastic bottles?"

"A coffee shop where you pay what you like."

"I see," I enlarge Po Toi on my map. "Not the kind of thing local traders are likely to embrace."

"Maybe we're being cynical."

"Anything else?"

"Only that when colleague asks the kid serving him about the philosophy behind the place, he's given short shrift."

"What nationality is your colleague?"

"Hong Kong Chinese."

"What makes you think I'll do any better?"

"You don't have to," a sternness returns to Redmond's voice. A sternness I last heard when he was crushing an insect. "This is only a backup plan, remember?"

"That's right," I tell him, checking the ferry times. "One to keep on the backburner, just in case."

CHAPTER TWENTY-TWO

Jeanie Lau and Horatio Lam walked slowly along Central harbour front, taking care only to talk on the stretches between ferry piers. They ignored the green water that churned beside them complainingly and the skyscrapers opposite that caught the sun in their myriad glass panels and flashed it their way at inopportune moments. While waiting for Lam, Jeanie had noticed that the digital display running up and around the ICC tower claimed it was 34 degrees and not yet 10am. Things were hotting up.

"You look tired, Ms Lau," said Lam, "if you don't mind me saying so. You were up late waiting for your guests to return?"

"Part of the job."

"We're neither of us getting any younger."

"Speak for yourself."

"And you had a health scare recently?"

"You'll have a health scare if you don't cut out the small talk," she told him, ensuring there was just enough humour in her voice to keep communication channels open.

"Forgive me," Lam stopped to encase his rubbery features in a crimson handkerchief. "When both daughters leave for British universities," he whipped the cloth away like a magician performing a trick, "it can be hard to let go of paternal duties."

"We're the same age," Jeanie reminded him, "and Paul not much younger. The difference being he has a small child to think of. We both of us appear to have our affairs in order."

"For now at least," Lam agreed.

"How is he?"

"Superficially?"

"There's nothing superficial about Paul."

"He appears to be angry, confused, but accepting of the fact that if you set fire to an occupied building, it's hard for the authorities to show much sympathy and understanding."

"Has he been asked about motive?"

"He hasn't said as much, but it's been assumed the arson attack was an impromptu protest against his hapless situation. The fact that the crime doesn't appear to have been premeditated will stand in his favour."

"But he'll still be deported?"

Lam stopped, shielded his eyes and looked at her, checking she was serious.

"Of course."

Again, Jeanie stopped herself from snapping back. Lam's pedantry was part of his fairness, and fairness was what she needed.

"Would you like an ice-cream, Inspector?" she asked as they approached a booth selling drinks and snacks to tourists and commuters.

"Not for me," he told her. "Sensitive teeth."

"Sensitive teeth?" Jeanie hooted. "And you, a hardened Hong Kong policeman."

"Not so loud," Lam frowned, cupping a protective hand around his caramel-coloured tombstones.

"You're going to have to learn to relax, Horatio," Jeanie said, as she paid for her ice-cream and they drifted towards an unoccupied bench.

"Oh really?" Lam raised his eyebrows. "Is that how you extract information from your clientele?"

"You make it sound so seedy."

"What are you thinking, Jeanie?"

"I'm thinking that one of the boys—"

"Boys?"

"Calling them men suggests a level of – anyway, one of the boys thinks Paul knows a lot more than the rest of us about recent events."

"Those events being?"

"Jonathan Falk's disappearance and the death of Nick Powell."

"Or is it the other way round?"

"Precisely. What of Nick?"

"There's no record of him being held in police custody. Communications with the mainland authorities are less transparent but I still believe I would have heard one way or another if he was being detained by them."

"I see," Jeanie nodded, licked. "And does Paul have a lawyer?"

"On the way, apparently – one of the best in the business."

"That's something, although…"

Jeanie gazed off into space. Lam checked his watch, coughed politely. He had work to return to.

"Penny for your thoughts?" he ventured.

"I'm wondering if inviting the Falks back here would do more harm than good."

"They're cut up Jeanie," Lam reminded her. "And we don't have a clue where Nick is yet."

"It's Paul I'd like them to meet," she explained. "He's a good boy – and he's got nothing to lose."

"What about that rock you mentioned, sent to someone called Colin?" Lam gave his face a last wipe. "Any more thoughts?"

"Probably a red herring."

"Sounds like it belongs in the harbour."

"Some other harbour," Jeanie smiled goodbye. "Far away."

Fortunately my travel plans have taken me to Aberdeen harbour – far enough removed from the cop-loving landlady of the supposedly pro-Dem Brolly and her new pet, though if they'd arranged to meet an hour earlier they might have caught me coming off the Cheung Chau ferry with a human shield of retirees destined for the department stores of Central. Redmond takes me as far as the shoreline ATM before I board, extracting the three thousand dollars that has been transferred to him from his employer, and impressing on me the gamble *Hong Kong Uncensored* is taking in supporting my quest for the truth.

"Here," he passes me his metallic Dictaphone. "It's an old-fashioned one. Just press 'play' and 'record' together."

"Wow," I grin. "I'm getting the crown jewels."

The heat has stirred people from their slumbers at a precociously early hour. Up ahead we see a crimson Cameron Silverback trying to control a teetering bicycle waylaid by heavy shopping bags. He looks like an exotic bird dragging a mantrap back to its nest. It's Redmond's cue to do one.

"Remember," he tells me. "This isn't about you, or me – this is about covering a cause in an impartial, well-informed way.

You're making me trust you, Nick. I hope I can rely on your discretion?"

"Absolutely," I fold the three thousand and tuck it into the top pocket of my backpack.

"Need a hand?" I smile at Cameron as I breeze past him, but he's too out of breath to reply. Boarding the ferry, I feel empowered by my good fortune. All I have to do is find Ray, convince him to pow-wow with the commies – if only by phone – and I'll get them off my back, and Sky back onto it.

At Aberdeen I ask the young woman in the ferry ticket office whether today begins with a 'T'.

"No."

"Does tomorrow begin with a 'T'?" I ask

"Yes, tomorrow begins with a 'T'"

With his prestigious background in journalism it's no surprise to discover that Redmond has his facts straight – there's no chance of me getting to Po Toi until 10am tomorrow. A plan to hire a boat and claim the cost on expenses has already been pre-empted and ruled out by my frugal benefactor in favour of an all-night stay on a floating restaurant in the harbour.

"Eat and drink as much as possible," Redmond explained. "Then find an empty storeroom to fall asleep in. If they wake you up, apologise and say you've got a medical condition."

"What if I wake up in China?"

"Then you've eaten and drunk too much – those things are static restaurants, not cruise liners."

I take refuge in a sports bar until it's time for food, finding a dark corner in which to sup slowly on a steady succession of ice-cold beers. The other customers are also single men; each committed to one of multiple TV screens intent on aggrandising hyperactive, colourful, but ultimately futile pursuits happening somewhere else in the world. In order to blend in, I find my own screen and claim it with a penetrating gaze straight out of the football manager's handbook. I lose track of time. As Beryl used to at the Brolly, the waitress brings me drink after drink. At 9pm I decide it's time to eat.

After a minor altercation with a mooring rope, I hop onto the free boat that takes diners to and from the bright lights and gaudy paintwork of Aberdeen's water-bound restaurants. Their bright red facades – Imperial Dynasty meets '70s kitsch – bring to mind gypsy caravans and narrow boats glimpsed on childhood holidays, but on a much larger scale. Fiery Chinese characters add atmosphere but are impenetrable to me. Only at the last minute do I focus on the neon capitals above the biggest of the eateries: JUMBO KINGDOM. Most people choose to get off here but I'm not most people. As I stress repeatedly to the young deck-hand, I will not eat fucking elephant, whether it's a traditional delicacy or not.

"Where you go then?" he asks. "We go back now, everyone gone."

"What about that one?" I demand, pointing to a modest-sized vessel moored amongst a clutch of smaller craft. He says something to the skipper, laughs and off we go.

The junk is decorated with a lot more subtlety than the floating restaurant. In fact, on closer inspection, I see that its luminescent allure owes a lot to the reflection of JUMBO's audacious display in the plate glass windows of its raised and castellated stern. Food is the main thing in any case and aboard the junk I spot a husband and wife team preparing fresh fish with sweet chilli sauce and local veg in a blackened wok above a gas stove. Perfect. We get as close as we can to the junk and I heave myself on deck.

"Do you have any beer?" I ask.

So focused are they on preparing the speciality of the house that my hosts at first seem startled by my sudden arrival. They quickly recover themselves. The wife offers me a seat at the only available table and a large bottle of Tsing Tao is plopped in front of me by her smiling husband. The fact that Astrid is Swedish and Eric is Dutch only strikes me as significant after a good night's sleep under the stars.

"Morning," says Eric, joining me on the poop deck around 8am.

"Morning," I hunch myself into a sitting position, dispensing with the sheet someone has draped over me in the night. My mind is veering between existential breakdown and doomed counter-revolution. Did I eat? If so the food didn't soak up much of the booze.

"Sorry to be dense," I say to Eric, who has put down his carrot juice and begun an exercise routine designed to show off his strong yet supple physique. "But this *is* a floating restaurant, isn't it?"

"Restaurant?" Eric laughs. "I'll tell Yolanda you called her boat a restaurant."

"Yolanda?"

Eric manages to look surprised without his cool ever being threatened.

"You *are* a friend of Piers and Yolanda, right?"

I'm spared the temptation to lie by Astrid's return to the quarterdeck. Safe to say she's no longer smiling.

"Email from Yolanda, 'Glad you're having fun. Sorry, no idea who Vivian Letterby is. If he keeps repeating the same politically incorrect jokes you better make him walk the plank.'"

"I can explain…"

Fortunately, the aforementioned Piers and Yolanda have listed their renovated Chinese junk as Airbnb accommodation; unfortunately the rate is two thousand Hong Kong dollars per person, per night – excluding meals. I think Eric would have let me off but as I wave for a water taxi to take me back to Aberdeen, the look on Astrid's face tells me I'm not going to get out of here without paying. God knows what filthy jokes I told them – I struggle to remember a single gag in normal circumstances. I tell myself I needed this blowout, wave goodbye, and am shuttled at a painfully slow rate of knots towards my morning ferry to Po Toi.

CHAPTER TWENTY-THREE

The Po Toi Islands don't strike me as the obvious place to plan the revolution or counter-revolution or whatever you want to call it, but maybe that's because I've never done any serious plotting of my own. From what I can see from the boat, the main, eponymous island is formed from the same pinkish granite as Cheung Chau but unlike my final resting place has few trees and little shade beyond that offered by a low-lying pubic scrub. Don't plotters need dark corners to scheme in?

I plonk myself down at a plastic table outside the first restaurant I come to and order a drink from an apathetic matriarch. My fellow passengers are hikers and set out with their walking poles and sun visors, chatting excitedly about the change of scene. I imagine they will end up back here for food before the ferry returns to Hong Kong in the early afternoon. Strays and dawdlers will be stranded on Po Toi until the day after tomorrow. I wonder where they'll be accommodated – there doesn't seem to be much in the way of human habitation here. Unless a little-known mega city sits in the north of the island, I should be able to complete my search for Ray by lunchtime.

"How much?" I ask.

"Thirty."

I lower my sunglasses.

"I can't pay what I like?"

"You pay thirty."

"You're sure?"

"Thirty dollars."

Guess I'm in the wrong place. I decide my pint of iced tea is worth every cent for services to my receding hangover.

"Here you go, madam. I will need change."

I follow the single trail into the body of the island, the walking party ahead never completely disappearing from view. The erratic buzzing of a drone alerts me to its presence high to the east. Someone is aiming for a panoramic sweep of the island. Funny how these things always sound like they're about to crash but rarely do, tempting us to underestimate their powers of intrusion, or compare them favourably to asthmatic pets. Rather than scrabbling for a loose rock to fling at it, I simply retrieve my baseball cap from my backpack and lower its peak sufficient to obscure most of my face.

Reaching the vantage point offered by the Kwoon Yat pagoda, and having sweated out most of my bodily impurities, I decide I'm chasing ghosts. The exposed paths and descending rock formations are of interest to the walkers sitting here eating their packed lunches, but I can't see any likely hiding places ahead unless my old friend has gone underground. I double-back towards the ferry pier and investigate some creaky-looking eateries on the single sandy beach. They look like traditional, family-run affairs, although the waiter who idles out to take my order has a disconcerting touch of the urbane about him.

"Yes?" he asks.

"Is this the best place to get a plate of fried squid in chilli sauce round here?"

"No. That would be Mary Fu's, near the pier," he points back to where I had my iced tea.

"But am I right in thinking I can pay what I like here?"

"You are," he sighs, "but rich whites are expected to pay a little more."

"What makes you think I'm rich?"

"You're here on a Tuesday. Only rich dudes can afford to take days off during the week. Plus you dress scruffy. I read that a lot of rich dudes dress scruffy."

"Who am I to argue with your prejudices?" I decide the moon-faced kid isn't worth it. "Just bring me some fried squid in chilli. Please."

I squint out to sea, searching for a sign beyond the plastic litter sparkling on the shoreline – perhaps a modest breach by the mythical whale that upset the Macau ferry. Like Ray, that whale doesn't seem to mind taking on the big beasts. A risky undertaking, yet I want to reassure Ray that all he needs to do for his benevolent old boss is to clarify things with Panda and Salamander; reassure them that he's more of a rogue than a radical. They will in turn tell Sky that any pressure exerted on her was down to a simple misunderstanding. Then we can all relax.

"Who's in charge here?" I ask the waiter when he returns with my plate of food.

"This is a collective," he says. "Do you want me to explain the concept?"

"That won't be necessary," I tell him. "No offence, but I assumed you were too young to be managing this operation. Perhaps I'm wrong? You see, I have something urgent to discuss with your bedfellows."

The kid reddens but holds his nerve.

"Maybe you can speak to Ms Lee, if she's not too busy."

"Ms Lee?"

"Yes, she is also young. How does that make you feel?"

"Perfectly fine," I smile. "In fact, I might be ready for a beer."

"They're warm," he warns me. "Warm English beer for sweaty English man."

"Well as you're fetching it for me you can tell Ms Lee that I need to see her. My name is Powell – Nick Powell."

"Oh yes," the waiter nods knowingly. "We've heard all about you. You're kind of like Mr Bean crossed with Ah Q, yes?"

"Who?"

"He's a British TV comedy character whose characteristically—"

"The other one."

"Sorry, we were told you were well-read. Ah Q is a quixotic character from Chinese literature. A kind of holy fool, if you like."

"What I'd like is for you to fuck off and speak to Ms Lee. And yes, I know all about Ah Q – it's your tone I'm having problems with."

Content to have finally provoked me, the waiter retreats into the nether regions of the restaurant, skirting trollies loaded with dirty plates and smeared glasses from a distant rush hour. Five minutes later he reappears and calls over.

"Okay, Powell," he scowls, "Ms Lee will see you now."

I get up and intercept him in the shadows, pausing when we're nose to nose. Again his round face darkens, transforming his pimply features from Lunar to Martian landscape.

"What's your name?" I ask.

"Clarence," he tells me, still managing to exude smugness.

"Ever worked in a real kitchen, with real kitchen staff?"

"No."

"They're dangerous places," I explain. "Lots of knives. I'd watch that tongue of yours when this is all over and you're working in a Chinese prison chopping pak choi."

"Maybe I'll see you there?"

"I wouldn't count on it. Where is she?"

Clarence nods towards a chipped and cracked door that could do with a fresh coat of aquamarine. There's no handle but it proves as light as driftwood when I push against it. The stifling space I enter is a storeroom in which a small table and chairs are penned in by industrial-sized tins of sweetcorn and pineapple chunks, blackened pots and pans, and defunct fans and aircon units. A muted television is fixed to a bracket near a gummed-up window. I'm immediately stung by smoke emanating from Ms Lee's cigarette. She waits for me to recover then takes another drag, stubs it out and points to a seat opposite.

"There's your beer."

I sit down and finger it. Warm, as promised.

"I'm Nick," I say, holding out my hand.

"Winkie," she says, unexpectedly.

Ms Lee's determined features can't hide her youth; nor can the indie girl demeanour disguise the seriousness in her large, brown eyes. I look down to check that her hand has met mine; the pressure she exerts being almost imperceptible. When I release her digits and regard her again she winks.

"Don't get any ideas," she says. "Tear gas…"

"Hence…"

"The nickname," her voice is soft, but carries an authority that suggests she doesn't have to raise it very often.

"Occupy?"

"Yes – Sunday 28th September 2014. The day the authorities decided to up the stakes."

"It was just down the road from us," I tell her. "We'd only been in Hong Kong a fortnight."

"You didn't go?"

"My wife…was working. I wasn't sure what to do. The propaganda was all about western infiltration. I didn't want to look like an old colonial – or a spy."

"Sounds like you had a valid excuse."

I can't tell whether she's being sarcastic or not.

"And what do you think of this?" Winkie gestures towards the TV with a second, unlit cigarette. They're usually so clean-living, these millennials – Winkie must have decided that nicotine was the least disruptive stress-reliever available to her.

"Very noble," I tell her, glancing up at the silent images of protestors on yet another march.

"Three weeks until the deportations begin," Winkie reminds me. "And there's Hong Kong kids out there saying no."

"Maybe they're worried it'll happen to them next?"

"Very funny," Winkie lights her cigarette. "You think China's gonna let the best brains leave its third richest city?"

"I guess not," I stroke my chin. "And I can't imagine Hong Kongers joining the Africans fleeing climate change and the Syrians fleeing war on the boats to Europe."

"Why not?" Winkie slams a fist on the table. "You don't think we're tough enough?"

"I just mean culturally—"

"You want to see my fucking scars?" Winkie begins removing her black sleeveless T-shirt. I've already noticed a war wound meandering south from her collarbone, like the Nile on Google Maps. "Want me to strip for you, Powell?"

"No, no, look, I'm sorry – I didn't mean to be disrespectful. All I want to do is have a word with your friend Ray and get out of here."

Needing a break from Winkie's smouldering rage, I look back at the TV. Now it's my turn to lose my cool.

"Is that…? It can't be. What the fuck?"

Paul, handcuffed and surrounded by a braying pack of press photographers, is being hurried into the High Court building in Admiralty by a couple of uniforms. His lawyer is right behind him. She stops on the steps of the courthouse, flicks some escapee strands of violently red hair away from her eyes and begins talking to the assembled media. It's Lennox.

"Turn it up," I snap at Winkie. "Turn the sound up."

The remote control is lying on the table beside her cigarettes. Winkie picks it up and flings it at me. I thumb the volume upwards.

"...would like to extend his thanks to everyone who has supported him at this extremely difficult time. Paul Coyne is not a bad man. He is not a criminal. He is not an arsonist. He is simply a father who has been driven to the edge of despair and beyond by a system that first denies him access to his young daughter, and then tells him he must leave Hong Kong altogether. My firm is ready to contest the crown's case against Paul on his behalf and on behalf of the thousands of other expatriates – men and women – being so cruelly driven out of Hong Kong, and thus separated from their families, at this dark time in the territory's history."

"Jesus Christ."

"You know her?"

The camera pans to a small group of supporters holding placards in support of my old friend. The news moves on. I silence the TV.

"I can't say I know her, no. Maybe once. In another life."

"I don't have time for your riddles," Winkie tells me. "We have things to arrange. Try to help you while you sit here drinking beer."

"Believe me, I'm only drinking it to be polite. And I have things to do too...so is Ray here, washing pots next door?"

"No," her tone turns cautious, "but he is not far away. Ray prefers to be by himself, after everything that's happened."

"Fine, I can understand that," I finish my drink. "So where is he then?"

Winkie looks at me through the cigarette smoke, trying to work something out.

"You sure you want to meet him, Powell?"

"We're friends," I explain. "I just need a favour, for old time's sake. To ask him to talk to some other friends of mine and—"

"You're not armed?"

"Armed?" I'm getting impatient now. "Of course not."

"Very well," Winkie dismisses me with a feathery waft of her hand. "Wait outside with Clarence. I will call him."

Thankfully there's no sign of my pseudo-intellectual server when I step back into the restaurant. A couple of walkers have returned prematurely, knocked out by the midday sun and ready to idle away the three hours before the ferry chugs them back towards their creature comforts. I inspect the contents of a kitchen-bound trolley, removing a couple of items – just in case.

"Powell," Winkie's voice brings me to attention and I return to her office. "He's at the lighthouse."

"The lighthouse?"

"Go south at the pagoda. Southernmost tip of the island."

"Any message for him?"

"Yes," she pauses, chews her lip, winks twice. "Ask him if he's ready to trust us again."

"Okay."

The squat Po Toi lighthouse isn't much to look at by British standards, or perhaps on a hot, white-bright day like today with calm blue water all about, it's the invention itself that strikes you as redundant. No sign of Ray – it would be unlike him to stay close to a building for long in any case. He seems to perceive them in the same way animals view cages. The tourists, those that made it this far, have been and gone. A sign points me in the direction of "Palm Rock", and sure enough, there's Ray – standing atop a bunch of rocky fingers, looking out to sea.

"I have to hand it to you…" I say as I approach, but the words are lost on him.

To distract myself from a darker thought threatening to gatecrash my consciousness, I concentrate on how Ray's appearance has changed since we last met – his shiny red and blue running shorts and vest no longer flutter about his slight frame. He has filled out; appears to have more muscle to him. I'd forgotten that as a man in his early 20s my young friend is still growing; that only now in my late 30s has my own body come to rest.

"I need to talk to you Ray," I call up at the fingers, treading carefully along the cliff edge below them.

"Talk?" Ray says. "All you do is talk, boss."

Physically at least he moves towards me, finding unseen creases in the elephantine rock that allow him to descend in stages like a mountain goat. I step back, towards the path – giving him plenty of room.

"I need to ask a favour, Ray," I tell him.

He nods; shifting from one Nike to another – always warming up, always ready to run.

"Those people you saw on Lamma – the big Chinese dude and the skinny white chick. They want to talk to you."

"No," he sighs. "They don't want to talk to Ray."

"What then?"

"They want Ray to do something. They think he should have done it already."

"What?"

He says nothing. His eyes look black, the bags below them more suited to a speed freak than a cross-country runner.

"Tell me what they want you to do," I repeat, but all Ray does is grab my forearm and squeeze it far too tightly for my liking. I'm dragged, staggering, towards the scattering of marble-sized stones that mark the narrow cliff edge. I quickly realise that there's no negotiating with zombies – my only hope is to provoke Ray into dialogue.

"It was you, wasn't it, Ray?" I ask him quietly. "When I saw you just now, on top of the fingers, I knew it was you who pushed Jonathan off Lion Rock. You killed him, Ray. And before I die, I want to know why."

CHAPTER TWENTY-FOUR

Once Lennox had disappeared into the courthouse, the crowd of fifty or so protestors, their police chaperones and the media assigned to see what would happen next declared an unofficial truce, reminding Jeanie of those she had read about in the Europeans' Great War. If Inspector Horatio Lam had been there she might have asked him if her Brolly crew could take on his officers in an impromptu game of football on High Court plaza. It was good to relax. There was no point being hyped up the whole time, in the manner of her younger self, but nor was there any excuse to lose focus. There was a rebellion brewing in the ranks.

"Miss Jeanie."

It was one of the Italians, Carlo – a tall, handsome boy and an obvious ringleader.

"What is it?"

She lowered her heavy wooden placard and propped it against a metal crush-barrier. Ditzy had found the remains of the tables and chairs they'd chopped up outside Think Tank and used them to fashion signs that morning. Jeanie had helped the girls with their English. She had chosen a Beatles' quote for her own placard: LOVE IS ALL YOU NEED. It seemed fitting, what with Paul being from Liverpool. Frank had suggested another '60s classic, LIGHT MY FIRE, before his sign had been wrested from him under considerable duress.

"We wish to see…the Peak," said Carlo.

"Crap view from up there," Fenton told him, lowering his politically incorrect BRITS ARE HONGKONGERS TOO. "Too many clouds, too much pollution."

"They just want your money," Frank agreed. "Hold you hostage like gorillas in the mist. Force-feed you Big Macs and make you buy thousand-dollar trainers."

"Arrive Hong Kong three day ago," Carlo persisted, gesturing at his duo of shy friends. "Stay at your beautiful hostel, Miss

Jeanie – *grazie mille*. But no sightseeing, no food, no girls – only walk three kilometres to town hall and now we shout here for many hour. Is very good…is fun…but…"

"Don't you know we're all connected now?" Jeanie asked. "Wherever you are in the world you have to stand up for your rights."

"Let them go, Jeanie," Kim suggested, touching her arm. "You can't expect everyone to care as much as we do. It's not fair. Besides," she pointed at the other Hostel-dwellers who were in a circle sharing sushi and soft drinks, "the Chinese girls will stay with us for the novelty value, and the Spanish boys will stay because they fancy me."

"Stereotyping again, babe?" Frank yawned and stretched.

"Very well," Jeanie sighed. "Thank you Carlo, enjoy the Peak. Remember, you can always get a ferry somewhere more—"

"Si, si," Carlo broke into a broad smile. "We know – go Tung Chung Mall, Cable Car, Ocean Park – very good culture – ciao, ciao."

He grabbed his companions and they rushed off before their host could change her mind. Jeanie turned to Frank.

"Where are Bob and Barbara?"

"Who?"

"The Falks – Jonathan's parents."

"I think they went to grab some food," said Kim.

"Okay," Jeanie scanned the barricades – a gaggle of local and international reporters were laughing along to the banter provided by two middle-aged performance artists, one in a pith helmet, the other wearing a tin hat and smoking a cigar. The circus had come to Hong Kong. "I don't want the Falks talking to the media," Jeanie told them.

She noticed Fenton edging towards the press pack wearing an expression that usually preceded an outpouring of venom in the Brolly.

"Fenton!" she called after him. "There's a time and place to speak to reporters. Now isn't the time. We don't have a cohesive message because—"

"We don't know what's going on," Frank concluded.

Just then, Jeanie spotted Star signalling from the courthouse steps. A series of star jumps had seemed the most appropriate way to gain her boss's attention, but the barmaid had grown so skinny on failed romance it was hard to make her out against the bricks and mortar.

Bob and Barbara had returned, looking a little dazed, and were seeking a trashcan into which to deposit the foamy fish balls they'd been hawked.

"Come on," said Jeanie, taking their rubbish and entrusting it to Fenton, "I want you to meet someone."

"I'm coming too," said Kim, hoisting her handbag over her shoulder.

"Fine," Jeanie pointed to Frank and Fenton. "You two stay here with the kids."

"And don't get into any trouble," Kim added, to complete the wind-up.

In a concrete garden within the court complex they found Lennox smoking a thin, purple cigarette. Her power-suit hung off her. She'd lost weight but none of her bearing – taller than ever, angular in all the right places, and with that long red hair that made little kids stop her in the street and ask if she was a mermaid. But there were bags instead of glitter beneath her eyes today.

"How are you?" asked Jeanie.

"Bloody exhausted," Lennox smiled weakly.

"This is Bob and Barbara Falk," Jeanie introduced her impeccably groomed guests.

"Forgive us," said Bob, "we're a little jet-lagged."

"But happy to see that Jonathan has such good people around him," Barbara added.

"A pleasure to meet you," said Lennox. "I can't imagine how tough it's been for you."

"Whatever happened to our son," Bob reached for Barbara's hand, "we're ready to accept it. We just want to know the truth."

"How do you see the case unfolding?" Jeanie asked Lennox.

"Given the circumstances," Lennox dropped her cigarette and toed it out, "the trial will be held next week. They want to get it out of the way before the expulsions start properly."

"And how's Paul's defence?"

"We have one good character witness, Sophia – a domestic helper who saw what Paul had to tolerate during his last assignment, when he…you know," Lennox scrambled for the right mime, "dangled that child."

"Will that be enough? Sophia's testimony?"

"No," Lennox admitted. "We need to work out what Paul was doing between leaving his last employment and setting fire to the bookshop. That is, who he was with and what they were planning."

"Hasn't he told you?" asked Bob.

"He's confused, and I don't see the sense in confusing him further. The courtroom isn't the right place for ambiguity."

"You're talking about Nick, aren't you?" Kim asked her, avoiding an ex-husband reference so as not to overcomplicate things.

"Yes."

"You haven't heard from him?"

"No."

"Wait a moment," Barbara spoke up. "You mean Jonathan's friend Nick – the young man who killed himself?"

"We're no longer sure he did," Jeanie explained. "We think Nick is alive, that he might know something about Jonathan's disappearance, and that he's undoubtedly in trouble."

"I'd bet my bottom dollar on that," Lennox told them.

"What does Paul say when you ask him about Nick?" Kim asked.

"He rambles, for the most part. I've made notes but there's not a lot to work on. Tells me Nick's being chased by communists."

"Communists?" Bob snorted.

"Exactly. I can't always tell which era we're in. One minute Paul's talking about Liverpool's football club winning some cup or other, the next he's asking me to find someone to play Estragon in his new production of *Waiting for Godot*."

"As the English say, he's all over the shop." Jeanie shook her head. "Nothing consistent in his statements?"

"There's one word that keeps coming up – 'ray'. When he says it he moves his hand across his face. Quickly, like this. Gets a strange look in his eyes. I don't know whether he's referring to a childhood friend, a Liverpool midfielder or a shaft of sunlight from happier times."

"Anyone know a Ray?" Jeanie asked, searching her extensive memory of names and faces.

Lennox checked her watch. "Look, I have to go back in, see Paul before they lock him up again. Any message?"

"Just that we're here for him," said Kim. "And will be until we sort this mess out."

Frank and Kim took the Lamma contingent towards the ferry while Jeanie and Fenton shepherded the rest of their coterie to the Brolly. There, Jeanie commandeered a television from the restaurant next door and they watched an English language studio debate show in which an icy female politician, a senior activist in a Che Guevara T-shirt and Inspector Lam were asked to play up to their designated roles as representatives of a divided society. The politician was game, but soon found herself on the wrong side of an unusually rowdy audience.

"Paul Coyne – an impoverished, unpredictable and dangerous man, with an alcohol intake eight times over the recommended limit – is exactly the kind of person we need to deny citizenship to in the new Hong Kong," she explained.

But her confident start was undermined by a gif-friendly clip of a tearful Paul sharing a few words with reporters as he was led into court in handcuffs.

"I don't care where I live," he sniffed. "I just want to be with my daughter."

The studio audience hissed. The young presenting team panicked and handed over to the activist, but his diatribe about a Hong Kong free from Chinese influence failed to provoke any reaction from those present. It was left to Lam to offer a less predictable view.

"When I was a child," he began, "there were riots in Hong Kong. You're too young to remember, most of you. But people died, and some of them shouldn't have died."

For a moment it looked like Lam was going to let the charged atmosphere in the studio arrest his own emotions, but he pulled himself together and carried on.

"The police? There were good police, bad police. British police, Hong Kong police. Good police on both sides, bad police too. True, the British were in charge. That's why I joined up. So I could represent my people. A lot has changed since then. Now Hong Kong Chinese people in charge. Not an easy situation, but the rules are easier for an old cop like me to understand now – treat people equal, wherever they come from."

Here, the young male presenter jumped in and rode the wave of populism he sensed in the audience around him.

"But what if the rules are skewed against certain elements in society?" he challenged Lam. "For example, the Deportation Act fails to take into account the family circumstances of the people due to be removed from Hong Kong in a fortnight's time."

Jeanie beamed as Lam allowed himself to be comprehensively outflanked, ending the debate with a benevolent smile on his face as if to say: "I'm just a humble cop, you have to decide where to go from here". This was the type of policeman she'd read about in British children's books. Perhaps in retirement he could do his beat in Sai Ying Pun, keeping an eye on the neighbourhood cats and calling in for a cuppa and a chat at the end of his rounds?

Later, on Lamma, Kim woke from her half-sleep and rolled over to check the time: just after 9pm. The day had exhausted her but catnapping had allowed her brain to relax enough to expel a small but crucial memory. Frank wasn't on the mattress, wasn't in the flat. She dressed quickly and headed outdoors. She found him where she'd left him – at the wine bar, spending their money on drinks for the supporters they'd rounded up to protest for Paul that day. On entering she had to dodge a hyped-up Scampi, who was telling anyone who would listen about his prominent role in Britain's poll-tax riots of the early '90s. Kim didn't like the way the cadaverous Molly Ransom had sidled up to Frank since she'd left them to it, but this was no time for petty jealousies.

"Frank," he spun unsteadily on his stool.

"Hello gorgeous, drink?"

"We have to go."

"Why?"

"I've remembered something."

They brushed off the protests of their fellow drinkers and ducked outside into an unusually starry night. Before Frank knew it he was being led past glum-looking fish and al-fresco diners towards the ferry pier.

"Whoa," he stopped them. "We're not going back into town?"

"We're going to Yau Ma Tei."

"That's at least an hour and a half away. Why the hell would we want to go there?"

"Because that's where I taught Harmony to play guitar."

"Harmony?" Frank wracked his brain. "Harmony, Harmony, Harmony."

"Changed her name to Winkie after Occupy."

"Shit, of course – Winkie Lee. I'd forgotten she was one of your pupils."

Frank grinned, then remembered that none of this answered his central question.

"But why—?"

"Because in one of our last lessons I asked her to think about her most complicated relationship and write a song about it."

"So?"

"She called her song, 'Ray.'"

CHAPTER TWENTY-FIVE

Unlike Jonathan – whom I suspect Ray pushed to his death while the American's back was turned – I have the advantage of facing my tormentor with my rear to the abyss. It's an advantage I intend to exploit fully, even as small stones skid under the well-worn soles of my trainers and fly over the island's natural ramparts with barely a squeak of protest. Ray's hands continue to pinch my biceps like a pair of wire cutters and the strain is beginning to show. Each time I manage to propel myself back towards the path I find the meagre gain I've made has drained me of more and more energy for the same reward.

"Tell me, Ray," I insist, "tell me why you killed him."

"He disrespect the banner. The banner our people fix to Lion Rock so all Hong Kong know our message. He call protestors stupid, naïve, hopeless, and other words. I didn't mean to push him, then—"

"Bullshit."

It's incredible how few people take advantage of the propulsive power of cursing. I swear by it myself. When I'm out running, a steady stream of "Come on you fucking loser" gives me the bite and venom required to go the distance without stopping to light a cigarette. On this occasion the cack of the bull allows me to get level with Ray, and while he has youth and fitness on his side, I have a fair amount of righteous indignation to burn off.

"You don't work for them," I wave back towards the town, the restaurant, the kids. "You don't work for me. No, I understand everything now."

Ray is finding it hard to hide his surprise – how he graduated from spy school is anybody's guess. He responds with a feeble attempt at an insult.

"You not so clever as you think," he says. "I hear your wife say so to Big Bitch."

"Leave Lennox out of this – she wasn't there the night we met. Only Paul and me were sitting half-drunk at the edge of that park like a pair of sitting ducks, ready to give you a pass for the expat cell you'd been told to infiltrate. Yes, you were running from your triad buddies, but they'd already started working for the government. They were the same thugs who pretended to be angry shopkeepers in Mong Kok when they started beating up the Occupy kids, weren't they?"

"I try to get away from them," Ray looks down, allowing himself a second or two of reminiscing. "That was not pretend. But they catch me and—"

"And soon you knew which side your bread was buttered," I remind him. "Once your bosses told you Jonathan was a spy, you either had to kill him or they'd kill you to make sure the information never went further."

He doesn't deny it. He doesn't deny anything.

"My new boss tougher than you, English," he concedes. "When they find out I don't kill you too, they beat me."

"I'm sure they'll do as much to Panda and Salamander if they fail too."

For now, Ray seems to have given up on hurling me into a watery grave, but as that fear recedes, another quickly takes its place. I realise why Winkie asked me if I was armed – Ray is dangling a black, shiny pistol loosely at his side. He couldn't have had the ugly, blockish thing secreted in his running kit; more likely he has weapons hidden around the island. It's clear the time to underestimate Ray has gone, but I've no intention of serving him my head on a platter.

"Make it quick," I tell him, "for your old boss."

I slump to my knees, dust rising to my shoulders. My mouth is dried out again. I can feel Ray's nervous energy swarming above me like a stack of mozzies partying by a stagnant pool. My words have unsettled him, as I knew they would – he's lost his zombie cool and won't find it as easy to kill me now as it would have been in the shadow of the lighthouse. Ray does something to the gun and it replies with an obedient click-clock. Sounds like an expensive bit of kit – like something a rich kid might plug in at Quantum's to make his guitar sound more psychedelic.

"You want make prayer?" Ray asks.

"It's been a while," I spit a gob of sweet nothing to the side. "Any recommendations?"

"My people believe White Lotus," he tells me.

"Your people? I thought you were a poor little orphan boy, like me."

"My other family."

"I see," I nod, non-judgementally. "And I assume this White Lotus is quite a compassionate…cult?"

But Ray's playing for time is taking off in another direction.

"You know, you had good wife," he says quietly. "If you stay with her, be good man then all this problem—"

Had he been a shark I would have pierced the glassy membrane of Ray's most conveniently located eye, as recommended in all good adventure books, but as Ray is a runner I stab him through the right foot with the stainless steel fork I've stolen from Winkie's Pay What You Can restaurant. He doesn't cry out. There is simply a sharp intake of breath as I watch the blood begin to blossom through the mesh roof of his lightweight shoe. Then I roll to one side and begin running as fast as I can.

"I told you before," I yell back at him, "don't talk about my wife."

Should I get the chance to return to Hong Kong as an old man or wandering spirit I imagine metal cutlery will have been phased out in favour of the traditional, and more effective, chopstick. For now, I can only be grateful to the humble fork.

Having run a hundred metres and mounted the nearest mound of scabby terrain, I look back at Ray while catching my breath. He hasn't even sat down to tend his wound. His runners and one bloodied ankle sock have already been removed. The second, far whiter sock is about to be peeled off. The fork is lying beside his pistol, looking less like a lethal weapon than a temporary inconvenience. Shit. He waves up at me, as if we were scouting a hashing trail together and he was required to reassure me that everything was tickety-boo. There's only one man I've seen run as quickly barefoot as with the latest New Balance or Nikes. That man has discarded his shoes and is now going through a well-versed warm-up routine of stretches and rotations that I expect to last no more than thirty seconds. All I can do is decide on the direction I'm taking – away from the restaurant, in the vague direction of oblivion – and set off like a flightless bird giving it one last try.

At 3pm I watch the small public ferry push away from the island through a hole in a thorn bush. The next scheduled departure from Po Toi is in forty-eight hours. The tourists on board the ferry will soon be regaling their extended families with tales of isolation and derring-do while sipping bubble tea and applying after-sun. I have cuts and bruises all over my red-raw face and arms from the improvised evasion techniques that have so far restricted Ray to two single shots, one of which met the unforgiving earth and the other the cloudless sky. The chances of me surviving for another forty-eight minutes seem remote, the night an implausible fantasy. But Frank and Kim weren't to know that as they rode a metal coffin up to the eighteenth floor of a Yau Ma Tei apartment block.

"You don't think she'll be asleep?" Frank asked, checking his watch. "It's almost 11pm."

"Asleep?" Kim looked at him as if he'd lost his mind. "You know that Hong Kong kids don't sleep, right? I was thirty before I stayed unconscious for six hours straight."

"Was that after," Frank smiled roguishly, "you know, our first night?"

"Maybe," the lift doors opened just as Frank lunged for her. "It was a long time ago, that's all I can remember."

The apartment Winkie shared with a shifting cast of college friends was off a dejected corridor lit by circular, fly-filled ceiling lights.

"This is why we moved to Lamma," Frank reminded her as they waited for the door to be opened, which it eventually was by a young stoner in jeans, T-shirt and baseball cap.

"We're here to see Winkie," Kim explained.

The kid nodded, led them into the deserted lounge and then disappeared back into his room. Kim tried to stop him.

"Excuse me…?"

Frank was busy studying the interior. The thrift store furniture was interspersed with African tribal masks; splashes of colour were provided by the spines of non-fiction guides to contemporary politics and popular protest. A modest array of hash pipes was roughly aligned on a coffee-table between mismatching leather chairs.

"Nice digs," he said, "pity about the caged windows."

"They have cats," Kim explained.

Frank sniffed. "Yep, thought I got that too. So where's Winkie?"

"I'll check her room. You look down the sides of the chairs."

"What for?"

"I don't know," Kim clenched and unclenched her fists. "Use your imagination."

But even Frank's poetical imagination couldn't conjure up much with squished juice cartons and tobacco crumbs, though the eight dollars in coins were almost worth pocketing. Fortunately Kim was soon back in the room.

"Po Toi," she said, looking red and flustered.

"What does that mean?"

"It's a place, a tiny island. Or rather the largest in a group of tiny islands."

"Winkie's not here?"

"I told you – she's on this island, with the others. It's far enough away for them to plan their next move without getting hassled by the authorities."

"Far enough away for Nick as well?"

"Maybe."

The stoner returned to show them out. He hadn't said another word but now sported a goofy expression. In the elevator Frank asked Kim what happened next.

"We get the *Christina*."

"You're kidding."

"We get Fenton to meet us at the marina, take him with us."

"You're mad."

"We need to get to Po Toi, track down Nick – get the gang together, or else—"

"What?"

"We'll lose you all."

Frank saw her face folding with emotion and felt bad for shouting. Then he noticed something else.

"Your lipstick… It's smudged. Tell me you haven't just…?"

And still they hadn't reached the bottom floor. Kim found a tissue, dabbed her lips and folded her arms across her leather jacket.

"I don't believe it," Frank began pacing around like a caged tiger. "How many other times have you—?"

"That's what he wanted for the information."

"Little piece of shit," Frank slammed the muted metal with his palm.

"We didn't have time to fuck about, Frank."

"Fortunately not, or you might have stolen his virginity. I mean, Jesus, Kim."

"Well, what about you and Molly Ransom?"

"What about her?"

"What were you talking about in the bar tonight?"

"Fucking hell," the lift door began to open. Frank helped it on its way. Outside it was still warm. Grungy types looked them up and down, amused by their age and demeanour.

"What are you looking at?" Frank yelled at a passing Goth.

Kim was busy flagging down a green cab.

"Get in," she told him. "We can get therapy later. In the meantime, we have to help those who are more fucked up than ourselves – like it says in the Bible."

I've always had a soft spot for Kim. Naturally, I fetishized her when we first met – which expat didn't? The funky rock chick with the kickass riffs raised in the strip joints of Wan Chai where Frank first encountered her, in his own words, "bathed in neon". Not strictly true. She finished school and college and her background was comfortably middle-class; how else would her uncle end up owning a yacht that size? No, Kim wasn't born into the rock 'n roll life – hers was as carefully engineered as most career paths in Hong Kong.

At least Kim was frank about her backstory. Yes, I suspect she might have persuaded Frank that I'm less of a man than he is, but all will be forgiven and forgotten if she succeeds in navigating her oversized lifeboat here in time to rescue me. Of course at this point I've no idea that anyone is looking for me – anyone besides Ray that is, and even if I had I wouldn't have fancied their chances.

"Come out, Powell," Ray calls. "We speak more. Lots more I need say to you."

My pursuer is talking the same talk, walking the same walk as he was two hours ago, but he's fooling no one. If I'd been chasing someone from one clump of cover to the next in broiling temperatures; someone who was older, far less fit but literally running for their life, and who periodically stepped out of a bush and hurled a rock at my head, I'd want to kill them twice over by now.

The truth is, Ray shouldn't have to wait much longer. The only genuine cover I can hope for here would be in the form of a couple of fat tourists, from a country allied with China, and this side of the island is completely deserted. Ray's voice travels over and beyond me. I sneak out of my lair and begin running back towards the restaurants. Even if Winkie is prepared to sacrifice me to win back Ray's trust, the whole community can't be in on it, surely? Visions of being burnt inside a giant wicker man spring to mind, unhelpfully.

I look at my feet pounding up and down on the dry, bare earth. It never fails to fascinate me, this desire we all have to self-propel – the drive to move forwards and onwards, beating out a rhythm with our bodies despite the scant reward promised at the end of the race. Perhaps we all hope to leave an echo of ourselves in places such as this, where the scholarly etchings of primitive geniuses – protected behind glass and incorporated into the official walking tour – can never match the whispering wonderment of the rock and sea and belligerent nature around us. These places will outlive us; beat us in almost every aspect of our existence. All we can do is tap-tap-tap, puff-puff-puff, tap-tap-tap – can we come in and stay for a while?

Another shot is fired, shattering a rock yards ahead of me, and sending a perfect little diamond of shrapnel into my shin for safekeeping. Ray's message is clear: even if I make it back onto the path towards the snooty waiters and café mommas that pass for civilised company here he has me covered and will floor me before I can get within earshot of Clarence's withering putdowns.

The island's birdlife has left us to our panting and our firecrackers. Most of them are windsurfing out at sea, dipping and soaring around a collection of underwater shadows; perhaps a rescue squad – or heavenly delegation – of porpoises, or porpoi, sent by Sky. Even if the birds are oblivious to me – the floundering bi-ped up here – their presence succeeds in pointing me towards a rougher track that has one or two larger rock formations whose temporary purpose, I decide, is to keep me alive. Ironic really as one looks like a large tomb and the other an erect penis; suggesting – like so much else in middle age – that I should be handing over the baton. Nevertheless, thirty seconds later I'm experiencing the novelty of being in shade, indoors, slumped on a stone floor and trying to squeeze my heart into silence.

Having missed it on my first couple of laps of the island, the overgrown house appears to offer a last chance of sanctuary. Within its blackened hollows I can try one final time to resuscitate my mobile phone, then give it the toilet burial it deserves. I can also take a leak at the same time. No plumbing but no smells of feral habitation either. The rooms are huge. Yellowing wallpaper is freeze-frozen in the act of unpeeling itself. I'm inside a holiday home – or hideaway – built by someone with a couple of dollars to rub together a century ago.

Hope springs eternal, like well-water dribbling from rusted pipes protruding from a kitchen cupboard. If Ray knows about this place; at least two rooms of which appear to be watertight, why would he choose to stay in a poky lighthouse? The villa must represent a blind spot. After all, there's no front door to distinguish it from the surrounding flora – it would have been a mere blur to him as he paced the island, trying to salve his guilty conscience. I creep upstairs to the master suite. There's an iron bedframe and brick fireplace. It's a beautiful spot for an illicit affair amongst the treetops, if you're into that kind of thing. Just a shame there's no glass in the window. I peek out. And there's Ray below me, his gun barrel pointing at my head, grinning like a kid who's won the fucking egg and spoon race.

CHAPTER TWENTY-SIX

The *Christina* cut through the nocturnal waters like a sleek, fibreglass ghost. They had reclaimed her from the marina with a minimum of fuss; Kim having retained her uncle's membership card from the first round of protests when the forty-footer had acted as a useful nerve centre and photogenic marketing tool. The night watchman recognised the niece, and her story – coyly told – of wanting to take her boyfriend out for a moonlit cruise vanquished any doubts he may have had in a haze of embarrassment. Moments later she was sitting at the tiller and her paramour was casting off. The churn was for the most part milky grey but occasionally they came across patches of indigo-stained luminescence.

"Look at that," Frank put an arm around Kim and pointed at the water with his free hand. "Isn't it beautiful?"

"They call it sea sparkle," Kim told him. "But it's deadly. Like those girls who wear the diamonds at Happy Valley – the ones you pretend to hate."

"I'm a socialist."

"Right... Anyway, this shit is an even worse form of single-celled organism. Looks like algae, eats plankton, shits toxins. And you know who needs plankton?"

"Little fish, shrimps."

"And you know who eats the little fish and shrimps?"

"Our friends the dolphins, our cousins the whales."

"Exactly."

They scanned the water hopefully, looking for subterranean shadows, then forced themselves to focus on more realistic goals.

"How much further to Mui Wo?" Frank asked.

"About an hour."

"I know it's out of our way but it's only right we pick up Fenton too," Frank conceded. "Together we're stronger."

"Took you a while to work that out, didn't it?"

Frank uncoiled himself from the skipper. It was cooler than expected on the water and her body heat had felt pretty good, but a barbed remark was a barbed remark. He looked up at the stars. Not just the basic package tonight – there were probably enough to navigate by, if you had the know-how.

"So what," he asked, "you think Nick is a friend of this Ray person?"

"I'm not sure Ray has many friends," Kim speculated. "I've been trying to remember Winkie's song lyrics. She sang in Cantonese. In English, they'd be something like, 'the cause is your only focus/won't you lay down your arms/and find room in your heart for me?' Angsty, I guess you'd call them."

"Sounds like Winkie had a major soft spot for Ray."

"Maybe. They're kids. Who knows."

"But Ray was on Paul's mind even as it started to fragment. And if we assume Paul was helping Nick to lie low before he cracked, it stands to reason Nick's also got some sort of connection to Ray."

"Let's hope we find Nick in a better state than Paul."

Frank nodded but didn't seem convinced. She peered over at him in the half-light, trying to analyse his subtle shift in mood.

"What?" she asked. "Have I said something controversial?"

"Not really, babe," Frank rubbed his chin. "Thing is, I still can't fathom Nick's motives. What's he after? And what's he capable of? A man who fakes his own death – which is pretty much a shortcut to wiping out everyone you know – could be capable of anything."

"You told me he lost his parents in a car crash. Perhaps to him, everyone you love or who loves you has to disappear, in order for that love to be reinforced."

"I don't know…sounds like you've done one too many chakras on the beach."

"What are you doing?"

"Calling Jeanie."

"It's 4.30am."

"You think she's sleeping any more than the kids right now?"

"Well?"

"Answer-phone."

"Let's just concentrate on—"

"Shush...here we go... Hi Jeanie, Frank here. We're on our way to find this Ray person. The one Kim reckons might know where Nick is. Got some time to kill. Look, remember that rock that was sent to the Brolly? Can you call me back and tell me what's written on the envelope it came in? I know you like popping those Omega 3 tabs but I prefer doing puzzles to keep the old brain ticking over. Help me out, will you? Cheers Jeanie."

By the time they came to pick up Fenton from the quayside at Mui Wo, Jeanie had got back to Frank with the requested addressee: COLIN SWOON-PATS. The dawn was adding a tangerine glow to the lush hills around the unfortunate concrete aspect of the town. For years, Fenton had failed to appreciate what was on his doorstep at this early hour. These days, it was the perfect time to employ his reinvigorated brain, drained as it now was of a lifetime's worth of alcohol. Frank wasted no time putting him to work.

"Ah, yes, the anagram," Fenton muttered. "Isn't that the lowest form of wit?"

"Sarcasm."

"No, I'm being serious. In any case, it represents a form of trivial pursuit for which I have a soft spot somewhere near the white-hot lobes of my cerebral cortex."

"Is he still speaking English?" Kim asked as she manoeuvred them on their roundabout course to Po Toi.

"Who knows."

"Never sounded like a real name to me," Fenton sat himself down, got comfortable, then fished out his reading glasses. "I mean, who's called Colin these days?"

"You'll need to be quiet, won't you?" Frank suggested, passing Fenton a notebook and pen. "While you work it out, I mean?"

"So tell me more about Molly Ransom," said Kim, as Fenton began to cogitate.

Frank bristled. "Not until you tell me more about that bloody stoner," he retorted. "Like, were tongues involved?"

"Children, children," Fenton interrupted. "A simple question for these complex times. Did our friend Nick ever go by the name of Nicolas?"

"No," Kim said, turning the wheel. "Always Nick as far as I know."

"You're wrong, love," said Frank. "I'm sure I heard Lennox call him Nicolas once or twice. When they were still together."

"Sure?" Fenton cocked an eyebrow.

"Yes, I'm sure. Otherwise I wouldn't be saying it, would I?"

"In that case," Fenton cleared his throat and held up the pad, "I think I've solved the riddle."

"Anagram."

"Want to know what I have, as a successor to Colin What's-his-face?"

"We're all ears," Frank told him.

"STOP NICOLAS NOW."

"Interesting," said Kim, checking her charts.

"But surely out of date?" Frank countered. "Whatever we were meant to stop Nick from doing...well...he's done it."

"Why do I have a bad feeling about this?" Kim asked.

"I expect we'll find out soon enough," Fenton replied brightly.

The *Christina* reached Po Toi in time for breakfast but its occupants could see few signs of life as they dropped anchor beside the ferry pier. Today wasn't a day for outsiders. The next tourists weren't due for another twenty-four hours. Frank scanned the shoreline with a pair of vintage binoculars they'd found below decks. At first the beach seemed deserted. Then Frank found himself doubling back to a sentinel-like figure dressed incongruously in a paisley shirt and slacks.

"Is that someone signalling to us?" Kim asked.

"You could say that," said Frank, lowering the binoculars and answering with a single finger salute of his own.

"Let me have a look."

It took Kim only a second to identify the miscreant.

"Clarence you little shit," she yelled across at him. "Get someone out here to pick us up or I'll be posting a video of you farting your way through French horn practice on every social media platform out there."

"Why didn't you say it was you, miss?" Clarence called back. "We'll have you and those two old guys onshore in a jiffy."

There was only enough room for Frank and Kim to squeeze into Winkie's tiny office at the back of the restaurant. Fenton had to wait outside with Clarence. The two got on surprisingly well. Fenton complained about Chinese neighbours encroaching on his land and Clarence complained about western tourists encroaching on their island. Inside, the atmosphere carried greater tension.

"Yes, your friend was here," said Winkie, lighting a cigarette. "But he didn't find what he was looking for."

Kim sighed, shook her head.

"It's too late for denials, Harmony," she told the younger woman. "I spoke to the boatman who brought us ashore. He said gunshots had been heard overnight. We know that Nick is here. We know that Ray is here too. So you better tell us what the hell is going on before we get the cops involved."

"Kim Tang calling the police," Winkie allowed herself a half-smile. "That would be a thing to see."

"Tell us what happened here," Frank insisted. "You owe that much to Kim, don't you?"

Winkie took a last drag, shrugged and released a little more information as she exhaled.

"We didn't want any weapons here," she told them. "But Ray said he needed a gun for emergencies. He said if they came for us we'd have to defend ourselves, maybe even shoot ourselves, because otherwise the PLA would take us across the border and torture us and make us betray the cause on television."

"And you believed him?" asked Frank.

"It's not beyond the realms of possibility," Kim conceded. "But why has he started firing it now?"

"Have you considered that your friend may not be as innocent as he seems?" Winkie asked. "I've known Ray for a long time. He's more than a comrade. He's like a...brother to me."

"A brother?" Kim echoed, innocently enough.

"Yes," said Winkie, winking, "a brother."

"The thing with brothers," Frank explained, "is they're not always as brotherly as you'd like them to be."

"Where are they?" Kim cut through the philosophising.

"Up near the haunted house, that's all I know," Winkie said, spreading her hands. "I warned Powell not to go but he wasn't taking no for an answer."

"How many people do you have here?"

"Six, maybe seven – it's early."

"Wake them up," Kim demanded, "if they're not awake already. You might think you can survive in seclusion out here but we all know there's no genuine hiding places left in this world."

"I hope you're not calling us cowards, Kim Tang. Because when the time is right, rest assured we'll—"

"I'm not calling you cowards. I'm saying that sometimes you have to cooperate with your enemy's enemy for the benefit of your cause. Here's a way of reminding your activists of that. Call it a lesson."

"Don't worry, Miss." Winkie's tone darkened. "It's always good for them to see whose side their people are on, when it comes to the final reckoning."

CHAPTER TWENTY-SEVEN

As Ray squeezes the trigger I decide my last thought should be of Sky – such passion and honesty and who cares if she complained that I lacked female intuition? And then quickly change my mind. Lennox is still my wife. I admire her more than any other woman I've ever met, even though she's intimidated me for longer than I care to remember. But then Sky is the future. I should look to the sky and pray for an afterlife with her.

And then my friends arrive en masse, elbowing each other out of the way in my cramped cranium: loyal Paul, energetic Frank, irate Fenton (I really do), and I'm even more confused as to who to retain in my grey matter before it's turned to mush. It must be hell for people who have parents too. In the end I settle for a kind of split-screen set-up. In the end the shot obliterates the window ledge and allows a chunk of rouge-coloured plaster to slip down the side of the building like a warmed-up slice of glacier. I duck inside, half-expecting the building to collapse around me. It doesn't.

Four hours later the day is done, but I am still alive. Ray is toying with me. I can think of no other reason why he wouldn't have entered through the non-existent front door and taken me out for the crime of being in the wrong place at the wrong time repeatedly. I am still alive but Ray is far from finished with me. I can hear him pacing and puffing and panting outside. A cosmic force field separates hunter from hunted. And then I remember the virtual guidebooks I downloaded back on Cheung Chau. One reminds readers that it's hard to swing a cat in Hong Kong's new territories without passing through a psychic presence. Each island has at least one haunted house. In an island with so few dwellings, the chances are…

"You scared Ray?" I shout through the rotten wall protecting me, ignoring how tremulous my voice has become. "Scared the monsters are going to get you if you come in here?"

No reply.

"All sorts of gremlins in here!"

More pacing.

Okay, I admit it – by winding Ray up I'm being culturally insensitive. Triad culture is infused with superstition and I don't expect the cult of the White Lotus is any different. Triads are blood brothers; incense-lighting amigos par excellence, praying to the gods that they may be excused from their wretched business, or kept safe within its mad verisimilitudes. I change tack.

"Why don't you get out of here while you still can?"

Nothing.

"Believe me, I'm doing a runner as soon as I get off this island. First plane to Heathrow and then a new life in some suburb of a suburb somewhere near a suburb. This kind of excitement is no good once you're past thirty, trust me."

I strain to remember more from my brain trust tryst with Redmond. An old pirate was meant to have lived here with his family. They got sick and died. Does Ray think I have them in here with me? Or perhaps that I've corralled the spirits of my own long-departed family?

"I'm not coming out until you go," I tell him. "I'm like the grey-haired guy in that embassy in London... You know, Julian...um...what's-his-name...?"

Anaesthetised by the deadlock I allow my mind and body to relax and promptly fall asleep below the fractured window ledge. When I awake it's light and I can hear voices outside. The Cantonese speakers sound familiar. Is that Winkie yelling and Ray replying in equally strained tones? And who's that with them – the owner of an older female voice accustomed to dealing with hecklers? The English speaker gives the game away.

"Give me the gun, you little squirt."

It is unquestionably Frank, his companion doubtless Kim. All I wish to do is remain quiet and let them have their discussion, but on shifting position and inadvertently glancing into the interior of the bedroom, I'm quickly unmuted and perilously close to losing my cool. A long black-and-olive snake, as toned and shapely as a gym-fit female arm, is uncoiling itself before my very eyes. The snake's unhurried demeanour is contradicted by its darting tongue that appears to have been sniffing me out for some time, as if I were its morning coffee. Initially I find myself able to follow some hardwired prehistoric know-how and remain stock-still. Then the snake lunges at me and I get all Anglo-Saxon.

"Fuuuuuuuuuucccckkkkkk!"

This in turn provokes a reaction outside, though it's not the human sirens I'm expecting to hear rushing to my aid. Instead there's the echoing crack of Ray's pistol being discharged at even closer range than previously experienced. Then the childlike cry of a male in pain. Then there is a scramble over loose shale, shouts and screams, but still no rescue party rushing in to save me from my peril. After several seconds I open my eyes and look to the snake beside me, the rat it's snaffled almost fully secreted already, shake my head and ease myself upwards.

"At least you don't have to deal with humans," I tell it. "Things carry on like this and I'll be back here to see you for lunch."

Leaving the house, I find only half of the anticipated personnel, and they're not in the best shape. Clarence is slumped against an anthill-shaped rock, pressing a bloodied T-shirt against his left shoulder. He is white. Winkie, tending to him, is at least as pale. They barely glance at me as I leave my lair.

"Where are the others?" I ask.

"They've gone after Ray," Winkie tells me.

"They're crazy. He's armed and dangerous."

"Not any more." – Winkie points to a pistol lying in the dirt path between us. – "He ran out of bullets."

"I got the last one," Clarence smiles weakly. "Aren't you glad about that, ghost-buster?"

"Someone had to be the martyr," I tell him. "Did he say anything before he fired?"

"That it was you or us," Winkie snaps. "That you were going to expose us to the authorities. Ruin everything we worked for. That if we didn't kill you, we would soon be imprisoned in China."

"Then what?"

"Clarence made himself a hero."

"He doesn't sound convinced he made the right decision."

Winkie looks at me directly for the first time. It's not a comradely look.

"Your friends are up there." – She gestures towards the raised spine of the island. – "Go find them."

"What about Ray?"

"He's dead to us now."

It takes me a while to shake off the stiffness accumulated overnight but soon I'm running at a decent pace towards the pagoda. I'm watching Frank and Kim in the distance, fanning out across the narrow peninsula at the south of the island, heading towards the lighthouse, calling after Ray. I don't realise that there's someone within the shade of the pagoda until I'm almost upon it.

"Hello, Nicolas," says Fenton. I wonder why he's using the extended version of my name when he's so evidently short of breath. "You're looking well for a dead man."

"You look better than ever," I feel able to return the compliment.

"Cut out the booze and ciggies, lungs far from recovered though – as you can tell."

"You had a change of heart?"

"I fell into a drainage ditch, remember?"

"It's funny," I tell Fenton, taking the chance to do some tentative stretching. "I remember when Jonathan started smoking again, and you asked who amongst us would have the willpower to resume the habit after six months off."

"Very determined fellow was Jonathan," Fenton scans the horizon for our friends. "Had principles, or appeared to anyway. Never been a big believer in principles myself. They get in the way, like penguins at a party, or tie you down, like Gulliver's Lilliputians. Say your wife or – what's the modern parlance? – *partner* has let you down badly, or vice versa. The principled man – the man for whom love is a black and white affair – could end up very lonely indeed."

"I guess that's true."

"We both know it's true, Nick," Fenton's voice harshens. "Only by the time we'd worked it out, I'd already lost Miriam and you'd already lost Lennox."

Silence.

"How did Ray look?" I ask.

"Out of his mind."

"Come on then, we better go and help bring him in."

The barren nature of Po Toi Island has almost cost me my life; now the running shoe is on the other foot. Frank and Kim have Ray cornered near the lighthouse. With Fenton and me offering reinforcements, there is nowhere left for him to go. He has no alternative but to give himself up and Frank isn't holding back from telling him so.

"Hello Nick," he calls across. "I was just telling your friend here that violence never pays, isn't that right?"

"That's right Frank," I confirm. "Good to see you, by the way."

"You see I've got a bit of a temper on me. Everyone knows that." Like Fenton, Frank isn't totally comfortable addressing the dead guy directly. "Been accused of a lot of things – but there's a difference between getting drunk and arguing with your adversary, and hitting them – or shooting them."

Ray looks across at me with little-disguised contempt.

"You think I'm the bad guy, huh?" he challenges us as we close in on him.

Worried he is about to turn and lock himself in the lighthouse I rush towards my old ally, inadvertently causing him to belt – at no mean speed – towards Kim.

"Traitor!" he barges her out of the way and makes a break towards the harbour. Age and experience and a basic grasp of physics tell us immediately that none of us is capable of running fast enough to catch him.

"He's getting away," Frank yells. "We've let the kid get away."

But Frank is wrong. We're all wrong, because our calculations failed to factor in Winkie, whom we now see leading a group of a dozen young people, some armed with baseball bats, others with metal poles, up the hill towards us. Ray is sandwiched between young and old. If I didn't know what he'd done – what he might still be capable of – I might have felt sorry for him. Winkie shouts a jumble of imperatives towards Ray, then immediately follows up with some softer words. Her voice is breaking but her words never fail to carry weight.

Ray hesitates, using that fleeting, self-imposed reprieve to turn towards me and offer a strange kind of smile. I recognise his expression at once. This is the look he gave me when I lost it with him in the abandoned army base: superficially acquiescent, fundamentally defiant.

Then he runs in the only direction open to him – the sea. In three elastic bounds he mounts Palm Rock; then extending his quadriceps one last time he leaps from it and embraces thin air. For a moment I convince myself that Ray is going to continue running unsupported, like a hyperactive cartoon character, before pausing, scratching his head and doubling back onto dry land. But of course he can't do that, not in this life anyway. For a few more strides Ray gives the illusion of running purposefully, if not from A to B then at least towards a tangible destination, but now he is arcing down, down, running and falling and falling and running soundlessly into the waiting waves below.

CHAPTER TWENTY-EIGHT

By the time the next public ferry arrives at Po Toi the witnesses to Ray's accidental demise have long since vacated the premises. I imagine the latest batch of visitors restoring equilibrium to the wretched place by replaying the same oohs and ahhs as generations before them; marvelling at Palm Rock, giggling past the token haunted house, then ordering wholly predictable dishes from Mary Fu's restaurant while comparing unoriginal blisters on their inappropriately-clad feet.

The sky is a penetrating blue as the *Christina* ups anchor and relinquishes Po Toi's craggy charms and I'm soon advised to head below decks because of the sunburn I've developed while scurrying from one fascinating local landmark to another. Here everything is cream or white and Clarence the waiter is lying bare-chested, freshly bandaged, sweat-stuck to one of the parallel vinyl sofas running either side of the cabin. I ease myself onto the other.

"Thanks for taking that bullet for me," I say, out of politeness.

"It's just a graze," Clarence reassures me. "And besides, I did it for Winkie, not you. Someone had to show her what a psycho Ray had become."

"I'm glad we agree on something."

I notice Clarence has a book in his lap. Its author has a long, Spanish name. On the cover people are holding up placards. They could be in Central America. Somewhere like that. The title is written in Chinese.

"So what's your plan?" I ask him, as he's about to resume reading.

Clarence lowers the book.

"You seriously think I'd tell you?" he raises his eyebrows. "You really think because we both wanted Ray dead we're on the same side?"

"Now hold on," I try to raise myself on my elbows but find I'm also stuck to the greasy vinyl. "I didn't want Ray—"

We're interrupted by Frank who has been forced to fold himself in half while descending the shallow steps to the cabin.

"Not interrupting anything, am I?" he asks.

"No," I tell him. Clarence stays quiet, puts his head into his book.

I sit up on my sofa and Frank squeezes in beside me.

"How are you?" he asks.

"I'm okay Frank, a little dazed," I admit. "I appreciate you guys coming for me, you didn't have to."

"We're all screwed," Frank is brandishing a cracked tablet computer. He tilts it towards me and scrolls down a list of news headlines, most of which relate to the government's uncompromising stance on the deportation of undesirable expats. "We're best off sticking together."

"So you believe what I said? That Ray had a fight with Jonathan and Jonathan fell?"

"No reason to doubt you, though he never struck me as argumentative – one of those quiet Americans. You said they were rowing about politics?"

"Yes, it's in the air at the moment."

"You were crazy to hide the body," Frank lowered his head in respect of my insanity. "To pretend it was you, but love – or the absence of it – does strange things to people."

"How's Paul?" I ask.

"Surviving, with a little help from his friends," Frank paws at the tablet some more. "Perhaps you can think what you can do to help?"

Frank passes me the tablet and I read the title of the page he's loaded up.

FALK FAMILY APPEAL: Did you see Jonathan running near Lion Rock before he disappeared?

"Actions don't always speak louder than words, Nick," he continues. "Sometimes people need information. You know, to give them closure."

"Sure," I nod, hand him back the machine. "I'm going to do what's right, but first I have to go to Cheung Chau."

"Where you were cremated?"

"Correct," I grimace. "Got a few things I need to tie up there, then I'll be ready to meet the Falks, visit Paul."

"You have to stay undercover for good now, Nick," Frank puts a paternal arm around me. "You understand that, don't you? If you're picked up by the cops, god knows what they'll try to pin on you."

"Roger that."

"One more thing." Frank pats me on the back then stands to go. "Say you were being bothered by someone, and wanted them to disappear," he gives me a curious look. "Wouldn't know how to arrange that, would you?"

"Not a clue."

"Thought not," he looks relieved. "I know you're not a violent man, Nick, whatever the tea-leaves say."

"No," I smile weakly. "Just a very tired and sunburnt man."

I fall asleep after Frank leaves and only wake when I hear the *Christina* squelching against the rubber tyres of an unidentified jetty. Clarence is gone. A twist of bloodied bandages sits where he lay. Winkie's quietly authoritative voice reverberates through word-distorting wood and fibreglass. Clarence chimes in with a more upbeat smattering of nonsense from above. Where are we? I decide I want to say goodbye to them, but on mounting the stairs I find the deck hatch locked. Knocking does no good and once we cast off and Kim starts up the engine again I have to accept that I am both being ignored and kept prisoner by my friends. Is this what I stayed alive for? Turning over, I seek, and find, oblivion again.

Waking a second time I find the air is not so still; the hatch now being three-quarters open and the familiar accents of the Cheung Chau gulls merging with the happy screech of freshly-arrived tourists. Less reassuring is the suspicion that my bunched-up clothes and bag have been searched by one of my fellow travellers. Surely my cotton trousers have been more elegantly strewn around than I could have managed with my earth-scuffed hands?

"Last call for Cheung Chau," Fenton calls down to me, conveying enough Carry On camp for me to realise that quitting the booze may yet make him insufferable. "Plenty to see and do here – eat your own weight in fish-balls, pin the tail on the grouper, or visit the final resting place of…um…oh, he seems to have disappeared…"

"Coming," I shout up, pulling on a semi-fresh T-shirt. "This galley slave's ready for some concrete underfoot."

I'm forced to squint as I reach the deck despite the *Christina* being under the protective skin of the public pier. The sun is bouncing off the water and the smell of greasy snacks in paper bags and cigarette smoke from the malingerers on the pier hits me full in the face. Kim and Frank – through wheel and rope – are making sure we're close enough to the pier for me to step safely ashore.

"There she is," Frank nods towards the metal benches closest to us. "She's expecting you."

I shade my eyes, trying to identify who it is and hoping, hoping, hoping that it's Sky.

"We'll wait for you," says Kim.

"No, it's okay," I tell her. "You go. I'll get the ferry. Won't be more than a couple of hours. Meet you at the Brolly."

Kim and Frank exchange glances. It's a busy day and a queue of boats large and small is mounting up behind them. They know it makes sense.

"Okay," Kim nods curtly. "You've no phone. It's probably safer like this. We'll see you at the pub, with Jeanie."

"Good luck," Frank pushes me on my way; then quickly unties the mooring rope he's just fastened.

"Don't fuck it up," says Fenton, like an older brother.

The arm draped over the parallel silver tubes of the bench opposite is wrapped in a rambling rose realised in the deep indigo and electric red palette of the backstreet parlour. Sky looks up, tosses back her dark mane and fixes me coolly, her expression neither unfriendly nor otherwise. At least she's got rid of the suit and is back wearing jean shorts, Havaianas and her faded skull T-shirt. I look back and see the *Christina* chugging its way out of the crowded harbour. We're together alone again, thank Christ. I walk over and bend to kiss her on the lips. She acquiesces then pulls away.

"Your breath…"

"I know," I sit down beside her. "I haven't been looking after myself very well."

"Here," she passes me a can of beer from the plastic bag at her feet. "This should help."

"Thank you."

I lean in to kiss her again. She puts a finger to my lips.

"Who am I kissing – Viv or Nick?"

"Shit, I'm sorry." I shut down my advances, try to remain calm. "I'm Nick. Nick Letterby. I couldn't tell you everything because—"

"It would have been easier if I'd known you were Nick Powell," she interrupts. "That way I may not have chosen your wife as my silk."

"Your what?"

"My lawyer. They call them silks. The best ones are in London. The best ones apart from Lennox Powell, that is."

"Why do you need a lawyer?"

"Because I've decided to take a stand, Nick. Nicolas?"

"Nick."

"This act isn't only discriminating against low-earners and rabble-rousers. You're statistically more likely to face deportation if you're gay, whatever your income."

"You got a letter?"

"Correct. And Harriett didn't, because of her job. Our marriage might be done but that doesn't mean other gay couples should be split up by this law."

"I can see what you're trying to do, it's admirable, but surely—"

"And you?"

"What?"

"Have you received a letter?"

"Technically, I'm dead so…"

"Dead but with more rights than me." Sky gets herself a beer, puts a foot on the empty plastic bag to stop it escaping. "Because I'm queer."

"Bisexual."

"Okay, Nick," she smiles for the first time. "It's a sliding scale – only macho men like you and those in the Immigration Department struggle with that."

"So you're going to be a hero? A gay icon like George Michael or Ellen DeGeneres or…um…"

"You never thought about asking Lennox for help yourself?"

"You're kidding. She wouldn't piss on me if I was on fire."

"How about if it was part of a kinky sex game?"

"Funny. I've been on a sex strike. Except with you."

"There's our problem, poppet," she grimaces, cocks her head away from mine. "No more canoodling. Best behaviour from now on. If a journalist got wind of what we've been up to, it could wreck the whole case."

"This is why you were in a suit last time we met." I've almost finished my beer. "Because you were going to meet Lennox in town – it wasn't anything to do with Panda and Salamander."

"Who?"

"I have to go."

"So the man of mystery departs my life for good."

"You don't sound too upset."

"Is that what Nick wants, to be sure that he's made an impact, for good or bad?" Sky sighs, takes a ladylike sip of Tsing Tao. "One day – I hope – you'll accept life as it comes. Let it wash over you. Stop resisting. Stop complaining. Don't look for proof that you're alive – just live."

"I love you."

"I love you too," her words drag me back to her. I kiss her again, biting her lips softly until she pushes me away.

"Go and do what you have to do," she tells me.

"With pleasure."

I stride off the pier wiping fresh moisture from my sweaty features. This time I don't look back.

Everyone knows about the pirate's cave on Cheung Chau; of how Cheung Po Tsai stashed his ill-gotten Bitcoins and iPhone Xs in a stinky crevice to the south of the island. Few people know about the gweilo's bum crack, located just yards off the path that leads to this tourist trap. Here a desperate desperado might dispose of a suitcase marred with suspicious stains for an almost indefinite period – or at least until the summer when potential aromas from within and a very real influx of curious tourists from without are likely to prompt interest.

"Dropped my case," I smile at some surprised-looking visitors as I duck under a chain-link fence after dragging the evidence up a slope of sparkling sandstone, take the path they've just climbed up, and make my way via the most discreet route I know to an isolated cove at the north-eastern tip of Cheung Chau. Here there is a steep, overgrown pathway down to Tung Wan Sai beach.

So busy am I hauling my plastic echo chamber towards the bay that I can't keep a proper look out for snakes. The many-banded krait lives here. I remember Paul telling me about its lethal reputation. How would he react if I were found here, months from now, stone dead with a pair of fang marks in my ankle? Poetic justice? Maybe he'd get another snake tattoo to immortalise me in a way that Sky refuses to.

"Don't worry, Paul," I mutter. "We'll get out of this."

Thirty minutes later I'm hiking back up to the path, so relieved to have all my senses dedicated to snake-watching duty that I almost bump into Redmond who is standing with hands on hips outside the so-called North Lookout Pavilion, dressed in lightweight hiking gear.

"Having some kind of bonfire down there, Viv?"

"Jesus," I almost topple backwards into the arms of Medusa.

"Not very environmentally friendly, I must say," he furrows his brow and I follow his gaze down to the half-submerged suitcase. Together we watch large quantities of smoke billowing from its back entrance.

"Got a bit out of control," I explain. "Had to put it in the sea. Safety first."

"Safety first," Redmond nods, "and second, there's the small matter of the exclusive research undertaken on behalf of *Hong Kong Uncensored* on Po Toi."

"Fuck," I smile. "Of course."

"You hadn't forgotten about the story, had you?" he arches an eyebrow.

I clasp him by the shoulder.

"This isn't the kind of story anyone could ever forget," I tell him. "It's…what's the word?"

"Unforgettable?"

"That's right, where shall we go to discuss it? Your apartment?"

Despite acting dumb I know exactly where I'll be taken next. Redmond has a famously chaotic apartment perfectly suited to his writerly endeavours but unhygienic – if not downright hazardous – for guests. He checks his watch.

"Well, The Moon shouldn't be too busy at this time in the afternoon. Pint?"

"Thought you'd never ask."

CHAPTER TWENTY-NINE

Surprised to find the locks at my Fragrant Gardens flat have not been changed, I enter briefly to retrieve my last few hundred dollars from a fag packet hidden behind the fridge. This should be enough to thank Redmond for his patience and edge me a little closer to a more permanent state of oblivion. As my colleague has suggested, The Moon is relatively quiet and from a back table in the darkened indoor space we can watch the tourists trundle by with their face fans and selfie sticks while supping strong lager and clarifying the details of my fight to the death with Ray.

"He was one of their own, but he'd become unhinged," I stifle a burp. "They recognised that – Winkie and her people. If it hadn't been for them Ray would have escaped. And who knows what he would have tried next?"

Redmond is halfway to filling his notebook. It's one of those expensive, leather-bound jobbies designed for people with something to say. His pen is perpetually poised and he can write shorthand at the speed of sound. For a second I'm transported back to school – to those damned talented, charismatic boys whom I will never surpass.

"Two large whiskies," I call over to the heat-slumped barman. "*M'goi.*"

"So you don't think Ray was affiliated to any other groups?" Redmond takes off his specs and cleans them with a tiny cloth.

I scrunch up my nose.

"Hard to say."

It isn't really, but I've already decided that Redmond has more than enough material for now. There'll be plenty of time for me to tell the rest of my story when I'm in a less precarious position.

"Well thank you, Viv," Redmond smiles.

"You can call me Nick, you know," I raise my glass.

"Okay," Redmond adjusts his face. "To you, Nick."

Four lagers and three whiskies down and the flow of tourists outside has eased sufficiently for me to suggest the next stage of my plan.

"I have to pay a visit."

"Pissers are over there," Redmond gets it right on the third finger waggle. "S'funny, thought you'd just been."

"I have," I scan my drinking companion for wear and tear. I think he can hold it – he's big-boned and hollow-legged, like the Canadian boys in the war, "and now I need to take a little walk up the hill. You coming?"

"Course I am," Redmond looks deeply hurt that I might exclude him from this as yet unspecified mission. "Let's go!"

On the way up Peak Road, Redmond and I develop a deep and lasting bond based on an exchange of half-forgotten names and repressed circumstances pertaining to our former love lives, and a mutually beneficial buddying system that has us looking to the future with newfound optimism. All's going well until Sky answers her door, takes one look at us and unceremoniously bars entry to the flat.

"You two need to make yourself scarce," she tells us.

"He has something to tell you," says Redmond, being uncharacteristically forward. "He wants to marry you."

Sky allows herself a small, shy smile. "Who says romance is dead?"

"I'm sorry," I massage some errant head sweat. "We shouldn't have come."

"No, it's good you came," Sky insists. "There were two people up here looking for you."

"Don't tell me," I groan, "a large Chinese guy and—"

"—a pale European. You know them?"

"What happened?"

"The neighbours intercepted them. The numbering system up here fooled them."

"It's confusing," Redmond nods, trying to give an impression of sobriety, "and its origins are unclear. Some say—"

"Apparently they were about to bust into my place," Sky continues. "But they ran into the ex-Shenzhen police chief who has the big house up the road. He told them they were on the wrong track."

"Why would he do that?"

"He didn't like the look of them. He didn't get to where he is today by capturing fugitives."

"Come and have a drink."

"No."

"When will he see you again?" Redmond asks, pleadingly.

"In the next life," says Sky, closing the door.

"Never then," Redmond breaks it to me.

"Don't worry," I tell my crestfallen companion as we turn and begin to retrace our steps. "We'll get over it."

Back at the pub we find some familiar drinkers have emerged under cover of darkness, surfacing at The Moon like a collection of world-weary moths around a dim flame. Laurent is ordering Pernod; Fung is stretching his long, bronzed legs while phone-calling outside so it's left to Cameron Silverback to update us.

"Two people were looking for you, Vivian," he gruffs. "Funny sorts."

"I was telling Ed here," I nod at Redmond. "It's nothing to worry about. They're wanting news on a mutual friend, but there's not much to tell. Where did they go?"

"Back to the ferry. Assumed you were drinking in the city with your old crew."

My relief takes the form of another round of beers. Despite the humidity, Silverback insists we sit outside, away from the fans, so he can smoke freely and watch his subjects sweat profusely.

"Haven't broken the unwritten rule have you, Vivian?" he wants to know, realigning his moustache with his equally bushy brows.

"And what is that?" I ask, his seriousness releasing a bubble of hysteria somewhere deep inside me.

"And vat izz vaat?" Laurent mimics, slapping his knees in tribute to my irreverence.

"We don't tell new people about Cheung Chau," Silverback continues. "There's more than enough bloody expats here already."

"I'm sorry," I release an inadvertent squirt of laughter. I can tell Redmond is about to crack too. "And can you remind me, Cameron, why we need to be so protective of this island?"

"Because, damn it," Silverback strains to crush my mood. "This is a little bit of fucking paradise here."

I can't resist. I sigh and nod and look around at the traces of paradise available to us, like the hotdog shop opposite, and then after 1-2-3-4 point under the table and scream: "Centipede!"

Glasses fly then bounce or tinkle, cigarettes spin like Catherine wheels; guttural screams reach for the stars; hilarity and terror find common ground; the yin balances the yang; the whisky balances the beer, and the next thing I know the night is over and Redmond and I are walking back to Fragrant Gardens slugging from 7-Eleven cans of Tsing Tao Draft. And here the curtain may have fallen on my Hong Kong days had my newest and most loyal friend and I not heard the gut-wrenching howl of pigs about to be slaughtered.

Waking up the next morning all traces of smugness have evaporated. That's to be expected following such a colossal intake of booze. I lie back, scratch and wait for the existential depression to tear me to bits. But I soon discover that it's not imaginary ghosts who lie in wait for me today. There are living things out there ready to consume me.

I crawl into the lounge, following a hunch. Redmond is passed out on the sofa, an old mosquito net half-draped over his elongated body. Was he offering himself up as a replacement bride? The curtains haven't been drawn in here. The view to the pool is unobstructed. In the shallow end of the pool there is a large pig. Either side of the pig are Ken and Archie, who appear to be simultaneously trying to coax the pig out of its newfound habitat and keep it safely ensconced there until the proper authorities can intercede.

"Oh fuck," I shake Redmond. "What did we do?"

"Whaaaaaaaa?"

"Exactly. What the fuck did we do?"

I only manage to extract scant details from Miss Havisham before there comes a rapid-fire banging on the door. Apparently after hearing the porcine cry for help at around 2am, we had returned to the village, found the legendary "Hunger" Pang finishing a dishwashing shift and offered him our remaining dollars for his assistance. The three of us had then managed to enter the grounds of the slaughterhouse unobserved before identifying a pig ripe for liberation. How we chose this particular pig is unclear, but the fact they remained silent during and after being wrestled to the ground and dragged away by Pang – geed on by Redmond and me – is to their credit, and had extended their hours of freedom to this point.

"Hold them for as long as you can," I yell at Redmond; then dive back into my bedroom, open the window as far as it will go, and climb out onto the roof.

Houses in the New Territories are restricted from being built above three stories; Fragrant Gardens itself has a toy town aspect that makes roof walkers like me feel safer than they should. In any case, I succeed in sliding down some tiles and shinning down a drainpipe at the back of my block. After a final glance at Ken and Archie and the pig I disappear into the pristine shrubbery and re-emerge on the path outside. Sure enough, three miniature electric police cars, of the type permitted on a pedal-friendly island, are parked up outside the entrance to the estate.

"Here, Mister," I'm being hissed at from a nearby bush. Parting the fronds I'm permitted a glimpse into a strange world curated by a familiar face. Here beach detritus large and small has been arranged into a twisted take on contemporary art, or a satirical comment on the breakout spaces favoured by Google and Facebook to allow their employees to return to carefree childhood days.

A plasticised Wendy House and bulbous child's oven are adjacent to a grey and blue portaloo beside which a Spiderman-branded child's tent is surrounded by mystical tokens – from headless action figures and wheel-less cars to dried-out starfish and exotic feathers. In the centre of all this is the tourist-cum-asylum seeker I'd almost crashed into on my way to Sky's first and best embrace.

"Thank you," I smile at Cheung Chau's latest resident. "But I have to be on my way."

Leaving the grotto my words are immediately validated by the appearance of two young cops in crisp, light-blue uniforms, either side of me.

"Mr Nicolas Powell?"

They've barely enunciated my surname before I'm running for my life again. Here is the small beach where they used to wash the bones of children before burial. Here is the rock on which I used to read my book on quiet days. Here is the hot, frothing sea. Here is the water. Here is oblivion.

I had often wondered about the point of the police patrol boats you saw attached to the public pier on Cheung Chau. Invariably a phalanx of young marines would hop off and return with bags of McDonalds' meals for their comrades. Now I understood the reason for sustaining the boat and the crew. There they were, on deck, waiting. There was a life ring being thrown into the water. As I had long suspected, it was all about me.

CHAPTER THIRTY

Prison life is far from cushy – if you think Hong Kong apartments are small you should try their boutique cells, but at least from here I have the luxury of reflecting on and recording my story, which to my chagrin I find is not really my story at all but that of those I've met, loved and (only occasionally) hated since arriving in this Special Administrative Region.

Fenton is my most frequent visitor these days. From being far removed from impolite society, and preferring it that way, he now has a friend on his doorstep in Lantau. To extend his visits, or on the odd occasion when my life has been threatened by a fellow prisoner, he slips the guards some handmade wooden toys for their children and things are resolved pretty quickly. Usually Fenton is in a good mood, but occasionally a darker countenance – more reminiscent of his drinking days – emerges.

"It should be Paul in here, not you," he tells me, from the other side of the glass.

"What do you mean?"

"I apologised to him, at the Brolly, just before he returned to the northern swamp from which he emerged."

"You apologised? For what?"

"For threatening him, when those commies were holding us hostage. Know what he said?"

"No."

Fenton coughs theatrically, adopts a generic Liverpool accent.

"'That's okay mate, I'm sorry for shoving you into that drainage ditch.'"

"He didn't?"

"Denied it immediately afterwards, but I couldn't prise that smug smile off his face for the rest of the evening."

Jesus, had I driven Paul that far? Sure, I'd confided to him that I suspected Fenton had smelt a rat, but I hadn't imagined he'd act on the perceived threat. I decide to guide Fenton away from our mutual friend and ask him to repeat the tale of how the "commies" had fared after narrowly avoiding me on Cheung Chau.

Jeanie had it all worked out soon after the shattered crew of the *Christina* arrived at the Brolly, Fenton reminds me. To her, Ray's failure to enter the haunted house was both superstitious and suspicious. It seemed more like the actions of an impressionable young triad than a hardened pro-dem fanatic. And which side were the triads on in all this, if any, she asked? And who paid the triads to cause trouble in 2014? And who exerted the most influence on the Hong Kong government, explicitly or otherwise?

Panda and Salamander arrived at the Brolly just in time for Jeanie to break it to them that they had been chasing an agent provocateur far higher up the food chain than they were. They left with their tails between their legs; the Falks followed later that evening, far from reconciled to their son's death, but with a sense that he was less of a victim, more of a protagonist than they had ever imagined.

After bidding them a safe journey, Frank had sat Kim down and calmly explained to her that it was Molly Ransom who had attempted to have him deported in a vain attempt to win his affections and his artistic credibility via a last-ditch marriage proposal. She wasn't to be castigated; the islands of Hong Kong were a lonely place for a single mother, however privileged.

My visitor and I settle into one of our periods of companionable silence after this outpouring of news, both nodding approvingly in tribute to our matriarch's wisdom, then frowning a little upon recalling that she's now dating a police inspector, then forgiving her and nodding again. Fenton pulls the string attached to a little wooden elephant on wheels he's made and lets it skid across his side of the table. I take this as a signal to address the other elephant in the room.

"You did tell Lennox I'm ready to accept her deal, the one she offered through Chan?"

"Several times," Fenton keeps his eyes on the toy.

"I can't get through when I try to call her from here."

"She's been busy," Fenton looks up, surreptitiously inspecting me for traces of delusion, "since she won the court case for that pair of lesbos."

"Fenton…"

"Sorry, always forget the correct label. Anyway, after the domino effect that brought about – the exposure of the government campaign to defame foreigners and the postponement of the Deportation Act – she's been in great demand, here and in London."

"Always was a popular girl."

"She got you a hotshot lawyer," Fenton reminds me.

"I know."

"So what's the latest?"

"Five years for perverting the cause of justice and preventing the lawful burial of a body, three if I'm a good boy while I'm in here."

"You're happy with that?"

"No comment."

"Oh, didn't tell you," Fenton fiddles with the elephant's adjustable trunk. "I heard back from Miriam. Seems Taiwan wasn't paradise after all. She's booked a flight. Decided she needs to check on her veggies."

"Now I know the world's gone mad," I manage a smile. "Well, look after her this time. I better be heading back to…you know."

"Of course," Fenton picks up the toy, looks around for the guard who requested it, then back at me. "Same time next week?"

"Why not?"

Football has always been a mystery to me but the other prisoners have wanted to see the tall white guy perform on the dirt pitch within the double bind of tall, wire fences and all-encompassing mountains since I arrived, and I can only feign injury for so long. On the fourth Thursday of my incarceration I'm led out onto a vast space between two sets of bone-white goalposts like a cheerless mascot, or sacrificial goat.

Despite a profound lack of footballing ability, my mood is dangerously good. Martin Chan himself has been in to see me earlier, to let me know of mysterious developments in the harbour. Floating beside a piece of priceless ambergris, the bodies of two no-longer-deniable assets and the remains of a half-burnt suitcase have been recovered, as if coughed up by a whale clever enough to navigate the shipping lanes and make a home for itself amongst the islands of Hong Kong.

"And this will help me how?" I ask.

"The suitcase should help corroborate your story about how long Jonathan was stored, and what kind of state he was in, and the death of your detractors whilst you've been in detention suggests the presence of a mysterious—"

"—or not so mysterious—"

"—third party."

Chan puts his papers into a neat little pile and taps them on the tabletop officiously. I miss Ewan Chan of the Galway Chans. Why doesn't he ever come to visit?

"Fingers crossed then?" I suggest.

"Fingers crossed," he nods, departs.

From kick-off it's clear I'm being targeted by the two mean-looking brothers dumped on us earlier this week, each with their own bespoke duelling scars. Thanks to Fenton's bribes and my offer of free English lessons, relations with fellow prisoners have been reasonably good thus far, but all that's about to change. It's not just me the brothers are intimidating; they've clearly briefed my fellow players. No one in their right mind would think of passing me a ball. Yes, I can run like the wind but whenever I'm thrown a pork bun in the canteen the chances of me dropping it are so high that the prison bookies have stopped taking bets. Today the bastards are all seeking me out with the ball and every time I receive it – or try to run away from it – one of the brothers steams into me, leading with a shoulder and wiping me out.

Eat dirt.

Does it matter if they're triad or hired by triads or hired by someone else? Not really. I look over to the touchline, expecting to see a couple of prison guards watching over us, but there are no guards in sight; even the corner watchtowers appear to be deserted. I get up and dust myself down. Both my knees are cut; two fruity slices of red shining through the grey muck in which I am plastered.

"Don't pass me the fucking ball," I hiss at my teammates, but as I stroll as calmly as possible towards the opposition goal, lighting a roll-up on my way out of the game, I find the semi-deflated ball trickling within a few yards of my plimsolled feet.

I brace myself for what's coming – both of them at once this time. I'm catapulted into the air, narrowly missing the nearest goalpost and landing heavily beside the tattered webbing that makes up one side of the net. Here the opposition goalkeeper has been tidying away loose rocks and stones that might otherwise have ruined the flow of the game. The poor guy, sweating through his big padded goalkeeping jersey. I can tell he wants to help me up but fears the consequences should he do so. Don't worry, I want to say, I can look after myself. The brothers approach, laughing and high-fiving and scuffing up dirt, and failing to notice the fist-sized rock I've acquired and am gripping ever-so-tightly; the same kind of weapon I used to brain Lennox's ex-boyfriend – the one who couldn't fight back because he was training to be a doctor.

I think of Frank's quote, about how expats must survive on the edge of a precipice, as the brothers stand either side of me, preparing to feast on their prize. I don't pity myself, I don't pity us – I pity the poor Hong Kongers who have to look after us; who have to clean up the mess on perfectly sunny days like this when the heat makes you want to sink back down into the earth from where you came and pop up somewhere new. Too late.

HONG KONG ROCKS PRINCIPAL CHARACTERS

Nick Powell: Enigmatic narrator; estranged from wife Lennox
Lennox Powell: Hotshot lawyer; estranged from husband Nick
Paul Coyne: Disillusioned teacher; estranged from daughter
Poppy
Jeanie Lau: Longstanding landlady of the Yellow Brolly
pub/hostel
Ray Lim: Cross-country runner; lacks direction
Frank Taylor: Proud poet; partner to Kim
Kim Tang: Guitar tutor; partner to Frank
Fenton Wilkes: Reclusive craftsman
Jonathan Falk: Amiable North American
Sky Burgess: Island-dwelling free spirit
Harmony "Winkie" Lee: Defiant activist
Horatio Lam: Conflicted policeman
Ed Redmond: Conscientious journalist
Panda: Deniable asset
Salamander: Deniable asset
Martin Chan: Literary lawyer
Harpo Brills: Cantankerous photographer
Molly Ransom: Ruthless romantic
Clarence Ho: Pithy activist
Cameron Silverback: Bombastic barfly
Scampi: Hippy bookseller
Star, Ditzy and Beryl: Helpers at the Yellow Brolly
PANDA PUSSY: Heartless hasher
BIG BITCH: Heartless hasher

ADVANCE COMMENTS

Hong Kong Rocks is a story set in an alternative past; in part a whodunit, with the who and the it constantly in doubt. At the centre is a group of dissolute, middle-aged, expatriates, who are held more or less upright, or let fall, by surer, stronger, women. Dissolution, however, has its consequences, in conflict with either the newly introduced Deportation Act, or two cross-border goons, or both. And, as the tale reaches its finale, we cannot but agree with the narrator that Hong Kong is "hotting up".
—Philip Chatting, author of *The Snow Bridge and Other Stories*, Winner of the Proverse Prize 2014.

Funny and twisted, in Humphreys' spirited novel Nick and a garrulous band of expats are caught in the shifting societal landscape of Hong Kong. Nights drinking at the Brolly, missing friends, the Occupy movement, fear of deportation and the threat of discovery by Chinese agents, all loom large. As his freedom hangs on the edge of a precipice, Nick seizes on the absurdities, secrets and joys of a life lived with regret.
—Maria Roberts, author of *Single Mother on the Verge*, Penguin.

Hong Kong Rocks encapsulates the emptiness which grips Hong Kong with refreshing wit and philosophical resignation. Humphreys has successfully created a forlorn atmosphere. A decaying urban lifestyle slowly eats the protagonists away, while entwining their lives.
—James Tam, author of *Man's Last Song*, Proverse Prize finalist 2011.

FIND OUT MORE ABOUT PROVERSE AUTHORS, BOOKS, INTERNATIONAL PRIZES, AND EVENTS

Visit our website:
http://www.proversepublishing.com
Visit our distributor's website: www.cup.cuhk.edu.hk

Follow us on Twitter
Follow news and conversation: <twitter.com/Proversebooks>
OR
Copy and paste the following to your browser window and
follow the instructions:
https://twitter.com/#!/ProverseBooks

"Like" us on www.facebook.com/ProversePress
Request our free E-Newsletter
Send your request to info@proversepublishing.com.

Availability
Most books are available in Hong Kong and world-wide
from our Hong Kong based Distributor,
The Chinese University Press of Hong Kong,
The Chinese University of Hong Kong, Shatin, NT,
Hong Kong SAR, China.
Orders and enquiries: Email: cup@cuhk.edu.hk
Website: www.cup.cuhk.edu.hk

All titles are available from Proverse Hong Kong
http://www.proversepublishing.com
and the Proverse Hong Kong UK-based Distributor.

We have stock-holding retailers in Hong Kong,
Canada (Elizabeth Campbell Books),
Andorra (Llibreria La Puça, La Llibreria).
Orders can be made from bookshops
in the UK and elsewhere.

Ebooks
Most Proverse titles are available also as Ebooks.